WHO DAT
WHODUNNIT

Visit us at www.boldstrokesbooks.com

Praise for the Scotty Bradley Series

"Fast-moving and entertaining, evoking the Quarter and its gay scene in a sweet, funny, action-packed way."—*New Orleans Times-Picayune*

"A pleasant addition to your beach bag."—*Bay Windows*

"Greg Herren gives readers a tantalizing glimpse of New Orleans." —*Midwest Book Review*

"Herren's characters, dialogue and setting make the book seem absolutely real."—*The Houston Voice*

"So much fun it should be thrown from Mardi Gras floats!"—*New Orleans Times-Picayune*

"Greg Herren just keeps getting better."—*Lambda Book Report*

"When Herren introduced young, well-muscled former New Orleans bar dancer Scotty Bradley, he gave crime fiction one of its most engaging gay heroes."—*Booklist*

"Upbeat prose compounded of humor, caustic observations of Bourbon Street tourists and far-reaching subplots recommend this first book."—*Library Journal*

By The Author

The Scotty Bradley Adventures

Bourbon Street Blues

Jackson Square Jazz

Mardi Gras Mambo

Vieux Carré Voodoo

Who Dat Whodunnit

The Chanse MacLeod Mysteries

Murder in the Rue Dauphine

Murder in the Rue St. Ann

Murder in the Rue Chartres

Murder in the Rue Ursulines

Murder in the Garden District

Sleeping Angel

Love, Bourbon Street: Reflections on New Orleans
(edited with Paul J. Willis)

WHO DAT WHODUNNIT

by

Greg Herren

A Division of Bold Strokes Books

2011

WHO DAT WHODUNNIT
© 2011 BY GREG HERREN. ALL RIGHTS RESERVED.

ISBN 13: 978-1-60282-225-2

THIS TRADE PAPERBACK ORIGINAL IS PUBLISHED BY
BOLD STROKES BOOKS, INC.
P.O. BOX 249
VALLEY FALLS, NY 12185

FIRST EDITION: MAY 2011

CREDITS
EDITOR: STACIA SEAMAN
PRODUCTION DESIGN: STACIA SEAMAN
COVER DESIGN BY SHERI (GRAPHICARTIST2020@HOTMAIL.COM)

Dedication

This is for the SUPER BOWL XLIV CHAMPION
NEW ORLEANS SAINTS
Bless you, boys, and thank you.

"Ignorance—of mortality—is a comfort. A man don't have the comfort, he's the only living thing that conceives of death, that knows what it is."

—Tennessee Williams, *Cat on a Hot Tin Roof*

"What kind of Fascist state would deny a gay man a bridal registry?"

—Margaret Cho

"This stadium used to have holes in it, and it used to be wet. Well, it isn't wet anymore. This is for the city of New Orleans."

—Saints Coach Sean Payton,
accepting the NFC Championship Trophy

PROLOGUE

It was the best of times.

It was the craziest of times.

Well, what it *really* had to be was the end times, which was the only logical explanation for what was going on in the city of New Orleans.

Pigs grew wings and nested in the branches of the beautiful live oaks everywhere in the city. Some thought the pilot light in hell had gone out, so that icicles hung from the noses of shivering demons in the realm of the dark lord. Others starting watching the horizon for the arrival of the Four Horsemen, for surely the Apocalypse must be coming. Surely the earth was tilting in its axis. Maybe aliens would land in Audubon Park, or the Mississippi River would start flowing backward.

Anything and everything was possible, because the Saints were *winning*.

GEAUX SAINTS!

People who don't live in the South don't really understand how important football is down here. Football is more than a religion in the Deep South. I'm not sure why it is—my mom claims it's because the South lost the Civil War—but it's true. On Saturdays, when the colleges play their games, the entire region comes to a complete halt. People live and die by their teams— whether it's LSU, Ole Miss, Alabama, Auburn, Florida, Georgia or Tennessee—and how they fare on Saturday. I myself grew up cheering for the LSU Tigers—even though attending Vanderbilt was a family tradition on my mother's side. Whenever Papa Fontenot gives me crap for dropping (well, flunking is probably a more accurate word) out after my sophomore year, I give him a withering look and reply, "Maybe I'd have done better at LSU."

That always shuts him up.

But as much as we love football, here in New Orleans we've known nothing but shame for decades. Tulane, the only major university within the city limits, might as well not even have fielded a team, they were so hopeless. And the Saints, our NFL team, were probably the most hopeless case in the entire league. For forty-two years, the Saints (sometimes called the Aints) failed spectacularly. It took them over twenty years to post their first winning season. Yet somehow, we loved them. No matter how bad they were—and they were pretty bad most of the time—we kept on loving them and cheering for them. They were ours, and well, if they were losers, they were still OUR losers. The Saints were like that crazy uncle every family seems to have, you know what I mean? You don't stop loving him because he's a screw-up and a failure. You just keep loving him and hoping for the best, thinking *maybe someday he'll get it together.*

Even though he never seems to succeed—and sometimes, many times, he shoots himself in the foot.

But this year, things were *different.*

The fever spread through the city faster than bubonic plague. Each week, the excitement built as our sad-sack always-an-also-ran NFL team mowed down every team they faced. Every Sunday, at game time, the streets were as deserted and empty as they'd been those months after the floodwaters from the levee failures receded. For those few hours, New Orleans turned into a ghost town, eerily silent until a roar would erupt from the nearest bar—a roar that meant the Saints had scored.

By the time the team was 4–0, people were saying this could be the year we went to the Super Bowl. No one talked about *winning* the Super Bowl; just making it there was more than enough for us long-suffering Saints fans. As hopeful as we were, there was always that thought in the back of our minds—*Is this a fluke? Will the clock strike midnight and turn the Saints back into field mice from champions?*

But somehow, week after week, they kept winning.

People were talking about destiny.

And the city turned black and gold.

Even those people who didn't care for football were hanging Saints flags on their houses, writing FINISH STRONG on their car windows in grease pencil, and wearing jerseys on game days. Everywhere you turned on Sundays, all you could see were locals in Saints jerseys. Anything with a fleur-de-lis, the words "Who Dat," or the Saints logo on it just flew off the shelves. Even the gay bars turned off their traditional music videos on Sundays and played the games for crowds of jersey-wearing gay men, offering drink specials every time the Saints scored. One bar started calling vodka-and-cranberry a "Drew Brees."

Priests took to performing Sunday mass in Saints jerseys, and closing with a prayer for a Saints victory.

The fever was everywhere. It was bigger than Mardi Gras.

It was almost as though it was ordained somehow.

Some of the wins were not only improbable, they were impossible. Down by seven points against the Redskins, less than three minutes left in the game with the Redskins getting ready to kick a field goal to clinch the game—they somehow found a way to win. Down twenty-one points to the Miami Dolphins, they wound up winning.

Week after week, somehow the Saints just kept winning.

And eventually, the Minnesota Vikings came to the Superdome with the NFC Championship on the line, and a trip to the Super Bowl—the Promised Land Saints fans never once believed we'd ever see after wandering forty-two long years in the desert.

My name is Milton Scott Bradley, but you can just call me Scotty. I am a born and bred New Orleanian, and I bleed black and gold. I live in the French Quarter with my two boyfriends, Frank Sobieski and Colin Cioni. Yes, I have two boyfriends—but Colin's work takes him away most of the time. Frank and I have a private detective business—Bradley & Sobieski.

And that Sunday night, my parents decided to invite people over to watch the Saints play (for only the second time in their history) for a chance to go to the Super Bowl.

And it came down to a field goal—*in overtime.*

An entire city—no, an entire state—held its breath as a twenty-three-year-old kid who'd missed a game-winning kick a few weeks earlier trotted out onto the field with a chance to go down in New Orleans history as either a great hero or as the goat.

The ball was snapped.

All I could do was whisper "oh my God" as I watched him swing his leg. My eyes filled with tears of shock and joy as I watched the ball go up in the air, travel forty yards spinning end over end, and cleanly split the uprights.

And the entire city of New Orleans spontaneously erupted with joy.

By that time, I was emotionally exhausted and drained. With about five minutes left in the game, I just went completely numb. I've never experienced anything even remotely like that during a football game; it was weird, like I'd blown a circuit in my brain. I had alternated between joy and disappointment throughout the entire game, but as the game wound down I was numb from head to toe and felt nothing but an unearthly calm that frankly had me worried I'd had a mini-stroke or something. When the

Saints intercepted legendary Vikings quarterback Brett Favre with nineteen seconds left in the game, I could hear the cheers roaring and echoing from every direction outside. In my parents' living room, people were screaming and cheering, jumping up and down—but I just sat there on the couch, unable to believe what I was seeing, to process what had just happened.

When we won the coin toss for the overtime, I felt the electrical current that flowed through the entire city. Every hair on my arms was standing up.

Frank was hugging me so tightly I could barely breathe.

I was almost afraid to keep watching. My hands were clammy, my heart was pounding, and my chest was tight. My entire body was trembling.

I couldn't even think clearly enough to pray.

And when the field goal went through the uprights, the city literally exploded.

And I cried. I just sat there on the couch and cried as everyone in the room screamed and hugged. Outside, all hell broke loose as people ran out screaming into the streets of the French Quarter. Horns were blaring, and I swear I could hear the cannons down on the riverfront being fired.

"Oh my God." Frank grabbed me and dragged me to my feet. He put his arms around me and lifted me in a bear hug, kissing my cheek as tears flowed down both of our faces. Even though it was cold, we ran out onto the balcony with everyone else and screamed at the top of our lungs. We didn't form words—we couldn't just yet. We just screamed and hollered and laughed and cried and kissed and hugged.

People were dancing in the streets.

Fireworks were going off over Jackson Square.

The night was a blur from that point on. My memory is, frankly, spotty. I drank champagne and did shots with total strangers. I hugged and kissed people. I remember joining impromptu second line parades. I sang "When the Saints Go Marching In" or screamed the "Who Dat?" cheer until my throat was sore and my voice was barely more than a croak.

And I cried from the sheer joy of it all. I was so happy, so proud, so glad to be a New Orleanian, so glad to experience this incredible moment with everyone else in the city.

No city knows how to party and celebrate like New Orleans.

We live here because we love New Orleans and don't want to be anywhere else. We stayed after the flood because we could live nowhere else; and even a battered, almost completely destroyed New Orleans was still better than any other place. For a New Orleanian, there is nowhere else.

There is only New Orleans.

It would have been easy for the Saints to leave us in those dark days after the flood, and there was talk of it. It was heartbreaking. The Saints, even in the days when fans wore paper bags over their heads to the games and we referred to them as the Aints, were as much a part of this city's fabric as the Superdome, St, Louis Cathedral, and Mardi Gras. We loved our sad-sack Saints, even when we shook our heads and clicked our tongues over their bad luck. Some claimed it was because the Superdome had been built on top of an old slave cemetery—the team was cursed.

And when Katrina damaged the Superdome, the Saints played in San Antonio and in Baton Rouge at Tiger Stadium.

Was there ever a more opportune time, it seemed, for the Saints to leave New Orleans in their rearview mirrors, change their name, and start over again somewhere else?

But they stayed. They could have left but they stayed. And a grateful city, in its darkest days, in its bleakest hours, opened its heart and poured out an extraordinary and seemingly endless flow of love and gratitude.

And the team loved us right back. They gave us something

to be proud of, to look forward to, and they united the city when we had so little, when we were just hanging on by our fingernails and trying to get through the day with our dignity intact and our heads held high.

That day I was so keyed up and nervous about the game I couldn't do anything. I kept reminding myself *it's only a game, it's only a game* but it didn't work. All of my life, as big a sports fan as I am, I have never been so worked up over a football game, so tense, so nervous. When the Saints took the field, I had to wipe tears out of my eyes. They were tears of pride and joy—not just in my team, but in my city and we who live here—because we never, ever gave up on New Orleans. Because it would have been so easy to just give up. But we didn't—we didn't just walk away from one of the worst natural disasters in the history of the country. We stayed, and we fought and rebuilt in the face of so much negativity. Because our actions, so much more so than our words, gave the middle finger to all those who seemed to exult in the annihilation of our city—because New Orleans will be here long after they've all gone to hell and their corpses crumble to dust in their graves.

And now, after years of listening to naysayers pronouncing our city dead, or beyond redemption, being told it was hopeless, the Saints pulled off a miracle.

And they did it for us.

Frank and I stumbled home around seven in the morning, exhausted, drained both emotionally and physically. We undressed and got under the covers, our arms around each other. "The Saints are going to the Super Bowl," I whispered for maybe the thousandth time that night, still not quite able to believe it.

"I know," Frank replied, kissing the top of my head.

"I don't want to go to sleep," I said, "because I'm afraid I'll wake up and the whole night will have been a dream. It still doesn't seem real."

"It's real, baby." He kissed the top of my head again. "They did it. I just wish Colin was here to enjoy this with us."

"I know," I replied, rolling onto my side and closing my eyes.

My last thought before I went to sleep was *Wherever you are, Colin, please be safe.*

CHAPTER ONE
QUEEN OF SWORDS, REVERSED
A sly, deceitful, cruel woman

Contact made.

I stared at the computer screen while emotions swept over my body. Relief and joy were followed closely by irritation. The urge to reach through the computer screen and strangle Angela Blackledge until her face went blue and her protruding tongue turned black was much more powerful than it should have been. I closed my eyes, took some deep breaths, and centered myself.

Once the toxic feelings were gone, I opened my eyes and read the two words again.

Seriously, Angela, would it have killed you to say more— like everything is okay, or maybe when he's going to be coming home? You know, stuff we'd like to know?

I shook my head and sighed.

It would have to be enough, like every other time Colin was out there in some incredibly dangerous trouble zone, putting his life on the line to make the world a safer place for us normal, everyday people. When one of your boyfriends is a master secret agent, just knowing he was still alive has to be enough.

"He's alive," I called out to Frank as I typed *Thanks* and hit Send, wishing there was a way to connote sarcasm electronically.

Frank walked into the living room with just a towel wrapped around his waist. Shaving cream was lathered all over his face, beads of water glittering on his defined muscles. "Angela e-mailed, then?"

A smile spread over my face as my gaze traveled up and down his truly exquisite body. Frank, in his late forties, had the kind of body a man half his age would kill for. He was even hotter now than when we'd first met all those years ago, when I was still in my twenties and dinosaurs roamed the earth.

He stands about six feet two in his bare feet, with broad shoulders and a narrow waist. There isn't an ounce of fat on his thickly muscled frame. Every muscle on him looks carved out of stone. The ridges between his abs are so deep my fingers will fit there up to the first knuckle. Blue veins run over every muscle like a road map. His round, hard ass has to be seen to be believed— underwear models wished they had a butt so beauteous and awe-inspiring. He is balding and shaves his head down to little more than stubble. His jaw is strong and square. An angry-looking scar runs down his right cheek from almost the corner of his eye to the corner of his mouth. It gives him a mean, almost sinister look— especially when he scowls.

But when he smiles, his blue-gray eyes light up, dimples deepen in his cheeks, and the scar isn't even noticeable.

Fortunately, he smiles a lot.

"As usual, she didn't say much." I shrugged. "Her typical cryptic shit." I signed out of the computer and got out of my chair. "But I suppose if she told us anything more—"

"She'd have to kill us." Frank finished the running joke between us with a laugh. No matter how many times we said it, it never seemed to get old. He winked at me. "You look hot," he went on, giving me a wolf whistle.

"You think?" I looked down at what I was wearing—a pair of worn low-rise jeans and a black T-shirt that fit a little more snugly in the waist than I would have preferred. For that matter, I'd had some trouble closing the jeans.

I was going to have to start being a little more careful with my diet.

"I thought this was supposed to be a dressy thing—why are you wearing jeans?"

"Do you think Mom and Dad are going to be dressed up?" I rolled my eyes. "Besides, our branch of the family is always expected to be a freak show."

"Why are we going, anyway?" he asked as I followed him back into the bathroom. I leaned against the door frame as he started shaving. "Mom hates these command performances, doesn't she?"

"She's not the only one," I replied.

Dinner parties at the home of my paternal grandparents were always tedious affairs, where the only saving grace was the good liquor. Get-togethers at my maternal grandparents' graceful Garden District mansion were always a good time—you never knew what was going to happen, and that was part of the fun. But the Bradleys were the antithesis of the Diderots—boring, stuffy, and extremely concerned about appearances. Papa Bradley disliked my mother intensely—and the feeling was more than mutual. He blamed her for turning my dad into a "French Quarter bohemian"; she thought he was an uptight racist classist bourgeois bastard. On more than one occasion he'd said something offensive and Mom had blown up.

At the Diderot house, a lively family argument would ensue. Papa Bradley just curled his lip disdainfully and drank more Scotch, his disapproval of his second son's family written all over his face.

Frankly, I much prefer the Diderots. I try to avoid the Bradley side as much as possible. It's not fun to be part of the black sheep branch of the family tree.

Even my brother Storm's law degree and marriage to a Garden District blueblood didn't make up for the "sins" of our parents. My sister Rain, who'd married a doctor and was very active in all the correct Uptown charities, hadn't set foot inside the State Street house in years.

And I suspect Papa Bradley didn't like to admit to many people he had a gay grandson with two long-term partners and his own private eye business.

I can only imagine what he'd think if he knew I was also a bit psychic.

"But it's an obligation." I took a deep breath. "I don't want to go any more than you do."

Frank frowned at me in the mirror. He rinsed off his razor before going back to work on his neck. "I don't mind your Bradley relatives as much as you do."

"That's because they aren't *your* relatives," I retorted. As soon as I said it, I was sorry.

I'd never met any of Frank's relatives. I knew he had parents up in one of the Chicago suburbs, and a sister with a family in Birmingham. Other than that, he didn't talk about them. I quickly added before the vein in his forehead started throbbing, "Besides, much as I loathe my cousin Jared, he *does* play for the Saints"—*mostly on the bench*, I thought—"and they *are* going to the Super Bowl, so if Papa Bradley wants the whole family there to toast this momentous occasion, we have to go. It's just one evening." I sighed. "I guess this kind of thing means a lot to him."

"Do you think MiMi will get drunk?" Frank winked at me as he rinsed his face.

I glanced at my watch and raised an eyebrow. "It's six thirty—she's already been drunk for hours."

No one in the family really blamed MiMi for getting drunk. "It can't be easy being married to that horrible old bastard, If drinking keeps her from putting a bullet in his head, who are we to judge?" was what Mom always said whenever one of us suggested getting her help or possibly staging an intervention. She had a point. Hell, if I'd spent fifty years married to the old bastard, I'd probably have my first drink at lunch, too. Mom also liked to point out that she rarely made a spectacle of herself in public—although there was that one time at Galatoire's we weren't allowed to talk about. No one on our side of the family had been there to witness it. According to my sister Rain, whose friend Catsy Thorndike *had* witnessed it, MiMi apparently took off her blouse, climbed up on her table, and did a pole dance to the cheers of the other diners.

I'm quite sure it wasn't quite *that* bad. Catsy Thorndike is prone to exaggeration—and had most likely been pretty hammered herself.

"Colin's lucky he's wherever he is," I said sourly. "I know I'd rather be shot at than spend the evening on State Street."

"It's not that bad." Frank rolled his eyes at me as he went into the bedroom. A nice pair of navy blue slacks, a yellow button-down shirt, a pair of socks that matched the shirt, and a leather belt were laid out across our neatly made bed.

"You're wearing that?" I moaned. "Come on, Frank, wear jeans."

He dropped the towel and grinned. "Papa Bradley's wish is my command." He gave me a mock bow and winked as he pulled the pants on. "He doesn't have to know I'm going commando underneath, does he?" He zipped them closed.

I leered at him. "Unless I pants you over the after dinner cocktails, which isn't a half-bad idea." I let out a long-suffering sigh. "That should shake things up a bit, don't you think?"

"All Papa Bradley would do is get that sour look on his face and drink more Scotch," Frank pointed out. "And MiMi wouldn't notice."

"It would gross out Jared—which might make it worth it." I sat down on the corner of the bed.

"He's not that bad, is he?" Frank asked.

"You didn't grow up with him." Since I avoided that side of the family, Frank had never really gotten the full Bradley experience. Whenever Frank was around, that side of the family was always on its best behavior—because they didn't consider him part of the family.

The dinner was in honor of my first (and only) cousin on that side of the family, Jared. Jared was about five years younger than me, and as the only child of the oldest son, he was the Bradley Crown Prince. He was horribly spoiled and could do no wrong. Jared had been a football star in high school, gotten a scholarship to Southern Mississippi, and somehow managed to finagle his way into a spot on the Saints roster. He didn't get to play much, but the sight of the name BRADLEY across the back of a Saints jersey on the sideline was all Papa Bradley needed.

Jared was also a homophobe. I came out to my family when I was sixteen, and when no adults were around he always called me "fag."

Well, that and "pillow-biter"—and other words equally charming.

I really hate my cousin.

About ten minutes later, we were heading uptown in the silver Jaguar. The Jaguar is really Colin's car, but he leaves it in New Orleans for us to use since neither one of us have one. It's a sweet ride, actually—it's custom, with leather seats and all kinds of gadgetry I have no idea how to use. Angela had gotten it for him, which is the primary reason I don't like driving it. I'm always afraid I'm going to accidentally hit a switch and launch a rocket or something. On the other hand, Frank loves to drive it. So far he hasn't blown up anything, so I'm okay with leaving the driving to him.

But there's always a first time.

I shivered as we headed up St. Charles. "Turn the heat up," I instructed, trying to tuck as much of my head as possible into the collar of my black leather jacket. Most People Not From Here don't realize it actually does get cold in New Orleans in the wintertime. It's a horrible damp cold that cuts right to the bone and seems to settle into your joints.

And since our homes are built to be as cool as possible in the mind-numbing heat of summer, they're really hard to heat.

Frank obliged, then glanced at the clock on the dashboard. "We're going to be late," he commented.

"Good," I replied, looking out the window at the mansions passing by. "There's nothing worse than being the first ones there." I shuddered. "Ugh."

"You know, Papa Bradley isn't that bad, and MiMi is pretty harmless." Frank slowed the car as the light at Napoleon turned yellow, then red. "I really don't know why you don't like them."

I had to give Papa Bradley credit—Frank *was* welcome in his home. As a law-and-order conservative, he respected Frank as a retired FBI Special Agent. He was always cordial to him—although he never admitted we were more than business partners.

Still, for him that was something.

"Well, I do love them," I replied. "I just don't *like* them very much."

"You used to feel that way about Papa Diderot, too," he reminded me, shifting back into first gear when the light changed to green again.

I gave him a sour look. "Yeah, yeah."

Much as I hated to admit it, he *was* right. I closed my eyes and tried to remember a time when Papa Bradley acted like a decent human being. I had some vague memories of him tossing me in the air when I was a little boy, and the smell of his cigars and bourbon. *When did he turn into an asshole? When did I stop liking him?*

I honestly couldn't remember. There wasn't a clear line of demarcation, like there was with Katrina, dividing time into before and after. I just remembered the clear look of disapproval when I told him I wasn't going to be playing football at Jesuit High School, the way his eyebrows knit together as he puffed on his cigar when I told him I'd be going to Vanderbilt instead of LSU—the list of times I'd proven to be a disappointment to him was endless. I remembered him railing about the goddamned liberal Communists ruining this country, the lazy bastards on welfare, and the baby-murdering liberals, how we should just nuke Iran—on and on and on.

"It's kind of hard to love someone when you disagree with him about just about everything," I finally said. "I mean, he makes Ann Coulter look progressive."

Frank laughed. "I'll have to give you that one."

How many homophobic things has the old bastard said in front of me? I thought, trying to remember and giving up. He thought gays were perverts who didn't deserve any protection under the law—and my being one didn't change his mind one bit.

"It's a wonder Mom hasn't killed him," I said out loud, and smothered a grin as I remembered the last time he said something homophobic in front of me. It was Christmas Eve, and we were gathered around the gigantic tree in the massive front parlor of the State Street house. I couldn't have been more than twenty-two or twenty-three, still in disgrace on both sides of the family for dropping out of Vanderbilt. I couldn't remember what exactly was said to set him off on his homophobic tirade—most likely it was my cousin Jared, it usually was—but it was one of his nastiest to date. Mom—who had absolutely no problem with telling her own father off and getting into a screaming match with him—always tried to bite her tongue at the Bradley house.

But she didn't this time.

She very calmly filled her wineglass to the top, walked over to him with a huge smile on her face, and threw the wine in his face.

He gaped at her in shock—everyone in the room did.

"You miserable old son of a bitch," she said in her pleasantest tone. "I've had to listen to your fascist bullshit for years, but I will be damned if you are going to insult and demean my son in my presence on Christmas Eve. What would your Lord and Savior think?"

She left him blinking, his mouth open, and walked over to the Christmas tree. Before anyone could stop her, she gave it a good shove. It fell over, ornaments that had been in the family for decades shattering and splintering as everyone just gasped in shock.

She turned back to him with a smile, gave him the middle finger with both hands, and swept out of the room, with Dad and me right behind her.

She laughed all the way back to the Quarter.

In fact, she still enjoyed a hearty laugh every time that night came up.

I stifled a moan as Frank parked in front of the house. "Gird your loins," he said with a smirk. "We're here." He patted my left leg.

I love him, but he can be really annoying sometimes.

Papa Bradley's house is a massive two-story structure made of gray stone. The porch was only large enough to hold several people standing at the front door. There was a huge bay window to the right of the front door, where an enormous Christmas tree decorated entirely in black and gold sparkled. That wasn't the family tree, of course—this was for passersby to gawk at. A huge Saints flag fluttered from the roof of the porch in the cold wind. The paved circular driveway was clogged full of cars. In the island of lawn between the driveway and the sidewalk, a black iron fountain bubbled and splashed.

I took a deep breath and got out of the car, shivering as another blast of cold wind seemed to go right through my clothes and skin to my bones. I started walking to the front door as another car pulled into the driveway.

"Hey, boys." Storm waved as he got out of his black Mercedes. He walked around to the other side and opened the passenger door for his wife, Marguerite. We waited for them on the walk. Marguerite kissed us both on the cheek. She was pretty, tall and slender with long chestnut hair. I often felt sorry for her—I was born into this family, I couldn't imagine what it was like to marry into the insanity—but she always seemed to handle it fairly well. I linked arms with her and we walked up the steps to the verandah while Frank and Storm talked about the Saints' win over the Vikings.

As I pushed the doorbell, Marguerite whispered, "Three hours, max, before we can escape."

I suppressed a laugh as Louisa opened the front door. She'd been my grandparents' housekeeper for as long as I could remember, and I'd often wondered how much they paid her to overlook Papa Bradley's all-too-frequent racist remarks. She smiled at us. "Everyone's in the parlor," she said, taking our jackets.

I exchanged a look with Marguerite, who just rolled her eyes. The parlor meant before-dinner drinks. And that meant MiMi was probably already hoisting her third sheet to the wind. I sighed and walked up the hallway to the parlor.

There was a fire going in the fireplace underneath the massive oil painting of Jeremiah Bradley, who'd made the family fortune shipping sugar and coffee after the Civil War. (Papa Diderot *always* likes to point out that Jeremiah Bradley was a carpetbagger.) MiMi was sitting in a red velvet wingback chair, sipping an enormous martini with two olives nestled in the bottom of the glass. Papa Bradley was pouring himself what was most likely his third or fourth Scotch. My aunt Leslie was sitting in the matching wingback chair on the other side of the hearth, a glass of red wine in her hand, watching MiMi through half-closed eyes.

Leslie was married to my uncle Skipper, and in her mid-twenties, maybe. She was very pretty; in that well-kept way younger woman married to men living off trust funds always seem to have. She had shoulder-length fine white-blond hair, a cat-shaped face ending in a sharp chin underneath thick red lips Mom swore were injected with collagen, and glittering green eyes. Her nose was slightly too perfect to be natural, and her perfectly round breasts sat high on her chest. She was wearing a black off-the-shoulder dress that reached her knees but had a deep slit up each side. Her black stiletto pumps completed what my sister Rain would say was "a few pennies short of expensive" look.

Personally, I liked Aunt Leslie. When you got her alone, she had an earthy sense of humor and a raucous laugh—but in company she was glacial and reserved, rarely speaking unless directly addressed. Everyone assumed she married Uncle Skipper for his money—why else would such a carefully packaged young woman marry a drunk old enough to be her father?—but I think she was fond of him in her own way.

Besides, what was wrong with marrying for money?

She nodded at me as I kissed MiMi on the cheek. MiMi patted my cheek, and I tried not to recoil from the combined odor of Chanel No. 5 and stale gin. Her eyes were glassy, and it was going to take a major production to get her out of the chair.

I kissed Aunt Leslie's cheek and whispered, "Where's Uncle Skipper?"

The corners of her mouth twitched. "Throwing up in the bathroom, probably." She muttered out of the side of her mouth, her right eye closing in a wink only I could see.

Papa Bradley, a fresh glass of Scotch in hand, curtly nodded at me. "Milton," he said as he shook Storm's hand, ignoring Frank and Marguerite.

I closed my eyes and counted to ten before meeting Frank's

eyes. That was another reason Papa Bradley irritated me—he *insisted* on calling me Milton. Marguerite maneuvered her way to the bar and mixed herself and Storm martinis—taking a big gulp from hers before passing Storm his.

It was going to be one of *those* nights.

The doorbell rang again as Uncle Skipper staggered into the parlor. Like MiMi, he was well on his way to total incoherence. He gave me a big, crushing bear hug. "Scotty! How's my favorite nephew?"

"Good," I replied, wincing from his whiskey-soaked breath.

"What am I, chopped liver?" Storm sipped his martini with a good-natured smile.

Before Uncle Skipper could answer, Mom and Dad appeared in the doorway. Mom's gaze swept over everyone, and I could tell she was bracing herself. She was wearing a red cashmere sweater over black slacks, and black boots with heels. A single teardrop diamond hung around her neck on a gold chain—and even Dad was wearing a jacket and tie.

I felt enormously betrayed.

"You're looking well, Cecile," Papa Bradley boomed as he walked over to MiMi's chair, standing beside it and glancing down at her briefly. MiMi ignored him and smiled at my parents.

There was tension in the air as greetings were exchanged, and I found myself looking around, trying to figure out where the tension was coming from. These gatherings were always tense—to say the least—but this time felt different somehow, like something truly unpleasant was floating just beneath the surface, and all it would take was one spark to ignite an explosion that would be almost impossible to put out. I glanced over at Frank, but he was talking in a low voice to Storm.

Aunt Leslie reached up and grabbed my arm, pulling gently until I leaned down. "I'm so sorry," she said in a low whisper, "for what's about to happen."

"What's going to happen?" I whispered back, but she just shook her head and gulped down half of her wine.

Puzzled, I walked over to the bar and poured myself a stiff vodka and tonic. As I took a sip, Mom joined me and helped herself to a glass of red wine. *That's off, too*, I thought. *Papa Bradley always plays bartender, making hearty jokes that aren't funny about what everyone wants to drink.* But he stood still beside MiMi's chair, not saying anything, just sipping his own bourbon.

I was watching him when the door chimes rang again. He started a bit, looking over at the doorway nervously. *What's got the old bastard so spooked?* I wondered, glancing around to see if anyone else had noticed his nervousness. *What is going on around here?*

He relaxed a little as his youngest child, my aunt Enid, swept into the room.

Enid was what was politely called a "change of life baby." MiMi thought she had an intestinal tumor—and was quite shocked to discover she was pregnant. Enid was only a few years older than Storm. She'd never married, and had only recently left the house on State Street for her own apartment in the lower Garden District.

I'd always felt kind of sorry for Enid. She'd been a pretty little girl, but by the time she was in her teens she began gaining weight and had never looked back. She was small, barely over five feet tall, but at her heaviest she'd weighed in excess of three hundred pounds. A few years earlier she'd had that weight-loss surgery to put a band around her stomach. She was now down to a skeletal ninety pounds or so. When she was heavy, she'd always smelled slightly sour. Now she tried too hard to be glamorous. Her light brown hair was coiffed into a ridiculously complicated up-do, which probably meant she'd spent the entire afternoon at the beauty salon. She spoke in a girlish little voice that wasn't age appropriate and was kind of creepy. She was very fond of pinks and lavenders—she was wearing a pink silk dress with matching shoes and carrying a pink patent leather bag. When she was happy or pleased, she squealed in delight like a child and clapped her hands together. She frequently talked louder than necessary, always in that high-pitched voice. I felt sorry for her—it couldn't have been easy to be raised in my grandparents' house. She was always friendly almost to the point of pushiness, demanding and insisting on confidences, showering anyone and everyone she knew with cards and little gifts, lecturing others regularly on their bad behavior and how to be a better person. She was devoted to her cat, Harley, and her Christmas cards always featured the two of them.

My mother despised her with a passion she usually reserved for right-wing politicians, oil company executives, and racists.

She'd done poorly at Newman and flunked out of the University of New Orleans after two semesters. She would occasionally get a part-time job, which would last a month or two, and as far as I could tell she'd never dated anyone. And as Rain once said to me grimly, "Never tell her anything you don't want the world to know."

We'd been close when I was younger, but as I got older she started rubbing me the wrong way.

I hazarded a sidelong glance at Frank, who had a smile plastered on his face as she dashed toward him with a disturbing high-pitched squeal. She'd formed one of her unnatural attachments to him, regularly sending him heart-shaped cards with "thinking of you" in glittered script on the outside and her neat, precise printing on the inside—in pink ink, of course.

Frank gave me a "help me" look as she threw her arms around him and squeezed him and giggled. "Did you get my card?" she said breathlessly in her childish voice, and squealed. "Wasn't it just the cutest ever?"

I smothered a grin and avoided Frank's eyes. "Shouldn't you

be rescuing him from that freak?" Mom murmured as she sipped her wine. Mom disliked all the Bradley relatives, but Enid was at the top of her list. I wasn't sure why and was about to respond to her when she grabbed my arm in a death grip. I looked at her and was about to say something when her grip got tighter. Her face was drained of color, and her mouth was open slightly. She was staring at the doorway. I swiveled my head to see what had startled her so much and almost gasped myself.

My cousin Jared was good looking, much as I hated to admit it. He was standing in the doorway, wearing a black sweater with a gold fleur-de-lis embroidered on the chest over a pair of tight jeans. He was about six-three and weighed 230 pounds. He had the thick build of a football player, and his once-aquiline nose had a bump in it where it had been broken when he was in high school. His shoulder-length brown hair shone and was perfectly parted in the center of his head. He had wide blue eyes, but as far as I was concerned, his looks were ruined by his air of smug arrogance. But it wasn't Jared's appearance that rattled Mom so completely.

It was the woman on his arm.

"Tara Bourgeois," I managed to breathe out as Mom let go of my arm.

Tara Bourgeois was probably the most notorious Miss Louisiana in the history of beauty pageants. The previous year she had swept through the Miss Louisiana pageant on her way to infamy at the televised Miss United States pageant in front of a worldwide audience of billions. I didn't know her, but Frank and I loved to watch beauty pageants for their amazing camp value. (I was always disappointed when the talent portion passed without an accordion player.) We, of course, were rooting for Miss Louisiana as she made it through every cut, her bleached teeth glowing in her perfect smile under her perfect nose and her beautiful green eyes and long, teased and lacquered black hair.

And she made it to the final five—which, of course, was the all-important question segment. I personally love that part of every pageant, as the contestants try desperately not to offend anyone and try to think fast enough on their feet so they don't make fools of themselves. Frank and I leaned forward as Miss Louisiana was called forward and stepped to the microphone. The bland host with the big teeth and the televangelist hair pulled her question out and said, "There have been a lot of recent court decisions that have awarded gays and lesbians equal rights. Do you believe that gays and lesbians should be allowed to marry, and serve openly in the military?"

Her eyes got wide with panic—you could tell she wasn't expecting that, and I kind of felt sorry for her—until she stepped up to the microphone and said, "Well, I believe that everyone is made in God's image." She paused before adding, "But I believe marriage is between a man and a woman, and any judge who says otherwise shouldn't be sitting on the bench and presiding over the law in a Christian nation, and I don't believe it is God's plan to let gays and lesbians to serve next to our brave soldiers who are out there risking their lives every day for our freedoms." When the audience let out a collective gasp, she smiled and shrugged, "I'm sorry, I was raised a Christian and that's what I believe."

There was a smattering of applause, but it was drowned out by boos and catcalls from the audience.

Frank and I sat there, dumbfounded, unable to speak.

She finished as first runner-up.

That might have been the end of it, but an openly gay blogger who runs a celebrity gossip site called her some nasty names the next day on his blog, and it turned into a huge mess. Rather than backing down, she went on the offensive. Before long, evangelical Christian groups and the right-wing "Gestapo" (as Mom called them) were coming to her defense. She was eventually fired as Miss Louisiana because she was skipping required appearances as Miss Louisiana in order to promote herself as the new queen of the anti-gay movement, but she refused to take responsibility for her own actions. Instead, she claimed it was "the gays" who did it to her, and there was a huge conspiracy of radical homosexuals out to get even with her, and deny her her First Amendment rights to free speech. She was now commanding large speaking fees and had been hired by a national anti-gay marriage group, Protect American Marriage, as their spokesperson. She had also written a book called *My American Dream*, which was soon to be released, and was being promoted as the star speaker at an anti-gay marriage rally being held somewhere in Kenner over the upcoming weekend. Mom was trying to organize a counter-protest.

And here she was, walking into my grandparents' home on the arm of my cousin, in a skintight blue dress with stiletto pumps, her big pageant smile plastered on her face.

And now I knew why Papa Bradley had been so nervous— *he knew she was coming.*

I felt resentment and anger beginning to simmer inside me. It was one thing to listen to her hateful homophobia on national television—it was quite another to have her waltz into my grandparents' home like she owned the place.

I wanted to punch the smug look off Jared's face.

As my anger began to boil over in my brain, I realized Mom was walking quickly across the room toward the door. I heard someone murmur "oh dear God"—it might have been Aunt Leslie—but the rest of the room was quiet, everyone too stunned to say anything.

"Hi," Tara said, flashing her pageant smile as Mom reached her. She stuck out her right hand. "I'm Tara, and you are…"

"Someone who hates your homophobic guts," Mom replied, tossing the contents of her glass into Tara's face. Tara stepped back, her perfectly coiffed hair sparkling with drops of wine, her makeup ruined, and rivulets of reddish purple liquid dripping from her chin and streaking down her bare neck and shoulders into her deep cleavage. Her dress was ruined, a huge stain on the front of it. Her eyes narrowed and she slapped Mom. "You *bitch!*"

No one moved as Mom slugged her with a right hook she usually reserved for security guards at nuclear power plants. Tara went over backward and vanished from view into the hallway— except for her feet in her stiletto heels.

I couldn't help it. I laughed.

"Bravo!" Marguerite got out of her chair with a glare for my grandfather. "Storm, take me home. I have no desire to share a table with that"—she sniffed disdainfully—"piece of Kenner trash."

Frank managed to disentangle himself from Enid's clutches and nodded at me. There was a sort of stampede for the door. Jared was helping Tara to her feet as I went by them on my way to the room where Louisa had deposited our coats. Her nose was bleeding. Jared was murmuring to her, and she was crying. For a brief moment, I felt sorry for her—she was, as my sister-in-law had so snobbishly put it, Kenner trash. I would imagine it was a big deal to her to be invited to the home of a society family on State Street in New Orleans, and she'd hardly made the kind of impression she would have wanted to.

Then I remembered all of her speeches and public appearances, demeaning Frank's and my relationship as something perverted and abominable, and whatever sympathy I had for her went right out the window.

"I guess this is an improvement," I said over my shoulder at them. "At least this one isn't stripping on Bourbon Street—yet."

Frank tossed me my coat, his face rigid and red. He was furious—I could tell by the muscle tic in just below his scar. "Come over," Mom said as she and Dad went out the front door. "We'll have a *family* gathering."

The last time I saw Tara Bourgeois alive was when I paused in my grandparents' front door and looked back. She was seated in one of the hallway chairs with her head tilted back, and Louisa was holding a burgundy towel to her nose.

I shook my head and slammed the door behind me.

Chapter Two

Ten Of Cups

Lasting happiness inspired from above

"I still can't believe you slugged her," Frank said, a delighted grin on his face as he unwrapped his cheeseburger.

We were sitting on the huge sofa in the living room of my parents' apartment. The temperature was dropping, and a cold night wind was whipping around the building. The wind was rattling the shutters on the balcony doors, like it was trying to get in. The air was heavy and damp, which meant rain later. I was hoping the rain wouldn't start until we got back to our own place. I shivered just as the central heating clicked on. Mom wasn't a fan of central heat—she said it felt canned and stuffy, so she rarely used it. Usually, I agreed with her, but now I was glad to hear it come on. It felt like it was less than fifty degrees inside. My nose and ears felt like they had frostbite, and even the wool blanket I had draped over my legs wasn't helping much.

The hot air coming out of the vent just behind the couch was heavenly against my neck.

Mom had offered us leftover tofu lasagna, but we'd politely ordered burgers from the Quartermaster Deli instead. It was just the four of us. Storm and Marguerite had conveniently gotten a call on their way to the Quarter from friends with an invitation to dine at Galatoire's, but were coming by for drinks after they finished dinner.

I suspected they knew about the tofu lasagna.

I glanced at Frank out of the corner of my eyes while unwrapping my own mushroom bacon cheeseburger. He'd been unusually silent since we'd left Papa Bradley's. The entire trip downtown he hadn't said a word, but from the tic of a muscle in his jaw and the throbbing vein in his forehead I knew he was pissed off. I just let him stew. When Frank's angry, it's best to just let it burn itself out. He'd talk about it when he was ready.

But I couldn't help but think it was weird. Surely he wasn't that upset about Tara showing up with Jared?

"She's lucky that's all I did—she deserves much, much worse," Mom replied, viciously stabbing a piece of lasagna with her fork. "I absolutely *despise* people who use religion as their excuse for bigotry. What religion has bigotry and hatred as its core values? I may not be a Christian but I'm willing to bet I've read the damned Bible more than she has." She gestured with her fork. "*Homosexuality is an abomination?* I bet she eats shrimp and lobster and wears mixed-fabric clothes. Same-sex marriage is against God's plan?" She scowled. "But it's perfectly okay for that hypocritical piece of trash to get her nose fixed and her boobs done. So, what her precious Lord gave her wasn't good enough for her? She thought she could improve on her God's work? *She's* an abomination."

"I still can't believe Papa didn't warn us Jared was bringing her." Dad shook his head, a sad look on his face.

I felt bad for Dad. It wasn't the first time. I've never understood the Bradley side of the family. For that matter, it was impossible to believe Papa and MiMi could have supplied the DNA for Dad. Rain once theorized that either MiMi had an affair or he had to have been adopted.

If Dad didn't have a strong resemblance to Papa Bradley, I'd find that easy to believe.

"Because he knew damned well if we knew Jared was bringing that monster, we wouldn't have shown up." Mom took another slug of her wine. "And he wanted us all there, regardless of how we might feel, to worship at the shrine of St. Jared. And he certainly wasn't going to tell the Holy Child not to bring her."

"How did they even meet?" I wondered out loud.

Mom ignored me. "I am *never* setting foot in that house again, and I'm never speaking to him again unless he apologizes, and he certainly won't do that. And admit he was wrong? That he behaved in a way that was offensive? Maybe when monkeys fly out of my ass." She shook her head. "We should have cut him out of our lives years ago. He's always treated us like trash, anyway. The worthless drunk Skipper can do no wrong—and if he can't appreciate what a fine man you are, honey—" She kissed Dad on the cheek. "Well, then he doesn't deserve our love or respect. I know he's your father, darling—"

Dad gave her a sad smile. "It's okay, dear." He shrugged his shoulders. "He certainly went too far this time. I don't understand why he favors Jared so much."

"Because he's a football player," I replied.

"What does that have to do with anything?" Frank wiped ketchup off his chin and looked at me.

I smiled at him. Frank was born and raised up north and had lived in DC most of the time he was with the Feds. "It's a Southern thing," I said, for simplicity's sake. "Football is like a religion down here. Like how the whole city's gone nuts this season? How many other cities have gay bars televising the local team's games?"

Frank nodded. "So, because Jared's a Saint, Papa Bradley treats him different than everyone else?"

I rolled my eyes. "When I didn't play football in high school...I might as well have been a cheerleader in his eyes." Storm *had* played football—Papa Bradley hadn't missed even one of his away games all four years. When Jared got a scholarship to play football at Southern Mississippi—a school he would have pitched a fit over if any other Bradley had wanted to go there—it was like Papa Bradley had died and gone to heaven.

Making the Saints roster in try-outs (no team drafted him) was just the icing on the cake.

"He always favored Skipper," Dad said, taking a sip of his wine. "Whether Jared played football or not, he's always favored Skipper."

"Oh, Skipper's just perfect," Mom replied, her face hardening. "He doesn't need to have a job or anything—or even stay sober for more than twelve hours, or stay married to the same woman for more than three years, or be a good father, or do anything besides just exist, for that matter. He can do no wrong as far as Papa Bradley's concerned. And *we* can't do anything right." She laughed, shaking her head. "It doesn't make any sense, does it, Frank?"

"No," Frank said with a ghost of a smile. "Can't say that it does."

"And that Jared! What a miserable little bastard he is!" Mom started winding herself up again. Affronts to her family were not something she took lightly. "I mean, I suppose we can't really blame him for being such an insensitive troglodyte—it's not like Skipper was any kind of father to him, and that revolving door of stepmothers he had to put up with—I don't even know how many times Skipper's been married."

"Four," I said, taking a bite out of my mushroom cheeseburger and trying not to moan from pleasure. I was starving, and Quartermaster's burgers are ambrosia.

Mom frowned. "Are you sure it's only four? I'm pretty sure it's five." She put her fork down, and started ticking them off on her fingers. "His first wife was Darla—how long were they married? Not even a year? Then there was Bethany, and after she left him, that's when he married that Lebanese girl—what was her name?"

"Bethany," I said to Frank in a low voice, "is Jared's mother."

"Wasn't her name Noor?" Dad replied, wrinkling his forehead. "Or am I thinking of the Queen of Jordan?"

"It doesn't matter—she only lasted a few months anyway." Mom dismissed the third wife with a wave of her hand. "And then he married Marybeth, and now Leslie. Five. He's been married five times." She rolled her eyes. "But like I said, Skipper can do no wrong in Papa Bradley's eyes. He could burn the house down and Papa would just say, 'That's fine, son, I was tired of the place anyway.'" She smiled at Dad. "And here we are, still happily married after all these years, and all three of our children have turned out so well." She gave me a big smile. "That must really stick in the old bastard's craw." She looked at Frank. "Papa Bradley has always disapproved of me, you know."

"I can't imagine why," Frank replied, giving me a sly wink she didn't see.

Mom chose to ignore the sarcasm and took it literally. "I'm a bad influence on John. And of course, it's my fault Scotty's gay—the liberal, pinko communist way I raised him, you know." She scowled. "He's stuck in the McCarthy era. He thinks women should be deferential housewives and mothers, that blacks belong in the back of the bus, Mexicans should all be sent home, and all gays should go back in the closet. Can you believe an educated man, in this day and age, thinks being gay is something you *choose*?"

"I chose to be gay," I grinned at Frank, "when I was about five years old. When I saw Greg Louganis diving in the Los Angeles Olympics in that stars-and-stripes Speedo, I was lost to heterosexuality forever." I closed my eyes and clasped my hands together. "That body! That butt! That bulge!" I batted my eyelashes at him. "There was no hope for me after that."

"They do always say it's the mother's fault," Frank replied, and ducked for cover as Mom threw her napkin at him.

"Horse shit. I'm so fucking sick of that idiocy." Mom

exploded, her face a thundercloud. "Why would anyone would choose to be gay—"

"The great sex," I whispered, and Frank elbowed me in the side.

"To be discriminated against and treated like a second-class citizen? Would anyone choose to be bullied and called names in school? Would—"

Dad interrupted her gently."He was teasing you, dear."

"Oh." She gave Frank a black look before grinning and wagging her finger at him. "You're just lucky I love you, Frank."

"I know." Frank patted my leg. "Every day when I wake up I thank the universe for my incredible good fortune."

"I do the same thing," Dad replied, rolling his eyes as Mom slugged him in the arm.

We all laughed, and I was crumpling up my burger wrapper when the doorbell rang.

"That'll be Father Dan!" Mom jumped to her feet, heading for the back door. She called back over her shoulder, "He called when we were on our way home and I invited him over."

"I'll open some more wine." Dad got up and went into the kitchen.

"I really hate your aunt Enid," Frank said once Dad was out of earshot.

I opened my mouth and closed it without saying anything.

"She's a homophobe," Frank whispered as Dad came back into the living room, struggling with a wine bottle and the corkscrew. Frank jumped up and took them from Dad with a grin and winked at me as he freed the cork in two twists.

I just stared at him, my mouth open. Where the hell did that come from?

Aunt Enid was odd, sure, no argument there, but a homophobe?

Seriously?

"Thanks, Frank," Dad plopped back down in his chair with a sigh of relief. "It's like I have a mental block with corkscrews—I can never get them to work."

Frank sat back down next to me as Dad refilled our glasses. I gave him a look that clearly said *what did she say to you* and he just shook his head slightly, mouthing "later" to me as I heard the back door shut.

"Scotty! Frank!" Father Dan rubbed his hands together as he walked into the living room, Mom on his heels. He was wearing a black leather jacket, a black and gold Saints muffler around his neck, and a tight pair of black jeans. He leaned down and kissed us both on the cheek and shook hands with Dad before taking his jacket off.

I've known Father Dan Marshall almost my entire life— or at least as long as I can remember. I'm not sure how old he actually is, but he's most likely in his late forties or early fifties. It just seemed like he'd always been around, sitting in the living room getting stoned with Mom and Dad and arguing politics with them. He's tall, maybe an inch or so over six feet, and has always worked out regularly. He's striking more than handsome, with a long narrow face, even white teeth, and blue eyes. He's got a great body—when I was a teenager I'd had a huge crush on him. At the time, the incongruity of having sexual fantasies about a Roman Catholic priest never crossed my mind. He was always tanned, and his body was amazing—broad-shouldered and narrow-hipped, with a big round hard ass that always seemed to be straining the seams of his jeans. But the most striking thing about him was his hair. He had the thickest, most beautiful blond hair I've ever seen. He usually wore it long and parted in the center, but as he removed the muffler from around his neck, I noticed he'd gotten it cut short for him. It was parted on the side and stopped just above the ears, but there was still a lot of it. He was wearing a red and black plaid flannel shirt with the top two buttons undone, given me a glimpse of the smoothly muscled valley between his strong pecs.

He took the glass of wine Dad was offering with a grateful smile and sat down in a wingback chair facing all of us. He took a sip and opened his eyes wide. "Oh, that's good," he grinned, taking another sip. "I've been needing some wine for hours."

"A Chilean Merlot," Dad replied, refilling his own glass while Mom loaded a pipe with some of their best marijuana.

"It's perfect." Father Dan set the glass down before taking the pipe from Mom. He lit the bowl and took a long hit, holding it for a moment with his eyes closed before blowing a cloud out toward the ceiling. He coughed a few times, and took another drink of his wine. He passed the pipe over to me.

It's always a little unnerving to smoke pot with a Roman Catholic priest. No matter how many times I'd done it, I still hadn't gotten used to it.

I took a hit and passed it to Frank, who also took a big hit before handing it over to Mom, who dumped the ash and reloaded it for herself. I suppressed a giggle. I was smoking pot with a priest and a retired FBI agent, I thought, and had to bite my lower lip to keep from laughing out loud.

Damn, it was good pot.

"So, how did the meeting go? I'm sorry we had to miss it," Mom said, blowing out a massive cloud of smoke. She checked the pipe and sheepishly reloaded it.

"It went really well—much better than I could have hoped." Father Dan replied, sipping his wine. "According to our Facebook page, we should have about two or three hundred people at the counter-rally." He shrugged. "But you never know how many people that's really going to translate to, you know? I'm hoping we get more of a crowd than they do—that's pretty much been the case everywhere this ridiculous tour of hate has been. But this *is* Louisiana, so who knows?"

"This is the counter-rally at the Dove Ministry of Truth, I assume?" I asked, trying not to cough as I passed Frank the pipe. The Dove Ministry of Truth was a megachurch on Airline Drive in Kenner.

"That's another one I'd like to punch right in the face—that bitch Peggy MacGillicudy. What's it to her if gays and lesbians can get married? Who cares? If my marriage isn't strong enough to survive Frank and Scotty getting married, well, there's something else seriously wrong with my marriage." Mom spread her hands. "How are gays and lesbians responsible for the divorce rate in this country?"

"It's just bigotry cloaked in religion," Father Dan replied. "I for one am tired of having my faith perverted by people who don't understand the teachings of Christ." He rubbed his hands together.

"But you're a *priest*." Frank put the pipe down on the coffee table. "Doesn't the Catholic Church—"

"As long as I keep a low profile, the Archdiocese lets me minister to the LGBT community," Father Dan grinned. "Of course, I'm sure Archbishop Pugh thinks I'm trying to get them to renounce their sin. And what the Archbishop doesn't know won't hurt him."

"But isn't the counter-protest going to be pretty high-profile?" I asked.

"That's why I'm listed as the organizer," Mom informed me. "Father Dan's name isn't anywhere, and he won't be there."

I looked at his smiling face. Many times over the years I wondered why he simply didn't renounce his Catholicism—it would certainly have made his life easier. As a gay priest, the conflict within himself had to rip him apart sometimes.

"And if they want to have a 'protect marriage' rally in Kenner, well, I'm not going to let them go unanswered," Father Dan went on. "The Community Center, P-FLAG, Forum for Equality—everyone's getting involved."

"Why would they have one in Louisiana in the first place?" Frank asked. "There's already a constitutional amendment here banning same-sex marriage—no one's trying to repeal it, right?"

"That's right, Frank—it passed in 2004." Father Dan sighed. "The year the right clung to power by campaigning against the rights of gays and lesbians nationwide."

"And there's no chance of it being repealed any time soon, not with all the ignorant bigots in this state," Mom went on. "No, she's just trying to raise some more money for PAM. I mean, really, that's what this is all about—raising money. Peggy MacGillicudy has turned this into her job." She spat the word "job." "She's gotten all the Louisiana bigots to speak—although for some reason I can't fathom, the governor isn't going to be there. I can't believe he'd pass up a chance to bash the queers, but there you go. And guess who the star speaker of the day is?" Her eyes glinted.

I closed my eyes, remembering her with a wet cloth pressed against her bleeding nose in Papa Bradley's hallway. "Tara Bourgeois, of course."

"Tara Bourgeois, our very own homegrown homophobe." Mom took the pipe off the coffee table and took another hit. "You know her book is being released this week—she's going to be on all the big talk shows, and of course, they're going to be selling her book at the rally—she's donating all the proceeds to PAM." PAM stood for *Protecting American Marriage*—but not from divorce or adultery or any of the real threats to marriage. Nope, they were protecting it from the insidious danger of the homosexual. "I really do hope I broke her fucking nose."

"Violence is never the answer, Cecile," Father Dan said with a frown. "And where exactly did you run into Tara Bourgeois?"

Mom scowled and proceeded to fill him in on everything that happened at Papa Bradley's house.

While they were distracted—Father Dan occasionally

making "oh dear" noises—I whispered to Frank, "What exactly did Enid say to you?"

His eyes narrowed and his face flushed with anger. The nerve started twitching in his jaw again. "She told me Jared was bringing Tara. Before I had a chance to even say anything, she went on a tirade about how terrible it was the way the gays treated her, and picked on her, trying to keep her from exercising her First Amendment rights, and how she had a right to her opinion, and the gays of all people should know what it was like to be silenced and treated badly."

My jaw dropped. I was so stunned I couldn't say anything.

"I couldn't believe what I was hearing," Frank went on when I remained silent, "and at first I thought she was yanking my chain, you know? But she wasn't kidding, Scotty. She was serious, deadly serious. And she kept saying 'the gays, you people'— things like that. I couldn't believe what I was hearing." His jaw set. "I know she's your aunt, but I don't want that homophobic bitch to ever set foot in our house again. No offense, but I don't put up with that kind of hateful bullshit from my *own* family, I sure as hell am not going to from her."

I nodded—because I still couldn't speak. My mind was reeling.

Surely she had to have been teasing him. Enid was one of the first Bradleys to be cool with my being gay—some of them, I reminded myself, still weren't—and while we hadn't been close in years, I couldn't believe she could have changed *that* much. She used to go to gay bars *with* me, and had a great time. She used to lecture me for not being more active in the gay rights struggle. She'd volunteered for the NO/AIDS Task Force for years, delivering food to AIDS patients so ill they couldn't get out of the house.

How could she possibly defend a homophobic bigot like Tara Bourgeois?

To Frank?

To be completely honest, she'd only started getting on my nerves as I grew older—and came to understand her better. As my sister Rain once said, "a little Enid goes a long way." She could be fun to be around, with her childish enthusiasm and little-girl mannerisms—and she could be really funny. But what I'd always seen as her selflessness actually came with a price tag attached. If you didn't do exactly what she wanted you to when she wanted you to, all the little things she'd done for you in the past got thrown back in your face as an example of her moral superiority and your own failures as a human being.

And another part of her immaturity was a mentality Storm described once as "I can say anything about anyone any time no matter how awful, but if anyone teases me or is the least bit critical of me, well, YOU ARE THE MOST HORRIBLE PERSON THAT EVER LIVED!" I'd seen this behavior a few times—and it was directed at me once.

After that experience of uncontrollable hysteria with tears alternating with a blinding, venomous rage—I'd kept her at a distance for a long time.

But Frank really liked her. Whenever she needed his help, Frank was there in a split second, literally dropping everything to rush to her assistance. He liked her, laughed at her jokes, and was always available when she needed someone to have lunch with or go see a movie with. It worried me a little, but she always seemed to be on her best behavior with him.

Until now.

Shock slowly began to give way to anger. *How dare she?* I thought. If Enid had been right there in front of me at that moment I would have cheerfully strangled her. I leaned over and kissed him on the cheek. "No worries, Frank," I said. "As far as I'm concerned, she no longer exists."

The relief on his face made my heart hurt just a little. "Are you sure? I mean, she's your aunt—"

I cut him off. "You're my family, Frank."

"I love you." He put his hand on my leg.

I kissed his cheek again but told myself dear old Enid was going to get it from me with both barrels the next time she was unlucky enough to see me.

"You two are coming to the rally, right?" Mom said, bringing me back into the conversation.

When she'd first mentioned it, I'd started thinking of excuses not to go. But now I was angry, and I wanted to do something about it.

"What time do we need to be there?" I asked, and grinned to myself as Mom spluttered a bit before answering. Obviously, she'd expected an argument.

"Meet here at eight in the morning." Father Dan smiled at Frank and me. "We need to strategize our plan of attack."

"Dear, remind me to leave eggs out so they'll be nice and rotten for Saturday." Mom patted Dad's leg. "Miss Bourgeois is in for a nice surprise."

I smothered a laugh. Mom's aim was perfect. If she had a clear shot, Tara was going to get a rotten egg square in the face.

"Such a pity," Father Dan said, shaking his head. "I went to high school with her mother, you know. Marilou was such a nice girl, with a big heart. If only—" He broke off.

"People change, Dan," Mom replied with a sigh. "More wine?"

Isn't that the truth? I thought angrily.

I was going to make Enid sorry she'd ever opened her mouth.

CHAPTER THREE

TEN OF WANDS

One who is carrying an oppressive load

I woke up around eight thirty the next morning with a mild hangover.

It wasn't the worst one I'd ever had—I didn't feel like death would be a welcome release. I was just slightly nauseous, with a mild headache. Frank was dead to the world beside me, sleeping on his side with his back to me. His body heat was great.

The apartment felt like a refrigerator. We'd turned the heat off when we'd staggered home—the apartment had been stuffy and dry, and we both sleep better in the cold.

There's *nothing* better than snuggling underneath a pile of blankets.

It was raining. I could see that out the bedroom window when I turned away from Frank. I moaned to myself. It was another typically gray, cold, and drizzly January day in New Orleans— perfect for staying in a warm bed buried under blankets. I closed my eyes and tried to go back to sleep, to no avail, so I decided I might as well get out of bed and face the day.

I reached down to the floor and grabbed my sweatpants, pulling them on while still beneath the warm blankets. Frank grumbled and turned over onto his stomach, but didn't wake up. I sat up and slid my house shoes on, cursing as I realized there wasn't a sweatshirt in arm's reach. I wrapped my arms around myself and managed to make it to the dresser without making a sound. I threw on some sweats while my teeth chattered. I brushed my teeth and swallowed some aspirin before heading into the kitchen to make coffee and toss a bagel into the toaster.

I dialed our office number—we maintained a small office for the detective agency about a block away on Frenchmen Street—and checked the voicemail. No new messages. I grinned. *Still no need to leave the house today*, I thought as I walked into the big room that served as our dining room and living room.

I could smell the coffee brewing as I sat down to check my e-mail in the little alcove we used as a home office. The aspirin started kicking in, but my stomach was still a little queasy. I didn't think I'd been that drunk, but wine has a bad habit of sneaking up on you. At some point, I'd completely lost track of how many bottles had been opened. All I knew for sure was my glass had never been empty for long. Come to think of it, I couldn't remember much of the stumble—er, *walk* home from Mom and Dad's. I vaguely remembered Storm and Marguerite showing up—they'd been a little sloppy themselves. There was also a lot of spirited discussion—Storm felt the protest of the PAM rally was a mistake. "Asking for trouble" was how he put it, which of course put Mom into debate mode. Dad and Father Dan joined in while the rest of us listened and gulped down more wine.

My bagel popped up in the toaster as the home page for my e-mail account opened. I started to get up when I caught a headline out of the corner of my eye that stopped me in my tracks.

ANTI-GAY MARRIAGE ADVOCATE SEX SCANDAL!

And right next to the headline was an *extremely* unflattering photograph of Tara.

I started laughing and dashed into the kitchen with a very light step, my hangover completely forgotten. I quickly poured myself a cup of coffee and smeared cream cheese on the bagel. I took a big bite and managed to not spill the coffee as I hurried back to the computer, sliding into the seat and grinning at Tara's face. Her hair wasn't blond in the picture, it was a darker brown, and she was scowling at the camera. She didn't have on much makeup, and the lighting was incredibly unflattering. Her mouth was open. *Her teeth hadn't been capped yet, either*, I smirked, *and she probably hadn't gotten the boob upgrade, either.*

Almost immediately, I felt ashamed of my reaction.

Okay, she may be a small-minded mean-spirited homophobe, I reminded myself, but she's still a human being, and you should never enjoy the pain and humiliation of other human beings. That makes you no better than she is.

I closed my eyes and apologized in a quick prayer.

"Of course, that doesn't mean I can't read about it," I said under my breath. It *was* news, after all.

How many times had some high-and-mighty person who presumed to sit in judgment on their fellow humans taken such a fall and been exposed as the worst kind of hypocrite? There was the homophobic senator arrested for soliciting a cop for sex in the airport bathroom, the family values senator exposed for going to prostitutes regularly, and that homophobic televangelist who'd snorted crystal meth with male prostitutes before satisfying his lusts.

I clicked on the link and started reading. In spite of my better inclinations, I could feel my grin growing with every sentence.

Like Mom always said, the ones who preach the loudest have the nastiest secrets.

NEW ORLEANS, LA. Tara Bourgeois, the former Miss Louisiana who made headlines all over the country with her on-stage comments against same-sex marriage at the Miss United States pageant, and later claimed she lost her state crown due to a "gay conspiracy" against her, has appeared in at least one, and maybe more, private sex tapes.

A former boyfriend, Joe Billette, released one of the tapes to the press today, and claims there are "plenty more."

"I think it's just plain wrong that Tara has set herself up as this person of high moral character, lecturing everyone else about what is and isn't godly, when the truth is she's the last person who should be making judgments about other people's behavior and conduct," Mr. Billette said in a statement released to the press along with the tape. "She's portrayed herself in the media regularly over the past year as a good Christian who uses the Bible to make all of her important life decisions. As evidenced by her behavior in this tape, she is the worst kind of hypocrite. I couldn't allow the release of her book—in which she portrays herself as a 'warrior for Christ'—to pass without exposing her true character."

An unidentified source confirms that Billette and Bourgeois dated casually while she was preparing for the Miss United States pageant.

Bourgeois did not return calls requesting for comment.

Since the Miss United States pageant, Bourgeois has made a name for herself as a speaker at conservative events and rallies against same-sex marriage. She signed a six-figure deal to be the spokesperson for Protect American Marriage (PAM), an organization involved in fighting the legalization of same-sex marriage.

Peggy MacGillicudy, executive director of PAM, was also unavailable for comment.

The article then went over more of her history, her book, blah blah blah, and closed with:

Miss Louisiana pageant director Devon Sheppard released the following statement through the pageant attorneys:

"While we certainly harbor no ill will against Tara and wish her nothing but the best in her future endeavors, we are horrified at the contents of these and other tapes, which certainly were a breach of the code of conduct she agreed to when she entered the Miss Louisiana pageant. Our attorneys will be pursuing this matter further."

At press time, Trinity Press had also not released a statement.

"Hmm," I said to myself. "If she made those tapes while she was still Miss Louisiana, or even before, she can kiss her lawsuit good-bye."

I wonder what Papa Bradley thinks of her now, I thought, scrolling through the comments on the piece. While there was a supportive one every now and then, the vast majority mocked her—and some were quite nasty. The delighted grin on my face started to fade as I continued reading the comments.

> *Where does it say it's okay to make a sex tape in the Bible? She's nothing but a hypocritical whore.*

> *Stupid bitch is getting what she deserves.*

> *Maybe she sees herself as a modern day Mary Magdalene? Wait, Mary repented of being a whore…*

Finally I got so nauseous over the tone of the comments I closed the page.

Why do people have to be so nasty? I asked myself as I refilled my coffee cup. *Isn't it enough that her true nature has been exposed? Her hypocrisy? She must be so humiliated—and now no one's going to buy her stupid book. Maybe she is getting what she deserved, but how shitty she must feel this morning.*

I sipped my coffee. Mom was going to be absolutely delighted to hear about this—and the PAM rally was now pretty discredited, especially since Tara was the headlining speaker.

But that reminded me of what Enid had said to Frank at Papa Bradley's. In spite of myself, I couldn't help but smile. "Poor girl," I said, mocking her voice. "The gays were picking on her!" I laughed. "I wonder how she's going to blame the sex tape on the gays?"

I took a deep breath. I wasn't as angry I'd been, but something had to be done about what Enid had said. Much as I didn't want to deal with her, I was going to have to.

At the very least she needed to apologize to Frank.

I was jarred out of my thoughts by a knock on the front door. Assuming it was either Millie or Velma, I walked down the hall and opened it.

I certainly wasn't expecting to see my cousin Jared.

"Jared?" My jaw dropped. "What are *you* doing here?"

His hair was soaked, and he was holding an umbrella in his left hand. He was shivering, and as he pushed past me a cold wind blasted through the door. "I need your help," he said briskly.

"Well, come on in." I said sarcastically. "There's coffee in the kitchen." I walked over to the thermostat and turned on the heat.

He stalked down the hall while I ducked into the bedroom. Frank moaned and shifted in his sleep while I grabbed a towel for Jared. *What the hell does he want?* I wondered as I tucked the blankets back around Frank's head. His eyes opened for a moment before shutting again. He rolled over onto his stomach and settled back to sleep. *And how did he get in without buzzing?*

Jared was sprawled on the couch, his legs spread wide. A cup of steaming coffee was on the table in front of him. He was wearing a pair of khaki trousers and a tight black sweater. He'd tossed his olive trench coat over one of the wingback chairs, where it was dripping onto the floor. I bit my lip, irritated. I tossed him the towel. "Make yourself at home," I snapped. He'd never set foot in my apartment before. *That*, I realized, *is part of the reason I don't like him—the way he just automatically assumes everyone else is here to serve him.*

He rubbed the towel over his head. "Thanks," he mumbled. "Nice place you've got here."

"I know," I said. He tossed the towel to me, and I pointedly used it to mop up the water from his raincoat. I picked the coat up and hung it up on a coat tree, putting the towel underneath it to keep another puddle from forming.

"So, you need my help." I kept my voice neutral as I took a seat in the dry wingback chair and crossed my legs, adding to myself, *and how galling that must be for you.*

"Yeah, this is a nice place," He ignored what I said, looking around appreciatively. "Much nicer than mine. But you gays are good at the decorating thing."

I felt my face get hot but bit my lip and didn't answer. I wasn't about to let him get under my skin.

We weren't kids anymore.

A ghost of a smile crept over his face. "That was offensive, wasn't it? I'm sorry." He shook his head. "I always put my foot in my mouth. I really don't mean to be offensive, Scotty. I'm sorry." He gave me an earnest look, like butter wouldn't melt in his mouth.

That look had helped him get away with almost anything when we were kids.

I took a deep breath, closing my eyes. "Why are you here, Jared?"

"Look, I want you to know I'm sorry about last night," he said in a rush. "I wasn't thinking when I brought Tara to Papa's. I'm not too bright sometimes, if you haven't noticed."

Trust me, I have.

"I mean, I'm not going to lie—I think what you and Frank do in the bedroom is kind of gross, but it's your business, okay?

If that's what y'all want to do, it's none of my business and more power to you."

He's apologizing, I realized with a start. *It's back-asswards, but he's apologizing.* "Okay." I sipped my coffee. "Apology accepted."

"So you guys shouldn't hold it against Papa and MiMi," he went on. "They didn't know I was bringing her—they didn't know I was seeing her. I told them I was bringing a date, and it never occurred to me you'd get mad." He rolled his eyes. "Well, how pissed Aunt Cecile would get."

I couldn't decide if he was stupid or just insensitive—and which option was actually worse.

"I didn't know Aunt Cecile had such a mean right hook." He grinned. "Man, I'm glad she didn't take a swing at me."

"Well, if she'd raised you you'd have known," I replied, unable to stop myself from grinning back.

"I've always envied you your mom, you know."

In spite of myself, I felt a moment of sympathy. The "revolving door of stepmothers," as Mom called it, couldn't have been easy for him.

"That's partly why I'm here." He stood up and walked over to where I'd hung his coat. He reached into the pocket of his trench coat and put something wrapped in a plastic grocery bag from Rouse's on my coffee table.

I inhaled. I could tell it was a gun—and the handle was sticking out of the bag. Across the bottom of it I could see the initials CDB carved into it.

CDB.

Cecile Diderot Bradley.

"Where did you get that?" I said sharply. "What are you doing with Mom's gun?"

"That's why I need your help, Scotty." He leaned forward. "I got it out of Tara's apartment. She's dead."

What? I stared at him in disbelief. *What is wrong with him? No one could possibly be that stupid, could they?* I struggled to hold on to my temper. "Wouldn't it have made more sense to have *started* with that information? Christ on the cross, Jared!"

He licked his lips. "I'm sorry, don't get mad. I've never had to deal with this kind of thing before, Scotty—I'm not like you, you know. I don't know what to do—that's why I came here."

It would have been annoying if it weren't true. "Start at the beginning." My voice was shaking. I couldn't take my eyes off Mom's gun. "And don't leave anything out."

"Well, after your mom decked her, obviously Tara didn't want to stay." He leaned back on the sofa and closed his eyes. "Once her nose stopped bleeding and she stopped crying, I took her home. She lives in Poydras Tower."

"Ugh," I said involuntarily, making a face. Poydras Tower was a condo/apartment high-rise built after Hurricane Katrina in the Central Business District, a few blocks down from the Superdome. It was hideously ugly—most New Orleanians thought it an unsightly architectural monstrosity. There had been a long, nasty battle over building it.

He ignored me. "So, we go up to her apartment and she's sniffling all the way up, you know? It was really getting on my nerves. I mean, it's not like she hasn't gotten hit in the face with eggs before, and it was just a bloody nose, for God's sake. So, in the elevator I told her to suck it up, and she got mad at *me*." He looked at me for confirmation that she'd behaved unreasonably.

He truly was a Neanderthal.

Unable to speak, I just nodded and he took that for agreement. "She starts yelling at me in the elevator, and so I start yelling back. By the time we get out of the elevator, we're really screaming at each other. All her neighbors had to hear us." He ran his fingers through his hair. "We finally get into her apartment, and she tells me she wants me to go home. I tell her fine, but my electric razor's in her bathroom, I want to get that, then I'll go, okay? So she lets me in, I go get my razor and get the fuck out of there. As far as I'm concerned, she can go to hell, right?"

"What the hell is *he* doing here?"

I hadn't heard Frank get out of bed or come down the hall. I started and stared. He was standing in the hallway, wearing just a pair of very revealing red bikini briefs. His hands were at his sides, clenched into fists. Veins were popping out in his arms, and the one on his forehead was also throbbing—which was never a good sign.

I smothered a laugh. Even though he's in his late forties, Frank still gets what we call "morning wood."

"Dude, put some clothes on!" Jared said, looking away quickly.

"Yes, Frank, why don't you put on some clothes," I echoed, raising my eyebrows. "Jared needs *our* help."

Frank made a noise that sounded suspiciously like a hiss and walked back to the bedroom. The underwear was riding up in the back, giving us both a nice shot of his right cheek.

"Do you want some more coffee?" I asked, getting up and grabbing my cup. "Might as well wait until he gets back so you don't have to tell it twice."

"Yeah," Jared muttered, his face a bright red.

"Oh, for God's sake," I snapped. "You're a fucking football player, Jared—you can't tell me you haven't seen other guys naked before—or do you not change and shower in the locker room?"

"Well, yeah, but—" He couldn't look me in the eyes.

I grabbed his mug and stormed into the kitchen. I took a few cleansing breaths. *He's so fucking infuriating*, I thought. I was adding sweetener to mine when Frank came up behind me, putting his arms around me and rubbing the stubble on his chin against the back of my neck. It sounds annoying, but I kind of like it.

"What is the asshole doing here?" he whispered before closing his teeth on my earlobe and giving it a playful nip.

"I'm not entirely sure," I replied, reluctantly pushing him away. "He showed up saying he needs our help, and he's got Mom's Glock somehow. He and Tara had a fight last night at her place—apparently she's dead and Mom's gun was there."

"What?"

"That's as far as he got when you walked in." I grinned at him. "Your, um, morning excitement made him a little uncomfortable."

"Good." He reached over me and got a big mug down. I stepped aside so he could fill it. "I don't know why you let him in the house—especially after last night."

"I'm glad I did," I replied. "We need to find out what's going on, and how Mom's gun got to Tara's apartment."

"Do you believe anything he says?"

I rolled my eyes and carried the two full mugs back into the living room, handing one to Jared, who mumbled thanks as I sat back down in my chair. Frank plopped down on the opposite end of the sofa from Jared.

"So, you had a fight with Tara last night," I prompted.

"Yeah," Jared said glumly, pointedly not looking at Frank. "And I went back to my place, right? I thought about hitting some bars or something—you know, *fuck* her for being such an unreasonable bitch, right—but I just went home and went to bed. When I got up this morning, I checked my e-mail and, well, I saw about the sex tape."

"Sex tape?" Frank's eyebrows went up.

"A sex tape of Tara's surfaced—it was all over the news this morning," I answered. "Go on."

"So, you know, I got kind of pissed." Jared looked at me. "You know, she's playing this whole 'I wanna wait till I get married' virgin shit in public all this time—I mean, I knew that was all bullshit"—he gave me a leer that made me want to throw up—"but you know, I took her to meet my family, and she's out making sex tapes? I wanted some answers, and damn it, I was going to get some, you know? So I went over there and let myself in with my key and there she was." He gulped. "Lying on the floor in the living room, blood everywhere. Someone shot her dead. And the gun was just lying there. I could see the initials on the handle." He gestured toward the gun. "And I thought, holy shit, Aunt Cecile came over here and killed her! So, I went in the kitchen and got a grocery bag and picked up the gun with it and hauled ass over here."

"Did you call the police?" Frank said in the dangerously quiet voice that I knew meant he was about to explode.

"Why would I do that?" Jared looked at him like Frank was insane. "Sure, I know the neighbors had to hear us yelling at each other last night, and I mean, there was Aunt Cecile's gun, and I figured the police might think, you know, that I did it, so I got the hell out of there."

"Okay, let's see what we have so far." Frank closed his eyes. "Tampering with evidence, contaminating a crime scene, hindering a criminal investigation—am I forgetting anything, Scotty?"

"Not reporting a crime," I added.

"Yes, thanks—I forgot that one." Frank turned his head to stare at Jared. "Those are the crimes you just confessed to us, Jared. Even if they don't charge you with murder, you can go to jail for any or all of those. I mean, *what* were you thinking?"

"You got to help me." Jared's eyes went from Frank to me. "That's why I came here."

I got up before Frank could say anything else. "Okay, I'll call Storm."

CHAPTER FOUR
THE MAGICIAN, REVERSED
The use of power for destructive ends

"You don't think Mom—" Frank whispered, looking down into his mug of coffee.

"I can't believe you can even ask that," I snapped, glancing around to make sure no one could overhear us.

Frank and I were in the coffee shop on the first floor of our building, Café Levee. Other than a young girl frowning at her laptop a few tables away and the dreadlocked girl with the nose ring behind the counter, we were the only people in the place.

As soon as Storm had arrived, he'd told us to make ourselves scarce. Rightly, Storm wanted us gone when he conferred with Jared. Besides, if the district attorney decided to press any charges against Jared—including murder—we were already on the hook as accessories after the fact since we hadn't called the police.

Jared was such an *unbelievable* dumbass.

Granted, he didn't have as much experience with stumbling over dead bodies as Frank and I did, nor was he a criminal attorney, like Storm. But had he never watched *any* movies or television shows about crime? What kind of *idiot* do you have to be to find a body, leave without calling the police, AND take the murder weapon with you?

I've stumbled over more than my fair share of bodies in my life, and it's never a pleasant experience. But not once—*not once*—had it ever crossed my mind to touch anything at the crime scene or not call the police or, heaven forbid, not report the body.

But maybe that was unfair. Jared thought he was shielding Mom somehow by taking the gun, so I should probably cut him some slack.

"Maybe he's taken too many hits to the head," Frank said, echoing my thoughts as he spread cream cheese on a toasted bagel. "Surely he wasn't born that stupid."

"He's never been the sharpest knife in the drawer," I replied, sipping my coffee. "He's always had this phobia about getting in trouble, even when we were kids. Why, I don't know." I stirred my coffee vigorously. "He was always the favored grandchild on that side of the family. He couldn't do any wrong as far as Papa Bradley and MiMi are concerned." I sighed. "I mean, at least with Uncle Skipper, you figure alcohol has killed most of his brain cells. I don't know what Jared's excuse is." I rolled my eyes. "Skipper. What man in his sixties still goes by Skipper?"

Frank laughed. "It's something straight out of Tennessee Williams."

"At least Papa Bradley doesn't make us call him Big Daddy and MiMi Big Mama." I grinned back at him. "Skipper's real name is Elwyn—so I guess you can't blame him for going by Skipper."

"Elwyn? Yikes." Frank made a face. "Why did they name him that?"

I laughed. "It's a family name. It's Papa's middle name, actually." I shuddered. "Makes Milton Bradley sound good, doesn't it?"

"Or Franklin Stanislaus Sobieski." Frank laughed, but got serious. "But what I really want to know is how Mom's gun got in Tara's apartment."

"Well, anyone could have lifted it—she just keeps it in the junk drawer in the kitchen." I sighed, idly stirring my coffee. "You know what it's like at Mom and Dad's—a revolving door of people all the time. And Mom probably doesn't even know it's gone." I shook my head. "You would think she'd be better about it, given her stance on responsible gun ownership, but there you go."

While Mom defended the Second Amendment right to gun ownership, she also believed in restrictions on ownership ("I seriously doubt the Founding Fathers thought everyone had a right to a semiautomatic"). She also didn't think it was out of line to hold gun owners responsible for the use of their guns in criminal activities. She was an excellent shot but had never kept a gun in the house until Papa Diderot gave her a Glock after the levee failure to protect us all from looters and criminals.

"What time did we leave there last night anyway?" Frank scratched his head and yawned. "Depending on what time Tara was killed, Mom might have a really strong alibi."

"I have no idea—I was hoping you'd know," I admitted. "I was pretty wasted."

"We both were—that was some serious pot," Frank reminded me. "I don't even remember how we got back home. Obviously, we walked, but after about two in the morning everything's a blank." He shivered as someone opened the front door, letting in a blast of cold air.

"Yeah—wine and pot are a lethal combination." I closed my eyes and tried to remember. The last time I remembered checking the time was around two thirty in the morning. "But if we don't know what time we left, Father Dan will. He doesn't drink."

"He doesn't?" Frank frowned at me. "He was sure drinking a lot of wine last night."

"Yeah, he was, wasn't he? I guess I meant to say he doesn't get drunk. At least I've never seen him drunk." I shook my head. "Maybe. I don't know. Should I call him?"

"Maybe." Frank yawned. "Sorry, my brain is full of cobwebs today."

I sighed. "I guess we need to go talk to Mom, find out

when the last time was she saw her gun—and who's been in the apartment since."

"And who else knew she had the gun. That's the part that gets me the most about this, Scotty." He shivered again. "Whoever killed Tara knows Mom well enough to know she has a gun, and where she keeps it. Someone wanted to frame her."

That thought had occurred to me, too. "I know," I replied, sipping from my coffee. "Someone we know. But who? Who would want to do that to Mom?"

"Mom has made enemies," Frank replied, not meeting my eyes. "She doesn't exactly have a problem with speaking her mind."

"But to frame her?" I shook my head. "No, I don't think so." Mom's activism had undoubtedly pissed off any number of people over the years—polluters, politicians, racists, among others—but I couldn't believe they would kill someone and frame her for it.

Besides, they couldn't have known Tara was going to show up at Papa Bradley's and have an altercation with Mom.

"No, I don't think whoever killed Tara was really trying to frame Mom," I said slowly. "I think the killer just needed a gun… and somehow had access to Mom's…but it definitely has to be someone she knows." I felt a chill.

We looked into each other's eyes. It wasn't that long ago we'd thought—no, *believed*—Colin had murdered my half uncles. We'd believed it for two years, until he finally came back to New Orleans and revealed the truth about that horrible Mardi Gras season to us, having finally gotten clearance from Angela to be honest with us. It had torn us both apart emotionally—followed a mere six months later by the levee failure, it had been a one-two punch I'd had doubts we'd survive.

"It's almost Mardi Gras again," Frank said, examining his fingernails.

"At least this time we know Colin's *not* involved," I replied, putting my hand on top of his. "He's on the other side of the world—and even if he was in town, he wouldn't need Mom's gun." I laughed. "Getting a gun is certainly never a problem for him."

"We don't really know where he is." Frank shrugged. "For all we know, he could walk in the front door any minute."

I was saved from answering by my cell phone, which started vibrating on the table. Storm's face grinned at me from the screen. I clicked "answer," and picked it up. "Hey, Storm," I said.

"I've called Venus, and I'm taking Jared down to the precinct to give a statement," he said, his voice low. "I've got the gun bagged—you didn't touch it, did you?"

"I'm not crazy," I replied, irritated.

"Good." Storm sighed. "Look, I need you to go over to Mom and Dad's—"

"I know what to do," I cut him off. "Find out who could have taken her gun. What time did you and Marguerite leave last night?"

"Right after you and Frank staggered out, about three thirty," he answered promptly. "Mom wasn't exactly in any kind of condition to get over to Poydras Tower and shoot anyone." He laughed. "None of us were. And Father Dan was still there when we left. So if you were worried about Mom, don't be. I wish she hadn't punched Tara last night, but no sense in crying over spilled milk."

I felt my entire body relax with relief. I'd never for one second believed Mom killed Tara—but that wouldn't exactly carry any weight with the police. It was good to know she wouldn't be a suspect.

"I'm hiring you and Frank to help," Storm was saying. "Jared doesn't have an alibi—of course, that would be too easy—but I don't think for a minute he killed Tara Bourgeois." He lowered his voice. "I don't think Jared's been to Mom and Dad's since he was a kid—he couldn't have taken the gun."

"Someone else could have taken the gun and given it to him," I replied. Frank raised his eyebrows.

"Scotty, I know you don't like Jared, but he's our client now, and he's our cousin." Storm's voice was chiding. "*Family*. So he deserves our support, got it? Now, I'll give you a call when we're done at the police station."

"Yeah, sure, whatever." I turned the phone off and gave Frank a brittle smile. "Looks like we have a new client."

Frank shrugged. "I figured that much. But I can't go with you over to Mom's." He glanced at his watch. "I've got practice in Biloxi."

I'd completely forgotten. Under the name "Frank Savage," Frank's a professional wrestler for the Gulf Coast Wrestling Alliance, and he had a title shot coming up on Saturday in Biloxi. "It's okay, I'll handle it. When you get home tonight I'll fill you in." I pulled on my black wool Who Dat cap and stood up, leaning down and kissing his cheek. "Have a good practice. Kick some ass, stud."

I stepped out onto the sidewalk of Decatur Street just in time to almost get knocked down by a cold blast of wind. I shivered and shook my head, grinning. It was one of the coldest Januarys I could remember—everyone was joking that hell had frozen over since the Saints were in the Super Bowl. I ducked my head against the wind and started walking.

Saints mania had swept over the city since the season had started way back in September. As I walked, everywhere I looked I could see Saints flags hanging from balconies. WHO DAT or SUPER BOWL BOUND or SUPER SAINTS or GEAUX SAINTS was written in black grease pencil on every available glass surface as far as the eye could see. Parked cars had Saints flags on their roofs, snapping in the wind. The city still seemed a little subdued from the game Sunday night—kind of like everyone was on day two of a massive hangover. Just thinking about it gave me a little lift in my spirits. I started walking faster. It was really cold.

I unlocked the gate and climbed the back stairs to Mom and Dad's apartment. It wasn't quite noon yet, so they might not be awake. I unlocked the back door and stepped into their kitchen. Coffee was brewing, and the heat was on. The warmth felt great. "Mom? Dad?" I called, slipping off my jacket and draping it over a chair.

Mom stepped into the kitchen. She was wearing a pair of black sweatpants and a gold Saints sweatshirt. "Scotty! What are you doing here?" She threw her arms around me. "This is a pleasant surprise!"

I hugged her back and kissed the top of her head. "Business, I'm afraid." I tossed my wool cap onto the table. "Is Dad up?"

"He's in the shower." She poured us both a cup of coffee. "Business? What do you mean? What's happened?" She looked into my eyes. "You're not in trouble again, are you?"

"Not me—Jared." I held the steaming mug in both hands, appreciating the heat.

"Jared?" She shook her head. "What has he done?"

"Better wait for Dad—no sense in having to explain twice."

She cocked her head to one side. "I don't know if I like the sound of that." I followed her into the living room, where she curled up in a reclining chair. She picked up a remote control and clicked the big-screen TV on.

"...has been positively identified as Marina Werner, daughter of Dick Werner, pastor of Dove Ministry of Truth, the megachurch in Kenner best known for its anti-gay stance. The police report that Ms. Werner, who worked as the treasurer for Dove Ministry and was also helping organize this weekend's Protect Marriage rally, was shot in her apartment yesterday morning between nine a.m. and noon. Kenner Police spokesman Jack Fournier states they are following up several leads, and have set up a hotline for anyone to call if they have any information."

"That's terrible," Mom said, a grim look on her face as she changed the channel. "You know, I don't believe anyone should be killed because of what they believe, but I'm not sorry that woman is dead. You reap what you sow, as her Bible says."

"Mom!" I said, my mind reeling. Tara's murdered, and now this woman?

"What? She was a homophobic bitch helping spread hate," Mom replied. "It always amazes me how so-called Christians have absolutely no clue what their religion is about. Have they never read the Sermon on the Mount? They almost make me *want* to believe in their stupid religion—because it's so comforting to think they're all going to burn in hell for eternity."

"And those megachurches are the worst," Dad said from behind me. He rubbed the top of my head. "Bilking people out of their money and promising salvation in return. What are you doing here so early, son?"

I tried not to smile. Mom and Dad firmly believed no one should get up before noon. It was actually rather surprising they were up so early. I took a deep breath. Might as well get right to it. "Mom, when was the last time you saw your gun?"

"The Glock?" Mom looked completely bewildered. She looked at Dad, who was equally puzzled. "We went to the shooting range Sunday afternoon, right? Before the playoff party—we were too tense and needed to blow off steam." She laughed. "It's amazing how much pretending you're shooting Brett Favre can improve your aim."

"It really does, son," Dad added.

"I'll have to remember that the next time I go shooting," I said, unable to stop myself from smiling. I was also unable to resist asking, "Are you going to pretend you're shooting Peyton Manning the day of the Super Bowl?"

"Of course not!" Mom looked appalled. "Peyton's from *New Orleans*!"

"What was I thinking?" I rolled my eyes. "So that was the last time you saw the Glock?"

"Why are you asking about my gun?" Mom got up and

walked into the kitchen. She opened the junk drawer and pulled out her gun case. She frowned. "That's weird—it feels light," she said as she opened it.

Her jaw dropped and she turned, holding the little case open.

It was empty.

She swallowed. "I—I don't understand. Where is it? I remember distinctly putting it back in the case at the range, and putting it back in the chest when we got home Sunday. Didn't I, John?"

Dad nodded. "I distinctly remember you putting it back when we got home."

"Someone stole my gun. I can't believe it." She sank back down into her chair. "Scotty, what's going on? How did you know my gun was gone?"

I filled them both in on Jared's visit earlier that morning. Their eyes got wider and their faces whiter as I talked. Finally, I finished. "How late was Father Dan here?"

Mom looked at Dad, who said, "Father Dan was the last to leave—around seven, wasn't it?"

Mom nodded. "The sun was up, I remember when he went out the back door. After you kids left, we started planning the protest."

I wasn't even aware I'd been holding my breath. "Well, Jared says he got to her place around eight this morning, so that should put you both in the clear." I grinned. "And what better alibi witness than a priest?"

"That doesn't change the fact that my gun killed someone," Mom replied, rubbing her forehead. "I feel responsible."

"You're not responsible, Mom," I said as Dad sat on the arm of her chair and put his arm around her.

"Yes, I am!" she snapped. "I have *always* believed gun ownership is a responsibility." She shook her head. "I've been meaning to replace the lock on the chest and just never got

around to it. If I had, that horrible woman would still be alive."
She paused. "At least it was someone like her and not a kid or
something."

I'd opened my mouth to tell her to stop beating herself
up about it, but the words died in my throat. "Mom—until the
killer's behind bars, it's probably not a good idea to act glad
Tara's dead."

"I'm not going to pretend I'm sorry, any more than I'll
pretend to be sorry that awful Marina Werner is dead." She set
her jaw. "That would be hypocritical."

"Marina Werner's dead?" Dad asked.

I nodded. "It was just on the news. Someone killed her
yesterday morning."

"Not a good time to be a hypocritical Bible-thumping
homophobic bigot," Mom remarked. "I'd be worried if I were
Peggy MacGillicudy."

"Maybe they're connected," Dad mused. "It makes sense,
doesn't it? Marina was one of the organizers of the rally, and Tara
was the main speaker. And they're both killed in a short period
of time."

"So, who at the party on Sunday night would have wanted
them both dead?" Mom scratched her head. "Besides you and I,
John?"

"Father Dan—but I just can't see Dan killing anyone, can
you?"

"No, I can't. I suppose any of the gays and lesbians would
have a motive—"

"Okay, enough—granted, it's all interesting—we're getting
off track here. We don't know for a fact the two murders are
connected." I steered the conversation back to the gun. "What we
need to do is figure out who could have taken the gun between
when you got back from the shooting range Sunday afternoon
and eleven p.m. last night," I said, shaking my head a little bit.
"Obviously, everyone who was at the party Sunday night could

have taken it." I walked into the kitchen and got the small spiral notebook Mom used to make grocery lists.

I flipped it open and wrote down our names and Frank's. "We're going to need to give the police a list anyway, so we might as well be ahead of the game," I explained as I kept writing names: *Father Dan, Dominique DuPre, Emily Hunter, Lurleen Rutledge, David Williams, Jesse Santana,* and stopped. I closed my eyes, remembering.

There had been other people here that night—people I hadn't really known.

I tossed the notebook and pen to my parents. "Those are the only people here I knew."

None of whom, I added to myself, *had any connection whatsoever to Tara Bourgeois.*

At least none that I know of at the moment, I added.

Mom scribbled down some names. "That's everyone who was here Sunday night."

"Who was here in the apartment yesterday?"

"Just us," Dad replied. "Until after the dinner party."

"Where I punched Tara Bourgeois in the nose," Mom went on. She moaned. "Thank the universe we invited everyone over last night! After that—and it was my gun—" She closed her eyes and shuddered.

"It would look pretty bad, Mom—that's what I've been saying." I commiserated, glad the seriousness was finally sinking it. "If Jared hadn't gone back over there this morning—"

"My goose would have been cooked." Mom shuddered again. "Time of death isn't an exact science…there's always a window."

"What?" I glanced at her. "How do you know that?"

"*Forensics for Dummies*," she replied with a shrug. "I ordered a copy from Garden District Books after"—she hesitated—"after the mess with Colin at Mardi Gras."

"*Forensics for Dummies*," I repeated, trying not to smile.

Dad tossed me the notebook back. I looked at the list of names Mom had written down. *Mike Mueller. Gary Musson. Ken Taylor. Gia Romano. Jamie Oliver. Cara White.* "I don't know any of these people," I said.

"Mike, Gary, and Gia are in Emily's band," Mom said helpfully. "Mike's lead guitar, Gia's bass, and Gary is the drummer. Ken is Gary's boyfriend. Jamie's a student at UNO we were hoping would hit it off with Emily."

"So, Jamie's a girl." I made a mental note. "And who's Cara White?"

"Lurleen's assistant." Dad replied. "We didn't know Lurleen was bringing her, but we didn't mind. She's a nice girl."

I closed my eyes and tried to put names with the faces. Ken and Gary were easy—they'd kissed every time the Saints scored. Cara was obviously the quiet young woman who'd stuck close to Lurleen all night.

Unfortunately, I'd been tense all afternoon like everyone else in New Orleans, so Frank and I had started smoking pot around two. We'd been totally stoned out of our minds by the time we got to Mom and Dad's.

Note to self: stop smoking so much pot.

I sighed and made a copy of the list, tearing it off and sticking it my pocket. "Who would have had the chance to take the gun?"

Mom and Dad looked at each other. "Anyone could have, really," Mom said with a helpless shrug. "Everyone's eyes were glued to the television. I wasn't really paying any attention to what anyone else was doing."

"And when Hartley made the field goal the whole place went crazy, remember?" Dad went on. "We were all screaming and yelling and hugging and jumping up and down. Some people ran out onto the balcony—"

"Frank and I ran down the back stairs and danced in the

street," I said, an involuntary smile creeping across my face. "It was chaos—and we left the gate open."

"We were all out on the balcony," Dad remembered. "For at least an hour after the game. We were all out screaming and yelling and cheering."

"And anyone could have gone back inside and taken the gun." I closed my eyes, picturing the chaos in the Quarter that night, the joy and exhilaration.

How could someone have thought to steal Mom's gun in the midst of all that emotion? The whole city had been celebrating. The streets of the Quarter were more crowded that night than they had been on any Fat Tuesday I could remember.

It didn't make sense to me—but I'd been caught up in the emotion of the moment.

Frank and I had even danced on the hood of a police car at some point during the celebration—a celebration that had lasted until the sun came up.

It had been chaos—and not just in the Quarter. The whole city had partied all night long, every neighborhood. At some point, Frank and I had been in a second line weaving through the mobs of people on Bourbon Street. Horns had blared, bands had played, strangers hugged and kissed.

I couldn't even begin to remember all the people I'd kissed.

The whole night still didn't seem real.

But someone hadn't cared about the Saints going to the Super Bowl as much as they had about getting Mom's gun.

"Someone came here that night intending to take the gun and use it." I opened my eyes, focusing on my parents. "It's the only thing that makes sense."

"Someone at our party," Mom said after a moment, her voice grim, "is a murderer."

Chapter Five

The Hierophant

The need for acceptance by one's peer group

I took the inside staircase from Mom and Dad's down to their combination coffee/tobacco shop, the Devil's Weed.

When I was a little kid, I used to love the inside staircase. The door to it was in the hallway of the apartment leading back to the bedrooms, and looked like a closet door. At the foot of the staircase was a door leading into the storage room of the shop—but there wasn't a knob or anything on the storage-room side. In fact, looking at the wall you wouldn't know there was a door there at all. There was a wall sconce directly just to the left. If you turned the sconce to the right the door popped open. Mom and Dad loved it because if someone ever broke into the shop they wouldn't know how to get upstairs—but they always locked the upstairs door anyway. I loved it because it was like a secret passageway in a creepy old black-and-white movie from the 1930s. Nothing gave me greater delight than to climb up on a chair in the store room and turn the sconce.

Now I hardly ever used it—I always took the back stairs.

I turned the knob on the door and pushed it open. The storeroom's lights weren't on, but there was plenty of light coming in from the open door to the store. I could hear the espresso machine running—Emily must have a customer.

My phone started ringing—my ringtone was Lady Gaga's "Telephone"—and I looked at the screen. A thrill rushed through my body. I clicked the red answer button on the screen. "Colin!"

"Hey, baby." His deep voice purred through the phone. "You'll never guess where I am."

"Beirut?"

He laughed. "I don't even want to know why you said that. No, I'm in a cab and we just passed the Metairie Road exit. I should be home in about ten or fifteen minutes."

My knees went weak, and I leaned against the wall. I couldn't believe my ears. "You're *home*?"

"Why do you sound so surprised? Angela said she'd e-mailed you."

That bitch, I thought. "All her e-mail said was 'contact made,'" I replied, trying not to let my anger at her creep into my voice. "She didn't say anything about you coming home."

"Don't get mad at her," he replied with a laugh. "To her, that means I'm on my way home. She forgets you don't know her code words."

I took a deep cleansing breath and let the irritation go. Once I was centered again, I couldn't help but laugh myself. "Are you sure you're not the psychic around here? It's like you read my mind."

"I just know my Scotty." His voice was low and seductive, sending a chill of desire through my body. He'd been gone for months. "I can't wait to get home. Man, I need me some hot lovin' from my boys."

"Frank's on his way to Biloxi—he has practice." I couldn't keep the pride out of my voice. "I'm glad you're back—he's got a title shot this Saturday."

Colin whistled. "Cool! I knew he'd do well with that promotion! So, he's a big star now?"

"Denny"—Denny Whistler owned Gulf Coast Professional Wrestling, the promotion Frank wrestled for—"says Frank gets more fan mail than any two other guys in the show combined, which is amazing—especially for a bad guy."

"Bad guys are more fun—and I'm sure it doesn't hurt that

he has the best body in the show," Colin observed. He let out a sigh. "But it's a bummer he's not home. I sure hope you're up for some fun this afternoon."

I thought about it for a moment. Depending on traffic, he was anywhere from about ten to twenty minutes from home. I could interview Emily quickly, and possibly get back to the apartment around the same time he got there. "Well, I'm not home right now—I'm on a case, actually. I have to interview a potential witness, but I should be back to the apartment around the same time you do if I hurry."

"A case?" That got his attention, which was typical. Colin loved his work. "What's the case?"

"I don't want to get into it right now," I replied, glancing out the door into the store. Emily was ringing up the espresso drink I'd heard her making, talking to a guy in a full-length trench coat with a gold wool Saints cap on his head. I added in a whisper, "The longer I spend talking to you, the longer it is before I get back to the apartment."

"Okay, then, back to work," Colin said cheerfully before whispering into my ear some of the things he was going to do to me when we were both home.

"See you in a bit," I breathed into the phone, clicking the call off. I leaned against the door frame and took a few deep breaths.

Damn, he could really get me going.

Emily Hunter was in her late twenties with dark hair shaved down to a military-length buzz cut. I'd never seen her hair any longer than that—she was meticulous about keeping it short. She had a round face and lovely oval green eyes. Emily always exuded positive energy—she was one of the most upbeat people I'd ever had the privilege to know. She'd come to New Orleans for Mardi Gras seven years earlier and stayed. She'd gotten a master's degree by the time she was twenty-one, and had spent a year in Mexico City teaching English at an incredibly expensive private girls' school. "I felt trapped, though," she explained to me once, "and it just seemed so wrong—all those spoiled girls at the school and all the poverty just outside the front gates—it was so unfair, and wrong, so I decided to save as much money as I could and do all the things I'd always wanted to do." Mom and Dad had practically adopted her, and she'd been working at the Devil's Weed for years. She had an amazing singing voice, but I hadn't had a chance to see her perform with her new band, Huck Finn. She loved to sing, and frankly had a better voice than most music industry superstars—but she had no ambitions to use her voice to attain fame and stardom. She sang because she enjoyed it. "And if I ever stop enjoying it, I'll stop doing it," she told me once.

"Scotty? You okay?"

I looked up and smiled at Emily, who was standing in the storeroom door. "Yeah, just give me a second. I was just talking to Colin—he's on his way home."

She gave me a knowing smile. "I can imagine. You want some coffee?"

I nodded, following her back into the store. "I also need to talk to you about something, if you've got a few minutes."

Emily filled a large cup from one of the large thermoses behind the counter, added some half-and-half and a package of Sweet'n Low before stirring it and handing the hot cup to me. I took a sip and let the heat radiate through my body. "You know exactly how I like it." I beamed at her. "Perfect."

"I've been making you coffee for going on seven years now," she replied with a wink. "I'd have to be an idiot to not know how you like it. And all appearances to the contrary, I am not an idiot."

She gave me her big grin. "What do you want to talk to me about?"

"The party Sunday night." I leaned against the counter.

Her face got dreamy. "Wasn't that *awesome*? I still can't believe we're in the Super Bowl." She shook her head. "It's so weird—I grew up in Chicago, but I never cared about football till I moved here. I still don't care about football outside of the Saints, though." She laughed. "I didn't get home until eight o'clock Monday morning, I just didn't want the night to ever end. Did you?"

I smiled. "No. Sometimes I still can't believe we're in the Super Bowl." I hesitated, trying to figure out the most diplomatic way of asking the next question. *Fuck it, it's Emily, just go ahead and ask, she's practically family.* "You didn't happen to notice if anyone went into Mom's junk drawer Sunday night, did you?"

She frowned. "The one in the corner? Why?" Her eyes got wide. "Oh, no, is something missing?"

I did a double take. "Mom's gun is missing—and it's not like it was a big secret she kept it there."

She scratched her head. "I don't remember seeing anyone in that corner, but it's possible, I suppose." She frowned. "And after the kick, everyone went nuts and it was just crazy—everything's really a blur after that. Someone could have taken it then, I guess. Why? Has something happened?"

She'd find out soon enough, so I didn't have a problem with telling her. "Someone killed Tara Bourgeois last night."

"Tara Bourgeois?" She made a face. "That homophobic bitch?" Her jaw tightened. "I'm not surprised—only that it took this long." She narrowed her eyes. "But what does Mom's gun have to do with—oh." Realization dawned on her face.

I sighed. "My cousin Jared was dating her, and he found her. Mom's gun was there."

"But how is that even possible?" she whispered. She looked confused, and her face had gone pale.

"Someone must have taken the gun during the party Sunday night, or sometime yesterday—but no one was in the apartment yesterday until late last night."

She nodded. "So, it stands to reason someone took the gun during the game."

"Did your band mates know about the gun?"

"You don't think—"

"Everyone at the party Sunday night has to be checked out, Em."

"I suppose you're right, but I can't imagine—" She gnawed on her lower lip. "I don't even want to think someone in Huck Finn is a killer. I mean, they're a great group, Scotty."

"How well do you really know them? You've only been in Huck Finn a few months, right?"

She sighed. "Yeah. I met Ken first—Ken Taylor," she added as I started scribbling notes. "Ken's not in Huck Finn, he's Gary's— Gary Musson's boyfriend, and he does a lot of our publicity for us. He works for a P.R. firm in the CBD. Destry asked me to sing with him one Saturday night and Ken was here." Destry was a longtime friend of the family. He taught music at NOCCA, and every Saturday night he sat in the Devil's Weed and played his guitar for tips. "After we were done, he told me he knew a band that needed a new lead singer, would I be interested? I thought why not? I've never been in a band—it'd be something new. And you know I'm all about new experiences, right? He set up an audition for me, and after I sang a few songs with them they hired me." She grinned. "Ken and Gary live over on Dauphine Street, Mike and Gia share a place in the Marigny." She grabbed her cell phone from her bag, stored under the counter, and read off their cell phone numbers, which I dutifully wrote down.

"What else can you tell me about them?"

"Gary's the afternoon bartender at the Saint, over on Magazine Street. Mike's a personal trainer at some gym on St. Charles Avenue, and Gia works at a tanning place." Emily shrugged. "Mike's originally from Alabama, I think, but Gia, Gary, and Ken are all from New Orleans, I think. Ken and Gary—they've been a couple for about five years, I think. Gia and Mike live together but they're just friends. I think Gia's bi but don't know for sure. Mike—I don't know about Mike. I think he's gay, but I've never seen him with anyone, male or female. I probably am just stereotyping because he's a trainer. He's in a good shape, takes care of himself, always dresses well. He might just be a—what's the word? Metrosexual?" She shuddered. "I hate that word."

I wasn't fond of it myself. "Do you know if any of them have a connection to Tara Bourgeois?"

Emily poured herself a cup of hot water and dropped a green tea bag into it as she pondered her answer. "No one ever mentioned her, no." She sipped the tea and let out a sigh of relief. "But we really don't talk about anything serious, you know? It's all about the music—at least for me."

"Did you know any of the other people at the party? Besides family, I mean."

"Well, Cara—Cara White, she comes in all the time," Emily mused. "Her boss, Lurleen, comes in every once in a while but she isn't very friendly. Cara's nice." She smiled. "She sometimes gives me a ride to Whole Foods when she's going, or picks stuff up for me if I can't go with her. And Dominique I know—we played at Domino's a couple of weekends ago. And Jesse? Was that his name? He came with Dominique. He's a bartender at Domino's. I don't know if they're a couple, but he flirted with me a lot when we were performing there. And of course I knew Father Dan. And David. But there was another girl—"

"Jamie Oliver." I supplied the name from my list.

"I'd never met her before. She was strange."

I didn't remember her at all, which was annoying. I made another mental note to stop smoking so much pot. "How do you mean, strange?"

"She kept to herself most of the night." Emily closed her eyes, remembering. "She didn't really seem into the game at all. I kept wondering why she was even there. She didn't really talk much to anyone, or drink much. She certainly didn't smoke any pot, at least none that I saw. So why was she there?" She snapped her fingers. "There you go. There's your person who wasn't into the game."

I smothered a smile. *She was there because Mom is trying to find you a girlfriend*, I thought but didn't say out loud. Instead I just shrugged and made a note next to Jamie's name: *Wasn't into the game*.

Just because Mom was playing matchmaker by inviting her didn't clear her of taking the gun.

Aloud I said, "I've long given up on trying to figure out why Mom and Dad invite people over."

"They do like to collect strays," Emily sipped her tea.

A ringing bell signaled the front door opening, and a young man in a Saints jacket and cap strode toward the counter. Emily looked at me, and I closed my notebook. "If I think of anything else I'll call," I said aloud, but she'd already turned to her customer.

I glanced at my watch. Colin would be at the apartment at any minute, so I walked out the front door. A blast of cold wind chilled me right to the bone immediately. I swore under my breath and started walking faster up Royal Street. Lady Gaga started singing from my coat pocket once I was safely across Dumaine, so I pulled my phone out.

"Hey, Storm."

"I'm on my way over to Tara's apartment," he said. "*You fucking moron, that's why you have a turn signal!* Sorry about that," he added quickly. "Stupid bitch in a white Lexus thinks she's the only person on the road. Anyway, they didn't arrest Jared, but he's riding over with Venus and Blaine, and I'm following. What did Mom say?"

I filled him in on the timeline, trying to walk faster. *Damn, it's cold.* The wind was relentless, and every so often I'd pass a pedestrian going the opposite direction, trying to swerve out of their way to avoid a collision. I had to stop at the St. Philip corner as a line of cars made their way toward Decatur. I debated ducking into the coffee shop on the corner for another cup of coffee—not that I needed more caffeine, but to keep my hands warm.

"And you've got the list of people who were there Sunday night?" Storm said. "Good, good, start tracking them down, talking to them. Do some background checks on them. Get Frank to help—I'll come by your place after I'm done here and we can have a powwow."

"Frank's on his way to Biloxi," I reminded him. "And Colin's back—he just called from the cab—"

"Excellent!" Storm enthused. *"You stupid fucking asshole!* Sorry—what was I saying?"

I switched the phone to my other, non-ringing ear. "I really wish you wouldn't scream at other drivers while you're on the phone with me," I complained. "And you were saying you're glad Colin is here to help me." I could have easily started one of those stupid sibling arguments with him—*Do you think I can't handle a case on my own?*—but I like to think that now that I'm in my early thirties I'm above that sort of thing.

As long as I just think it and don't say it out loud, I figure I'm okay.

"Sorry about the yelling." Storm's tone was sheepish. "And I know what you're thinking. Yes, I think you can handle it on your own without help. I'm just glad Colin is here to help only because you two can split the list and get through it faster, is all. If Frank weren't in Biloxi it would go even faster."

I smothered a grin. Apparently I'm not the only psychic in the family. I started across St. Philip Street. "I'm heading home to meet Colin now—"

"I know he's been gone for a few months, but don't get distracted." Storm ordered. "I'm pretty sure Mom's in the clear for the murder, but it was still her gun and I want to get this all cleared up as soon as possible."

"It's been more than a few months—he's been gone since August," I reminded him, checking both ways.

"Well, your bedroom gymnastics can wait another few hours," he replied. "This is more important."

Easy for you to say, I thought. Aloud I said, "Are you completely convinced Jared didn't do it?" I stepped up onto the curb in time to avoid being mowed down by a United cab.

Storm whistled. "Scotty, I know you and Jared have never gotten along, but given the time frame, there's no way he could have gotten the gun. And besides, during the party, he was kind of playing in the championship game? Against the Vikings?"

"Warming the bench, you mean."

"In front of eighty thousand fans and a television audience of millions."

"Your sarcasm is duly noted, bro," I replied. "Someone could have gotten it for him."

"Why would he need to get Mom's gun, though, Scotty? He has access to Papa Bradley's arsenal, not to mention Uncle Skipper's—and he undoubtedly has guns of his own." Storm clicked his tongue. "But no, Jared's not completely in the clear on this. I wish he had a better alibi than 'I was alone in my apartment all night.' And a word of friendly advice from your older brother, Scotty? Let go of the childhood grudges. I know Jared was a total shit when he was a kid, but we've all grown up since then."

"I'm quite sure I don't know what you mean—I was a really good kid."

He laughed so loud and hard I had to switch my phone to the other ear again. "Please. You were a spoiled little monster—you were just as bad as Jared, if not worse."

"Whatever. Talk to you later." I clicked the phone off and shoved it back into my coat pocket.

But as I hurried down Royal Street, much as I hated to admit it, I knew Storm was probably right. Jared wasn't the same spoiled, annoying child who seemed determined to make my life miserable when we were kids. He had his degree from Southern Mississippi—which was more than I could say—and not only played for the Saints but in the off-season ran a foundation to help underprivileged kids—and there was no shortage of those in New Orleans. He'd always been perfectly pleasant to me on the rare occasions we ran into each other—usually at family gatherings at Papa Bradley's.

But he knows I'm gay and knew Frank and I would both be there last night—and he brought that homophobic bitch anyway. Why would he do that? Could he have really thought it wouldn't bother us?

But he came to you when he needed help.

I bit my lower lip and turned the corner at Barracks. *Get over it, Scotty—he's not only your cousin but he's now your client. He didn't kill Tara. Presumption of innocence—and give him the benefit of the doubt.*

Another blast of wind almost knocked me over when I turned the corner at Decatur. From my coat pocket came the sound of cathedral bells—my notification I had a new text message. I pulled my phone out as I got to the iron gate of my building and grinned as I slid my key in the lock.

I'm home and naked. Where are you?

I laughed out loud and pulled the gate closed behind me. I ran down the narrow passageway to the back courtyard and up the back steps. I was just about to put my key in the lock to our apartment door when the door swung open and I was yanked inside. Colin spun me around and kicked the door shut behind him with his foot, pulling me into an intense bear hug.

He wasn't lying—he was naked and *really* glad to see me.

"I'm so glad you're home," I said an hour later. We were still in bed, but just lying there under the blankets with our bodies entwined. "And in one piece."

He nuzzled my neck. "You have no idea how glad I am to be back. In one piece." He stroked my chest with his right hand. "I think about you and Frank every night I'm away, you know."

I grabbed hold of his hand and brought it to my lips. "We worry about you. We all do."

"I'm sorry," he whispered.

"Don't be—you're part of the family." I laughed. "And pity poor Angela Blackledge if anything ever happens to you. Mom will hunt her down like a rabid dog."

Colin laughed. "She would, too. So, what's this new case?"

I sat up, pushing a pillow behind me to support my back as I explained. Colin's an excellent listener—part of his super-spy training, no doubt—and he didn't interrupt me until I finished.

"Tara Bourgeois, huh?" He ran his fingers through his sweat-dampened curls. "I can't say I'm sorry she's gone. How many people have been gay-bashed because of the hateful things she's said over the last year? She's done a lot of damage in the name of her 'faith.'" His eyes flashed. "It always amazes me how many people claim to be 'Christian' but everything they do or say denies Christ's teaching. I'm a Jew, and I know more about Jesus than she did."

"She was a miserable human being, but my cousin didn't kill her." Reluctantly, I got out of bed. "And I promised Storm I'd get started on talking to the people who were at the party—he told me not to indulge in bedroom gymnastics with you until we'd talked to everyone on the list."

Colin made a guilty face. "Uh-oh. We're bad boys." He rolled off the bed. "We'd better get moving."

CHAPTER SIX
THREE OF CUPS, REVERSED
Pleasure turns to pain

It took me a little less than fifteen minutes to get the addresses and phone numbers of Mom and Dad's football party guest list off the Internet. I cut and pasted them all into a Word document and printed it out. "What do you think, Colin?" I asked. He was looking over my shoulder. "Storm thinks we should split up— that way we can get through the list faster—and we'll be a couple of steps ahead of the cops."

He frowned as he slid his jacket on. "Interrogations are always better with two people," he replied. "One person asks questions, the other observes the reactions of the person being questioned— and it's always a good idea to have another perspective. I might think of questions or pick up on something you miss—and vice versa."

I didn't argue the point with him. For one thing, he's got a hell of a lot more experience interrogating suspects than I do. For another, I hadn't seen him in almost five months and didn't want to let him out of my sight for a while.

Storm could just get over himself.

"Okay then," I said, shutting down the computer. "Domino's is the closest place—and Jesse should be working. We can interview him and Dominique both—she lives on the top floor of the club. Well," I amended, "she used to. I'm not sure if she still does."

"Before the flood?" Colin asked.

I shut and locked the door behind me. I nodded as I started down the stairs, shivering. The temperature must have dropped at least ten degrees since I'd gotten home, and the air was getting heavier. I said, "You can deal with Storm, by the way. I'm not in the mood to listen to his bitching—and not splitting up was your idea."

"Coward. We're ahead of the police anyway," he said as we walked through the gate. A blast of cold wind almost knocked us both sideways. "Fuck me, it's *cold.*" He turned up the collar of his black trench coat and pulled his wool cap down over his ears. He grinned at me. "I always forget how cold it gets here."

I didn't answer as I wrapped my Saints muffler around my face until all that could be seen were my eyes. "It's been colder than usual this winter," I replied. "Everyone's joking that hell's frozen over."

He gave me a puzzled look as we started walking up the sidewalk. "Why?"

"The Saints are in the Super Bowl, dumbass," I replied with a laugh. "Granted, you've been out of the country for a while, but didn't you notice on your way into town from the airport? The flags on all the cars? Every one in jerseys or Who Dat shirts?"

"No—I was kind of tired from my flight and wasn't paying any attention. Seriously?" He shook his head. "The Saints are in the Super Bowl?" he asked, his eyes getting wide. He threw his head back and let out a whoop so loud other pedestrians stopped and stared. He threw his arms around me and picked me up, spinning me around until I was getting dizzy. Finally, when I thought I was going to puke, he set me down. He blew out a breath. "I can't believe I missed the whole damned season. The Saints are *really* in the Super Bowl?"

"I didn't know you were such a big fan," I said, weaving a little as we started walking again.

He just laughed. "I love everything New Orleans, Scotty."

He put his arm around my shoulders. "Was that the point of the party at Papa Bradley's?" He made a face. "Of course it was—it was in Jared's honor, right? And so the party on Sunday night at Mom and Dad's—it was to watch the Saints game?" He whistled. "I can only imagine what it must have been like in the Quarter that night."

"The whole city," I said as we turned up Barracks Street. The buildings sheltered us somewhat from the wind, but it was still cold. "I've never seen anything like it. It was the most exciting game ever, Colin. They're ahead, we're ahead, back and forth all night long—we were all screaming and hollering! It was like being on a roller coaster emotionally, up and down, up and down, and then it went to overtime—and when Garrett Hartley made the field goal that won the game, the whole city literally shook…everyone was jumping up and down and screaming and crying." Just thinking about it made me tear up again. "It was so fucking awesome." I wiped at my eyes. "The party lasted pretty much all night—impromptu second lines, everyone screaming 'who dat' all night—it was like every Mardi Gras rolled into one. Papa Diderot said it was like V-E Day, but bigger." I grinned. "I'd marry Garrett Hartley in a heartbeat. He's the cutest thing."

"Oh, man, I wish I'd been here." Colin sighed. "So who are we playing in the Super Bowl?"

"The Colts." I let out a delighted laugh. "So we really can't lose. I mean, it would be great if we did win, but even if we don't—well, Peyton Manning is from New Orleans. And his dad Archie played for the Saints for years, so the Mannings kind of belong to us anyway." I was bouncing as I walked. "And really— just *making* it to the Super Bowl is kind of enough for me— winning would just be icing."

"Awesome." He grinned at me as we reached the corner at Royal. "Damn, I'm sorry I wasn't here."

Domino's was on the 700 block of Bourbon, between Orleans and St. Ann, across the street from the Bourbon Orleans Hotel.

The sign, a big domino showing the 2 and 1 dots, was swinging back and forth in the bitterly cold wind below a huge Saints flag. We ducked our heads and walked faster.

The front doors were wide open, but just beyond that an iron gate was shut. We detoured into a huge room to the left. The walls were painted a deep burgundy, and several red couches were scattered around, with low tables placed in front of them. Against the far wall was the bar, with a huge mirror on the wall with bottles of liquor lined up on shelves. There were bar stools placed neatly equidistant from each other along the bar. Another big iron gate was closed on the wall opposite the street but I could see tables and chairs set up in front of a large stage. There were no customers in the place.

A bartender wearing the domino pattern on his shirt was polishing glasses behind the bar when we walked in. As we got closer, he looked up and smiled. I recognized him from the party. "Scotty, right?" he asked as we sat down on bar stools. "We met Sunday night. I'm Jesse."

My memory of him from the party was pretty blurry, and I made yet another mental note to stop smoking so much pot. Jesse Santana was a very good-looking guy. He looked to be about in his mid-twenties, with dark black hair he wore in a ponytail. His skin was dark and his eyes a rich dark brown. He was broad-shouldered and narrow-waisted. "I remember you," I replied, shaking his hand. "This is my friend, Colin."

"Ah, the one who was out of town." I started a bit as he shook Colin's hand. I didn't remember talking to Jesse much, let alone telling him about Colin. Maybe he'd talked to Frank. "Too bad, man, you missed out on a great night."

"That's what I hear." Colin smiled back at him.

"What can I get you guys?"

"Coffee," Colin and I said at the same time. We looked at each other and laughed.

"It's cold out there," Jesse commiserated. "I just made a

fresh pot." He shook his head as he put two glass coffee mugs on the counter. He turned and retrieved a full pot from a burner, filling our mugs before putting it back. "Cream? Sugar?"

After stirring the cream and Sweet'n Low into my coffee, I took a sip. It was good—most bar coffee was awful, and I said so.

Jesse shrugged. "I like coffee, so I make it good. What brings you guys out on such a cold day? Man, if I didn't have to work I'd have just stayed in bed."

I pulled a business card out of my wallet and slid it across the bar. Jesse picked it up and did a double take. "We came here because we need to ask you a few questions, Jesse, and since you're not busy…" I let my voice trail off.

"Detectives, wow." Jesse poured himself some coffee and took a sip. "I've never met a real private eye before." He winked. "Sure, go ahead. Ask some questions." He crossed his arms and leaned back against the cooler.

"Something was taken from the Bradleys' apartment on Sunday night, most likely during the party," Colin said smoothly, taking the lead. "So, we're talking to everyone who was there that night."

"Makes sense." Jesse nodded. "I didn't take anything, though, and I didn't see anyone take anything."

"You may have seen something and not even realized it," Colin went on. He was, I reflected, rather smooth. "We realize a lot was going on—and pretty much everyone was primarily paying attention to the football game, right? But I want you to think for a minute before you answer. Did anything seem out of the ordinary to you on Sunday night?"

"I…" He paused, wrinkling his forehead as he thought about it. "I don't know. I'd never been there before, you know?" He turned to me. "I'd never really met your parents before that night. I mean, I've seen them around, and I knew they were the Devil's Weed people, but we'd never really met."

"So why were you there?" I asked.

"Because I invited him as my guest," a voice said from behind us.

Before I could turn around, a tall, slender black woman raised a panel in the bar and walked through it. Dominique DuPre was more striking than beautiful. She had a long nose, high cheekbones, and a pointed chin. Her hair was styled in braids that hung down her back. She had long legs—she was well over six feet tall—and a small waist. She was wearing a cowl-necked black sweater over a pair of black wool slacks and low-heeled shoes. A gold cross glittered on a thin gold chain around her neck. She'd been in New Orleans for several years, opening Domino's just two years before Katrina came barreling up from the Gulf. There had been some trouble when she first opened the club—I'd heard rumors her ex-husband was a mob lawyer—but she kept a relatively low profile. During the time when the rumors about her were flying, Mom made a point out of befriending her, which was how I knew her. I liked her—she was an amazing singer and also was a pretty good photographer—and the best thing about her was you always knew where you stood with her. Dominique was not big on being nice just for the sake of being nice.

"Is this Colin?" She raised an eyebrow and smiled faintly. "Damn, boy, you're even better looking than I've heard." She held out her hand. She had long elegant fingers, and a French manicure. Colin delighted her by raising it to his lips and kissing it.

"Enchanté, mademoiselle," he said, his French accent perfect.

I refrained from rolling my eyes.

"You're quite a charmer," she said. "Jesse, would you mind getting me a cup of coffee? Put some Baileys in it, too."

Jesse stepped back and did as directed.

"Cecile is missing something?" She accepted a mug from

Jesse and took a long sip. "I can assure you, I wouldn't steal from her."

"Did you notice anything out of the ordinary?" Colin asked. "Anything at all that seemed off to you?"

She frowned, a few lines appearing on her forehead. "Well, it was a rather eclectic gathering of people, but one always expects that from John and Cecile—which is why one always goes. You never really know what you're in for." She laughed, a tinkling sound. "I'd thought about simply watching the game here, keeping an eye on things—we were packed to the gills that night—but I wasn't really in the mood to be around a crowd. I'd done two shows both Friday and Saturday nights, and so I felt something a little more intimate was in order for the game." She hummed for a moment, closing her eyes. "I don't really recall anything strange. I certainly didn't see anyone take anything."

"I don't mean to be offensive, Ms. DuPre—" Colin started but she cut him off.

"Dominique, please call me Dominique."

"Okay. Dominique, with all due respect, you hardly strike me as the kind of woman who would, um"—he had the decency to blush—"date one of your employees."

She threw her head back and a hearty laugh erupted. After a few moments, she wiped delicately at her almond-shaped eyes. "How delicately put." She reached over and patted Jesse's arm. "No, I am not dating Jesse, but I also didn't want to go to the party alone. I knew Jesse had no plans for the evening, and so Saturday after my second performance I asked him if he would escort me to the party. Being gallant, he agreed." She smiled at him, and he smiled back. "I am seeing someone else, but we're going through a difficult patch." Her eyes darkened. "But I feel confident we'll get back on the right track again soon."

Jesse snorted. "Not if that Bourgeois bitch has anything to say about it."

Dominique gave him a look that should have blasted him into smithereens. "Now, Jesse, they're not interested in my personal life."

"Not—not Tara Bourgeois?" I blurted out, getting an equally nasty look from Colin. "Is that who you're talking about?"

Dominique hesitated before leaning on the counter. "You're not really interested in hearing about my love life, are you?"

Before I could answer, Jesse said, "What the hell?" and grabbed a remote control from underneath the bar. He aimed it at the big-screen television mounted in the corner on the opposite side of the room. "Speak of the devil." We all turned to look. Tara's face was plastered across it, smiling weakly in her pageant dress, her black hair teased and hair sprayed into a huge bouffant around her head. As the little green line moved across the bottom of the television, her voice got louder.

"And I'm sorry, I think marriage is for a man and a woman, it's just how I was raised, but I don't want to hurt anyone's feelings or offend anyone but I was raised as a Christian with Jesus Christ as my personal savior and I believe, like all Christians do, that the Lord meant for marriage to be between a man and a woman..."

The television cut back to Jessica Johnson, a local news reporter. "To repeat, controversial former Miss Louisiana Tara Bourgeois was found shot to death earlier today—"

The television clicked off.

Dominique set the remote control down on the bar. Her hands were shaking. "I can't believe she's dead," she whispered.

Jesse put an arm around her. "Well, now things can get back to normal for you and Jared."

Jared.

I couldn't have heard that right.

"Jared who?" I asked, trying to keep my voice from shaking.

Dominique didn't look at me. "Your cousin, Jared Bradley."

Colin and I exchanged looks. "You were dating Jared?" Colin asked.

She nodded.

"Why?" I blurted out.

That elicited a bitter laugh. She looked up at me. "I wish I knew, Scotty." She shrugged, reaching for her mug of coffee and Baileys. "I have the worst taste in men, apparently. I always pick the wrong ones." She took a long pull at her drink, made a face, and put it back down on the bar again. She poured herself two fingers of Wild Turkey and tossed it back. She smiled. "As for Jared, well, I'd be a fool to stay with him now. It's just going to happen again. Once a cheater, always a cheater."

Colin and I exchanged glances. I was reeling in shock. I couldn't believe Jared was dating a black woman—*I* certainly didn't have a problem with it, but there were plenty of other Bradleys who would. Papa Bradley, for one—and Uncle Skipper for another, and I wasn't 100% sure MiMi would be all that cool with it, either.

He definitely would have lost his status as favored grandson.

"What exactly is going on with you and Jared?" Colin asked slowly, rubbing his knee against mine. I knew exactly what that meant—*let me do the questioning.*

"We met at a charity event here at the club," Dominique poured some more Wild Turkey into her glass. "We were raising money for Women of the Storm." She frowned. "Daughters of the Storm? Whatever—-you know that group. I got in touch with the Saints and asked them if they could send some players over—maybe some autographed jerseys for the silent auction, that kind of thing. Scott Fujita, Darren Sharper, and Jared were the ones who showed up. Jared and I clicked. He asked me out. I said yes." She waved a long finger at me. "I didn't know he was related to you, was John and Cecile's nephew. I didn't know he was originally from New Orleans. I just figured, since I never met his family or anything, that he came here when he was drafted for the Saints."

"And he let you think that, too," Jesse interjected. "No offense, Scotty, but your cousin's kind of a douche bag."

Before I could say *preaching to the choir*, Colin asked, "But you did eventually find out?"

She nodded. "During the Giants game—we always show the games here to get a crowd—this woman was sitting at the bar." She rolled her eyes and laughed. "She kind of looked out of place here. So I struck up a conversation with her. Turns out she's Jared's mother."

"Aunt Bethany," I breathed out.

Skipper and Bethany's divorce was legendary in the family. For one thing, it was one of the few divorces ever in the Bradley family—all of them, come to think of it, were Uncle Skipper's—and it was bitter and ugly. I didn't know the details, but the legal battle lasted nearly three years, and basically Papa Bradley wound up paying Bethany several million dollars for Skipper to have primary custody of Jared. Bethany had remarried, and had another couple of kids with her second husband. She now lived across the river in Algiers Point. I'd only met her a couple of times, but she made me uncomfortable. She made it very clear she hated anything with the name Bradley.

"You can imagine how shocked I was," Dominique sipped at her Wild Turkey. "But it was pretty clear why Jared never introduced me to his family—Bethany Cutrere is a racist through and through."

She's not the only one in the family, I thought, trying to imagine what would happen if Jared had ever brought Dominique to the big house on State Street. MiMi would get drunk—well, drunker—and Papa Bradley would have an apoplectic stroke. I'd never heard Skipper say anything particularly racist—but Aunt Enid definitely was. I shivered.

"We had quite a few fights about that," Dominique went on.

"But I got it, you know? I didn't like it, but Jared just wasn't ready to have that kind of battle with his family. And I loved him."

"You said 'loved,'" Colin observed. "Do you not love him anymore?"

"He's seeing—well, was seeing, Tara Bourgeois." Dominique finished her drink. "I don't know how long it's been going on—maybe he was seeing her the whole time he was seeing me, who knows? But when I found out last week, I kicked his ass out."

"Jared was the one who found her body," Colin said. "And Cecile's gun was there."

Dominique laughed. "And you were wondering if I took Cecile's gun to kill her with?" She tilted her head to one side. "I have my own gun. I didn't need to take Cecile's. I don't even know where Cecile kept hers."

"What about you, Jesse?"

Jesse was wiping the counter so hard he was probably taking the varnish off. "I didn't take Mrs. Bradley's gun," he muttered. "And I didn't have a reason to kill that woman. I didn't even know her."

"Oh, now, Jesse, you hated her, too." Dominique put her hand on his arm.

"One last thing—where were you both last night?"

Dominique smiled. "Well, I was playing hostess down here until around one thirty in the morning, and then Jared came by."

I almost fell off my bar stool. "Jared came by here?"

She nodded. "He stayed upstairs in my apartment until around seven this morning."

He had an alibi? Why hadn't he told us?

"How did he seem?" Colin asked.

She shrugged. "He'd had a rough night, he said—some family dinner thing. But other than that he seemed fine."

"And what about you, Jesse?"

If Dominique's revelation had knocked me for a loop,

I certainly was in no way prepared to hear Jesse reply, "I had dinner with David Williams and spent the night at his place."

"David?" I blustered. David was my best friend and longtime workout partner.

Jesse laughed. "I spent the night with him after the party, too."

Colin slid off his bar stool and placed a ten on the counter. "Thanks, you two. If we have any more questions, we'll come back." He smiled at them both. "The police will probably question you both."

Dominique barked out a bitter laugh. "Won't be the first time."

Colin waited until we were back out on the street before asking, "What did she mean by that?"

"A boyfriend of hers was murdered before Katrina—I don't know the details, but the story I heard was it was some kind of mob hit."

Colin stared at me. "Dominique is involved in the mob?"

I shook my head. "No, it had nothing to do with her—I think his father was the judge presiding over a mob trial, or something like that. Her ex-husband is supposedly a mob lawyer in Atlanta—but that's just a rumor."

He whistled. "We need to do some deep background on her."

"Can you believe Jared had an alibi and didn't tell me or Storm?" I still couldn't wrap my mind around it.

"He doesn't really have an alibi," Colin observed. "He could have killed Tara and come to Domino's from there."

"I don't think so." I shook my head. "I can't see Jared killing one girlfriend and then spending the night with another. And I can't believe Jesse—and David…"

"Why not?"

"For one thing, I would have never guessed Jesse was gay."

Colin laughed. "Don't tell me your gaydar is on the fritz. Where should we head next?"

"Okay." I consulted the list. "Ken Taylor's place is over on Dauphine, between Dumaine and Bourbon. Let's head there next."

A car pulled out of a parking space down the block, and I stepped back onto the curb.

"Look out!" Colin screamed as the car headed right for us.

CHAPTER SEVEN
TWO OF SWORDS
Indecision

I just stared.

It was like one of those horrible nightmares when you know something is going to happen—but you're frozen in place and can't move.

What is that driver doing? I thought.

It was inconceivable to me that he couldn't see he was heading for the curb and right where we were standing.

"Scotty!" Colin screamed from somewhere behind me.

The car was heading right for me and wasn't slowing down. If anything, it was speeding up.

In my daze, I couldn't tell anything about the driver, but he seemed male. He was wearing a black ski cap with the ubiquitous gold fleur-de-lis on the forehead—but he had it pulled down, obliterating his face.

It was a dark blue car, midsize, maybe a Honda or a Nissan or a Toyota.

It was also incredibly dirty.

There was a dent in the hood and a crack across the windshield.

Somehow all of those things registered in my mind as it came right at me.

The next thing I was aware of was someone grabbing me. I was lifted right off my feet and thrown backward. I landed on my heels and fell back as the car jumped over the curb—right exactly where I'd been standing—before swerving back onto Bourbon Street.

I heard a woman scream just as my body hit the sidewalk.

My head hit something hard and bounced.

And everything went black.

I was drifting through mist.

I was weightless, and I wasn't cold anymore—which was a really nice feeling.

Everything was gray, like it always was when the Goddess chose to speak to me. It had been a while—not since my last murder investigation—and I was a little relieved to know that She was still willing to appear to me. I'd offended Her the year of Katrina and She had turned her back on me, leaving me on my own. She'd forgiven me during my last murder case—primarily because I was in a position to help right an affront to another one of Her apparitions. After the wrong had been righted, the visions ceased—although I was still able to read the Tarot with some degree of success.

There was the familiar sense of love and protection wrapping itself around me, and a sense of peace and calm I always wished I could replicate when I wasn't having a vision. I always felt safe in this place She summoned me to—whether it was between worlds or dimensions, I didn't know, nor would I probably ever know.

There was a strange silence as I continued drifting down through the mist. I closed my eyes and let the smells intoxicate me—lilacs and lavender, roses and jasmine. I breathed the fragrances in deeply as the warmth worked its way through my body, banishing the damp and the cold.

I drifted down, and my bare feet touched soft earth.

I opened my eyes, and the mist began to dissipate. There was a glowing light to my right, reflecting off the fading mist. "Holy Mother?" I called softly. "Are you there?"

"Scotty." Her voice called softly from the same direction the light was coming from. I turned so that I was facing the soft glowing light, and the mist began clearing completely as She walked toward me. We were standing in a meadow, and the sun came out of the grayness, and its warmth caressed my skin.

As She drew nearer, I couldn't help but smile.

She was wearing a black Drew Brees jersey, with the big number 9 in gold in front. As always, I couldn't make out Her face clearly; it was always blurry and indistinct, unless She was appearing to me in a completely human form. Her bare feet were floating several inches above the grass as She moved closer to me.

"Does this mean we're going to win the Super Bowl?" I asked, gesturing at the jersey.

"Such things do not concern me," She replied with a wave of her hand. "What care I for your silly human games? The pride and self-absorption of mortals—sometimes it is too much to be borne! What does who wins a game have to do with the Great Plan, with the Eternal Cycle? What does it matter whether some mortal gets a job promotion, or some child gets a bicycle as a gift, or some teenager passes a mathematics test he did not prepare for? Such things do not matter, and in the endless passing of time are soon forgotten."

"I thought everything was connected," I replied. "Every event has an effect and changes the future—you've told me that enough times. When a butterfly beats his wings in China it has an effect here."

"Your mind cannot comprehend Truth as I can, Scotty. It is best if you do not ask questions you cannot handle the answers to."

"But, Great Mother—"

The air got colder. "Are you questioning me?" Her voice whipped around me. "Do you dare?"

"Of course not, Great Mother." I bowed at the waist. "I am

merely confused. I am, after all, merely a human." I gestured to the jersey again. "And seeing you in a Saints jersey, well, I could not help but assume there was a meaning in it."

She fingered the hem of the jersey. "Surely you know that when you see me, you see me in a form your mind can handle. Hence this oversized blouse made of this unpleasant fabric. But if it makes you feel any better—" She gestured with Her left hand, and the jersey transformed into a luxurious velvet toga in a stunningly beautiful shade of purple I'd never seen before. "Enough of this talk of silly games! There are much more important things for us to discuss." She gestured for me to follow Her. "There is great danger," She said, Her voice drifting back to me on the gentlest of warm breezes.

"Isn't there always," I muttered under my breath.

She stopped walking. "I chose you, Scotty. Out of all the mortals, I put my mark on you. I gave you a great gift, one that many would appreciate, that many would give their right arm to have. But there's always a price, Scotty."

"I know, Great Mother," I replied. "I do appreciate it."

"I doubt that you do." She turned Her back on me.

I followed her, and She waved Her hand as I came up alongside Her.

We were standing on a cliff, and far beneath us wasn't a valley, but a road I recognized as Airline Highway, with its box stores and fast food joints. There was a massive structure just on the other side of the highway from us—behind a vast parking lot filled with angry people carrying signs and shouting.

"There." She pointed.

"The Dove Ministry of Truth?"

"There is no truth to be found in that place," She whispered to me as the voices grew louder. I could barely make out the words—"No more hate! No more hate!"

"Is that the protest? The one this Saturday?"

"There will be trouble, Scotty, and it is up to you to make

sure that it doesn't happen." She continued, "This trouble, if it is allowed to come to fruition, will poison the next few years and lead to even more trouble, to great deaths and much destruction."

"You want me to convince Mom to not have the protest?"

As I watched, the front doors of the church opened and a wave of people came rushing out, heading for the protestors.

"Violence is never the answer, Scotty. It scars the plane— and those scars take an eternity to heal—and more evil comes into the world from those scars." She began to turn away from me as the mist began to rise again. Airline Highway, the sound of angry voices shouting, and the church disappeared into it.

"You must find out the truth before the violence takes control," She whispered.

And disappeared into the swirling mist.

"Scotty!" Colin's voice penetrated the darkness—and the pain.

It took me a few seconds to force my eyes open. My head was pounding, and it was cold. Slowly Colin's face swam into focus in front of me. Just beyond him I could see the Lucky Dog vendor in his white and red striped shirt across the street, and Oz just beyond him. Out of the left corner of my eyes I could see the front steps of Marie Laveau's Voodoo Shop. "What—what happened?"

"A car tried to run us down," he replied grimly. "I pushed you out of the way—a little too hard, I guess—and you hit your head on the wall." He pulled his cell phone out of his jacket pocket. "Let me call an ambulance—"

"No." I winced as I sat up, and closed my eyes until the wave of dizziness and nausea passed. "I don't need to go to the emergency room. I hit my head. No big deal."

"You could have a concussion—"

"I'm fine," I snapped. "I have a headache, that's all." I felt around the back of my head and felt the painful knot. "It's 2010,

Barack Obama is president of the United States, your real name is Abram Golden, my name is Milton Scott Bradley, we're on the corner of Bourbon and St. Ann, the date is January twenty-first, and I'm not seeing double." I forced a smile on my face to take the sting out of my tone. "I'm fine."

"I'd feel better if you got checked out," he replied dubiously. "Head injuries…" His voice trailed off, and he gave me a smile. "Okay—but if you don't feel better later, we're going to the hospital, no arguments. Is that clear?"

"Aye, aye, sir." I winced as I tried to get up. I must have landed on my shoulder wrong, because it also ached. "Help me up, would you, please?"

Colin shoved his big hands into my armpits and lifted me to my feet effortlessly. I always forget how strong he is. I leaned on him for a moment, hearing his heart beating and enjoying the warmth radiating off his body. It really was cold. He kissed the top of my head. "Come on, we'd better get you home."

I started to argue, but another wave of dizziness stopped me as I tried to stand on my own. "Okay." I swallowed. "Someone seriously tried to run us over?"

He nodded. "Yeah." He said it with a grim look on his face, which didn't bode well for the driver should Colin ever get his hands on him. "Headed right for where you were standing—if I hadn't pulled you out of the way—" His voice choked up.

I closed my eyes and tried to remember. The last thing I remembered was walking out of Domino's. I took another step and winced. "Man, my head and shoulder are killing me."

"We need to get you home," he said again.

"What about the investigation?" I protested. "We've barely started on the list."

"It'll have to wait." He shook his head. "Can you walk?"

I took a step without losing my balance or getting dizzy. My head was still throbbing, though, and my shoulder was screaming for Ben-Gay. I nodded. "Yeah, but stick close, just in case. Just get me home and you can go on without me."

"I'm not leaving you alone. What if..." His voice trailed off.

"Call David and have him come over to babysit me," I replied crossly. Colin and Frank both have an annoying tendency to try to cover me in bubble wrap, if I'd let them. I mean, come on—I'm hardly a hothouse orchid. "He should be home from work by now. He'll love the chance to mock me. And I can get the lowdown on Jesse, see if David confirms his alibi. You got the plate number of the car, right?"

"It didn't have one." He scowled as we started walking up St. Ann Street toward the river. When we reached the Lucky Dog cart, the vendor called over, "You all right, man?" He had a thick St. Bernard Parish accent. I nodded and gave him a weak smile. He just shook his head and started mumbling something about asshole tourists who don't know how to drive in the Quarter.

Colin went on, "It was a dark blue Honda—I didn't get much of a look at the driver, but I could see it was a man, and there was no license plate on the back either."

"He was wearing a ski cap pulled down over his face—a Saints one with the gold fleur-de-lis on the forehead. But why would someone try to run us down?" It didn't make sense. Okay, maybe my brains were still a little scrambled, but I couldn't think of any reason someone would want to run us down. "And you're sure it wasn't an accident? Maybe he was just drunk or something."

"No, it was deliberate, all right. He headed right for us—and he drove up over the curb before veering back into the street." Colin's face was grim. "He was definitely trying to run us down."

"But why would someone do that, Colin? It doesn't make any sense—none at all. Nobody knows we're investigating Tara's murder—hell, nobody even knew she was dead until the story broke just now. Unless—"

"Whoever it was might have just been after me," he finished the sentence for me. It was eerie how he could do that. "I'll call Angela—get her started looking into it. Maybe someone tracked me here—it's always a possibility." He looked away from me. "You know, it's always been a fear of mine—"

"Stop right there." I cut him off as we turned down Royal Street. Colin was careful to make sure I was walking on the inside. "Don't even go there, Colin. We don't know anything, so don't make any assumptions, okay?" I folded my arms, wincing as a lance of pain shot out from my shoulder.

"We have to face the possibility." He put his arm around me. "Maybe it would be better if—"

"Stop right there." I cut him off. "Yes, there's always a chance some lunatic terrorist or assassin or whatever might track you here. And yes, they might use Frank or me or Mom or Dad to get to you. That's a risk we're all willing to take." I poked him in the chest. "We lost you once before, and none of us are willing to go through that again. Understood?"

His eyes welled up, and he looked away quickly. "I know, but—"

"No buts."

"I have a lot of enemies, and there are a lot of people who would love nothing more than to put a bullet in me."

"Exactly—who'd want to put a *bullet* in you."

He put his key into the gate lock. "But run you down with a car? And a Honda, at that? That doesn't say professional killer, at least not to me. It's kind of amateurish, don't you think? I mean, I can hardly imagine some international gang of terrorists deciding the best way to get rid of you is to run you over on a public street with a beat-up old Honda." As we walked, the memory was slowly coming back to me. "There was a dent in the hood, and a crack in the windshield."

He didn't say anything else until we were inside the apartment. He helped me to the couch and placed a blanket over me, tucking it in around me. I bit my tongue. It was irritating, but if it made him feel better about going back out and leaving me, so be it. He got me some pain relievers and a glass of water. The pain had subsided to a dull throbbing. I gulped down the aspirin and the water. He sat down next to me. "Yeah, you're right," he finally said. "It does seem amateurish. But I'm still going to call Angela."

"You're not the only person with enemies, you know." I nestled down under the blanket. "I've made a few myself." I thought for a minute. "There's those neo-Nazis who worked for Willy Perkins, remember? And I'm not exactly popular with the Pleshiwarian fundamentalists we helped thwart last year. Or those Russian mobsters."

"True." He got up. "I'll call Angela—and Storm, let him know what's going on." He pulled his cell phone out and walked out of the room.

I closed my eyes and stretched out on the couch. It's not pleasant to think someone wants to kill you—but when it's reality you have no choice but to deal with it.

I was actually more concerned about the cryptic warning from the Goddess.

My relationship with the Goddess had become a little dysfunctional over the last few years—not that it had ever been normal. She'd first appeared to me during the Southern Decadence nightmare, when Woody Perkins and his band of neo-Nazis had plotted to destroy the French Quarter by blowing up the river levee. Before then, I'd primarily channeled my psychic gift by reading the Tarot cards. Sometimes She spoke to me through the cards, sometimes She just ignored me. During another case, She allowed me to communicate with the spirit of a dead man to help me get to the truth. But after the Mardi Gras case—when Frank and I thought Colin was a murderer, and She'd allowed me to go on thinking that—I turned my back on Her. Six months later Katrina came barreling in from the Gulf and She wouldn't even speak to me through the cards. In my bitterness and anger over the city's destruction, I was more than happy to be done with Her and the stupid gift once and for all. She'd come back during the Pleshiwarian case—along with Colin, who turned out not to be a killer after all—and our relationship had been a little contentious since then.

She never showed herself to me without a reason—and usually it was important. Something terrible was going to happen at the PAM rally and counter-protest this Saturday if we didn't get to the bottom of the Bourgeois case before then.

I was about to reach for the cigar box I kept my Tarot deck in when Colin walked back with a grim look on his face. "Well, Angela's going to put out some feelers—but she hadn't heard anything." He swallowed. "She's worried it might have something to do with my last mission—we thought it was over, but maybe not." I opened my mouth, but he held up his hand. "Angela thinks it very likely a professional would try to make it look like a simple accident. She's going to send us some backup."

"Great." I rolled my eyes.

"Don't be like that. She's sending the Ninja Lesbians—you like them, don't you?"

I'd met Rhoda and Lindy during the Pleshiwarian mess, and yes, I did like them. "I thought they worked for the Mossad."

"The Mossad owes Angela a few favors, and they know the city—and you, Frank, and the rest of the family. I think it's a good idea."

I sighed. "If you say so."

"We don't know what we're up against and it's better to be safe than sorry. I also called Storm, to let him know what's going on." He winked. "I made sure to emphasize not saying anything to Mom and Dad."

I blew out the breath I'd been holding in relief. Mom would have run every step of the way to my side, and would have been impossible to get rid of. Don't get me wrong—it's great having such a loving mom, but it can be a bit much sometimes.

When I'm fifty, I'll still be her baby.

"Storm's back at the police station—he's going to head over here when he's done there. They aren't charging Jared, by the way."

"Did you tell him about Jared's alibi?"

"Since they aren't charging him right now, I thought I'd let you have that pleasure when he gets here." He grinned, dimples marking his cheeks. "And David's on his way over. When he gets here, I'll try to track down these other suspects. What time will Frank be back?"

"Probably not until around ten," I replied, reaching under the couch and grabbing the cigar box. "I can do some background checking while you're gone."

He sighed. "I'd rather you just lie there and rest, but I suppose that'll be okay."

"I'll use the laptop so I can stay on the couch," I offered.

The gate buzzer rang, and Colin moved to the intercom. "Yeah?"

David's voice came through the wall. "It's me." Colin hit the buzzer to unlock the gate. A few moments later there was a rap at the door. Colin leaned down and kissed me on the cheek before opening the door. I heard them murmuring to each other, and the door shut again.

"You look like hell," David said with a big grin, sitting down in a reclining chair after removing his jacket. "I guess the gym's out of the question today?"

"Cute." I grinned back at him. David is one of the best friends anyone could ask for—particularly, as he liked to point out from time to time, since being my friend is dangerous. Thus far, he's had his nose broken, his car totaled, and his house shot up. But he can always be counted on, any time I need him—and for pretty much anything.

Of course, one has to put up with his sarcasm and teasing.

He leaned back in his chair and pulled a joint out of his shirt pocket. He lit it and took a deep inhale. "Can you believe it's open season on the anti-marriage crowd?" he said, blowing out the smoke and offering it to me. "Pity."

I hesitated, remembering my promises to myself to not smoke so much. I did have to talk to the cards, apologize to the Goddess, and do background checks online…none of which, I realized, would be impeded by being a little buzzed.

I took the joint. "Just one," I said, taking the hit.

"I can't say I'm sorry someone killed that Bourgeois bitch," he said, accepting the joint back. He took another hit before pinching it out and dropping it back in his pocket. "But Marina Werner, too? Now if only someone would shoot Peggy MacGillicudy, the world would surely be a better place."

I stared at him. The pot was relaxing me, and at the same time opening my mind a bit. *Of course, Marina and Tara both have been killed—the two murders have to be related.*

It couldn't be a coincidence that two of the movers and shakers for the Protect American Marriage rally were now dead.

And both were killed within a twenty-four-hour period.

"You're a genius," I said slowly.

"Underappreciated most of the time, but yes, I am." He grinned back at me. "So what happened to you? Colin said you were almost hit by a car."

"Yeah, I hit my head." I reached under the coach and got my deck of Tarot cards. I sat up and started shuffling. "I have a bit of a headache—had," I corrected, realizing the combination of aspirin and pot had taken the pain away. "Speaking of which, what's the deal with you and Jesse Santana?"

He started. "How do you know about that?"

I laughed and filled him in on Jared's possible involvement with Tara's murder—and Mom's gun. "When we were at Domino's, Jesse brought you up. Come on, spill."

"He's hot, don't you think?" David leaned back in his chair with a blissful smile. "Definitely next husband material."

As long as I've known David, he's really wanted to be in a permanent relationship. He's had a few false starts along the way—most notably being Carlos, this hot little Hispanic muscle boy who'd been transferred here right before Mardi Gras the year of Katrina. They'd gotten pretty serious, but that one-eyed bitch fucked that up. Carlos's company transferred him to Los Angeles while New Orleans lay in ruins—and they hadn't survived.

"I can't believe you're considering a bartender husband material," I teased. "What have I always told you about dating the help?" It was my first rule for Gay Life—you can sleep with bar staff but never date them.

He made a face at me and gave me the finger with both hands. "I'll have you know he has a master's degree and is just taking a break before going back to Tulane for his Ph.D., fuck you very much." He closed his eyes. "And that body…Christ on the cross. And he loves, loves, LOVES getting fucked—and he likes handcuff play, and—"

"Too much information, ew," I interrupted. "You met him for the first time at Mom's the other night?"

"Yeah. After the game was over we went bar-hopping and ended up at my place." He gave me a grin. "Other than to get a change of clothes and going to work, he hasn't left yet. And when he gets off work tonight, I'm going to see how he feels about being tied up."

I gave him a sour look. "I don't want to hear any more."

But for David's sake, I was glad Jesse's story checked out.

I got the cards out of the cigar box and started shuffling. David watched as I spread them out in a Tree of Life reading and started flipping them over.

A mean-spirited woman who commits evil in the name of God.

The death of one led to the death of the other.

Danger for a loved one.

"So what do they say?" David asked. He was one of the few people outside the immediate family who knows about my gift.

I leaned back and looked over the cards again. No, I'd read them correctly. It was a very clear message, much clearer than usual. The Goddess had clearly forgiven me my flippancy.

Danger for a loved one made me a little nervous. Which loved one?

I looked at David. I bit my lip. He could be trusted—he always helped with our cases without question. "I think you're right, and the cards confirm it," I said, explaining quickly the bare bones of the case.

When I finished, he stared at me. "Seriously? That douche bag Jared was dating both Dominique *and* Tara Bitch-wah?"

"But this"—I gestured at the cards—"this tells me the two murders are connected...which means—"

"You need to find someone with access to your mother's gun, and who was connected to both women."

"What if the connection was just trying to stop the rally?"

"Then you'd kill Peggy MacGillicudy—that would have put it to rest."

"So, it's likely she's in danger." I sighed. "I guess Storm's going to have to let her know."

"Talk about Sophie's choice," David replied.

CHAPTER EIGHT
THE HANGED MAN, REVERSED
Preoccupation with matters of the self

After a few hours of watching reruns of some horrible reality show set on the beach in New Jersey (David kept going on about how hot the guys were—which was certainly true. Unfortunately, they insisted on talking, which dramatically reduced their hotness quotient and appeal), I told David to go ahead and head home. It was going to start raining again at any moment and the sun had already gone down. My head had stopped hurting and I wasn't seeing double, so I figured I was out of the woods.

Besides, I wanted to get going on the background checks. It seemed rude to do them while he was there—since he was doing me a favor by making sure I didn't die or go into a coma or something. Lying on the couch under a blanket doing nothing while Colin was out doing the legwork didn't sit well with me.

I was also a little nervous about him walking around the Quarter alone. Intellectually, I knew it was dumb—if ever there was anyone who could take care of himself, it was Colin. His skill at just about everything never ceased to amaze me. There wasn't anything he couldn't do. He could fix a car engine and whip up a batch of the most delicious brownies you'd ever eat while engaging in a gun battle with a herd of bad guys—all of it without turning a hair or breaking a sweat.

Still, I couldn't help but worry about him.

As soon as David left, I retrieved the laptop and sat back down on the couch. I went online, and with the list of party attendees sitting on the end table, I started digging up everyone's past. It sounds a lot more interesting than it actually was. I was doing background stuff—employment histories, where they lived, credit checks, etc.—and creating dossiers on all of them. Once I had a "residence" history, then I checked local newspaper archives for mentions before broadening the search to any mentions of their names on the Internet.

If there's anything more boring than this kind of "legwork," I'd rather not know about it.

Every once in a while, something fascinating might turn up. But unfortunately, most people don't lead particularly interesting lives—and that was certainly the case with the people on my list.

Bearing that in mind, I decided to save Dominique for last.

I was beginning to wonder if it was actually possible to die of boredom when I heard footsteps on the back stairs. Hoping it was Colin, I typed *Lurleen Rutledge* into a reverse directory as the back door opened. A cold blast of wind whooshed through the apartment, blowing open some magazines on the coffee table.

"Shut the damned door!" I shouted, not looking up from the computer as I watched that annoying rainbow-colored wheel spin.

"Getting knocked on the head sure hasn't improved your disposition," Storm said, obligingly slamming the door so hard the entire building shook.

"Oh, it's *you*," I said, matching his tone as I closed the laptop.

"Glad to see you, too." Storm shrugged off his trench coat and placed his briefcase on the coffee table, sliding down into the same chair David had been sitting in. He glanced at the television. "*Jersey Shore*? Really? I thought gay men were supposed to have better taste."

"I'm not watching that crap." I put the laptop on the end table and sat up. "David thinks the guys are hot. I didn't bother changing the channel after he left." I picked up the remote and clicked the television off.

"Uh-huh." He propped his feet up on the coffee table. "How are you feeling?"

"Stir-crazy." I shrugged. "Other than that, I'm okay. No double vision and the headache's gone. My shoulder's still achy, though." I moved it and winced. "Toss me the Ben-Gay." He did, and I started slathering it on underneath my sweatshirt. "But I suppose I'll live. What's up with Jared?"

"Well, they aren't charging him—yet." Storm got up and headed to the liquor sideboard, pouring out two fingers of Johnnie Walker Black Label. He emptied the glass and set it back down. "Ah, that's better." He sat back down, shaking his head. "I haven't felt warm all day. Anyway, something's not right with his story. If he weren't on the Saints roster I think he would have been arrested. I don't think he's being completely honest, and when your lawyer is thinking that, you can be sure the cops are thinking it, too."

"He *didn't* tell you everything." I closed my eyes. The Ben-Gay was working its magic on my shoulder. "He might have an alibi after all—he wasn't home alone all night." I filled him in on what Dominique had told us. "So, it depends on the time of death, doesn't it?"

"The preliminary report says she was killed between two and four a.m." His face turned purple. "And that stupid son of a bitch has a goddamned alibi and didn't say a fucking word when Venus told us the tentative time of death. I'm going to strangle him."

I shook my head. "Well, he's not exactly a genius, Storm. He's trying to keep the whole thing with Dominique a secret, and since he knows he didn't kill Tara—"

"Innocent people go to jail every fucking day on a whole hell of a lot less circumstantial evidence than they have on him right fucking now!" Storm interrupted me angrily. "I can't fucking believe I wasted my entire afternoon helping that idiot! I should double my fee—not that he'll ever pay my bill anyway."

"Eh—just send the bill to Papa Bradley." I shrugged. "My guess is Jared would prefer no one in the family ever finds out he's been seeing a black woman." I couldn't help but laugh. "Can't you just hear what Papa Bradley would say about that? I'd pay good money to see the look on his face when he finds out."

Storm laughed with me. "Yeah, that would be priceless, wouldn't it? You almost have to feel sorry for Jared on this one, don't you?" He let his face go slack and said, in a perfect imitation of Jared's voice, "Arrested for murder or tell Papa I've got a black girlfriend?" He laughed again. "But honestly—this is the one instance where I don't think Papa Bradley would care about the black girlfriend. You know how his mind works—besides, as long as Jared doesn't *marry* her..." He shook his head. "A Bradley, arrested for murder? That just won't *do*."

"True." I shifted, wincing as my shoulder protested. "But the good news is Jared doesn't need you anymore, right?"

"Thank God." Storm blew out a raspberry. "God help me from having to defend him in court...the ballistics came back already, too. Apparently they put a rush on it, because it usually takes days. It was definitely Mom's gun that killed the Bourgeois woman." He put his hands together and looked up at the ceiling. "And thank you, God, for making sure she has an alibi. It wouldn't look good for Mom, especially after slugging her last night in front of a room full of witnesses." He sighed. "Mom's righteous anger is going to get her into serious trouble one of these days."

"She's never going to change, you know."

"I thought people were supposed to mellow with age," He rolled his eyes. "But I think we can safely rule out anyone else in the immediate family for this murder, praise be to Jesus." He winked at me. "We have the same alibi as Mom and Dad, and Rain's in Hawaii. And no one else in the family had access to the gun."

"Jared didn't, either," I reminded him. "Someone at the party must be the killer, Storm—how else could Mom's gun be involved?" I took a deep breath. "Did you know Marina Werner was also murdered? They found her this morning—apparently she was killed yesterday morning."

His face registered his confusion. "Who the hell is Marina Werner?"

I sighed. "Marina Werner's father is Dick Werner—the pastor of that megachurch in Kenner, Dove Ministry of Truth or whatever the hell it's called. She was putting together the anti-gay marriage rally Tara was speaking at Saturday—well, her and that Peggy MacGillicudy woman."

He whistled. "That's an interesting twist."

"Don't you think the two murders might be connected? I mean, it can't be a coincidence, can it? According to the news report I heard, she was killed yesterday morning, and they didn't find her body until *this* morning." I frowned. "So, whoever took Mom's gun Sunday night easily could have committed both murders." I got up and walked over to the printer. I collected the pile of printouts. "I've been trying to find someone with a connection to both women online, but haven't really had much luck."

"You won't," Storm replied. "That'll take old-fashioned legwork. What all did you find?"

"Well, I didn't find a whole hell of a lot on anyone, really." I sighed. "But I didn't get through everyone yet, and I was just getting to Lurleen Rutledge when you got here. And Dominique DuPre—I was saving her for last." I gestured at my laptop's dark screen. "What do you know about Lurleen? Or Dominique, for that matter?"

"Lurleen?" He got up and poured himself some more Johnnie Walker. "Not much, really. I know she's a widow—she was married to Dudley Rutledge, who used to own that overpriced gallery over on Royal Street. He died a few years back. I've met her a few times—she's nice, I suppose, but other than that?" He tossed the Johnnie Walker down in a gulp. "Not much. Any particular reason you're interested in her?"

"No, just being lazy." I sighed. "I was hoping I wouldn't have to do the background check. I didn't know she was married to Dudley Rutledge." I thought back. I'd never known him, but everyone who lived in the Quarter was familiar with the Rutledge Gallery—it was one of the bigger galleries on Royal. It was on the corner directly across the street from the police station. "He died before the levees failed, right?"

"Yeah, I think it was sometime that summer. She sold the gallery, made a fortune." Storm sat back down. "Marguerite's mother was related to him somehow—I think his mother and her mother were first cousins or something. That's how we knew him. I bought a couple of ridiculously overpriced paintings from there a few times to make Marguerite's mother happy." His face darkened, like it always did when he mentioned Marguerite's mother. Storm always swore Phyllis Hebert was a shrewish virago with talons for fingernails. I've always found her to be a rather nice and charming woman.

But then, if Storm were *my* son-in-law...the man could try Mother Teresa's patience.

I riffled through the printouts. "Nobody seems to have a connection to both women, but Gia Romano competed against Tara for Miss Louisiana." I frowned. "But I can't see losing a beauty pageant being a motive for murder."

"Well, they knew each other—that's a connection," Storm pointed out.

"Yeah, but it might be nothing—they were just in the pageant up in Monroe together." I shrugged. "I don't know how pageants work, but I've never really bought the way the contestants always act like it's a big happy family and they all get along."

Storm laughed. "Like sororities. On the surface they're 'sisters,' but dig a little deeper and it's a nest of vipers." He snapped his fingers. "I'm curious what you'll find on Dominique, to be honest. I've heard some rumors around the courthouse about her."

"Rumors from around the courthouse?" I hid a smile. If Storm was to be believed, the courthouse—and City Hall, for that matter—were hotbeds of gossip. "I swear, it's a wonder anything gets done around there—sounds like all you people do is sit around and spread rumors."

He scowled and gave me the finger. "You want to hear it or not?"

"I'm all ears."

"There was a story back before the storm—" He sat there, gazing at a spot high on the wall, but finally just gave up. "No, I don't remember. Jackie will remember." Jackie Fennell had been Storm's secretary practically since the day he passed the bar. He'd inherited her from another criminal attorney who'd had a heart attack while lunching at Galatoire's. He always said she picked him rather than the other way around, and he was damned lucky to have her. A model of efficiency, she also was an incorrigible gossip with a memory an elephant would envy.

He made a face and shook his head. "I can't really remember much from before the storm."

"Well, she's Jared's alibi, but we need to confirm that with him." I couldn't help but laugh. "I wonder if he'll 'fess up once he's confronted with the truth."

"I'll follow up with him—trust me," Storm replied grimly. "If he weren't so big and strong I'd slap him around."

I pictured it and laughed out loud. "Yeah, well, probably not a good idea, big brother. Was the story you heard that her ex-husband is a mob lawyer in Atlanta?"

"It's interesting, but no, that's not it. I think the mob *was* involved somehow, though." He pulled out his phone. "Let me give Jackie a call."

My cell phone beeped on the desk behind me. I started to

push myself up from the couch but my shoulder exploded with pain and I collapsed back onto the cushions. "Damn, that hurts," I muttered as Storm left a message for Jackie.

He disconnected his call and gave me a concerned look. "Are you okay? Do you want to go to the emergency room?"

"No, I don't need to go to the emergency room." I winced and moved my shoulder gingerly. "I just wrenched it, and I guess I need to be careful with it for a few days." I got up slowly and took a deep breath. My phone had stopped ringing. I walked down the hall to the master bedroom—there was some Vicodin in the medicine cabinet left over from when Frank had an abscessed tooth a few months earlier. I shook one out and washed it down with some water. I glanced at myself in the mirror and was startled to see how pale I looked.

No wonder Colin was so worried, I thought as I made my way back down to the living room. I picked up my phone on the way—the missed call was from Colin, but there was no message. I eased myself back down on the couch and covered my legs with the blanket. "That's better." I gave him a wan smile. I leaned back and closed my eyes. "What I don't understand is how the killer got into Poydras Tower—isn't that a security building?" The Vicodin was starting to kick in.

"There's supposed to be a doorman on duty, but the night she was killed there wasn't anyone working the night shift. According to the building manager, they haven't been able to find anyone to work the night shift yet—and the security cameras aren't working—there was some kind of glitch in the system that hasn't been repaired yet." Storm rubbed his head. "So, it has to be assumed Tara's killer knew her well enough to know about the lack of security."

"Or the killer checked it out ahead of time—which means premeditation." I opened my eyes.

"It wasn't a spur-of-the-moment killing," Storm replied. "Stealing Mom's gun to use proves that." He started drumming his fingers on the arm of his chair. "But the building is locked up at night. Visitors have to call up and be let in. So, she either let her killer in, or the killer had his own keys."

"Well, she gave Jared keys. There's no telling how many other people she gave keys to." I thought for a moment—which wasn't easy. The Vicodin was making me loopy. "What about that Joe Billette guy? The one who made the sex tapes? Did he have keys?"

"How would he have gotten Mom's gun?" Storm pointed out. "I mean, Mom's gun pretty much rules out everyone who wasn't at Mom and Dad's for the game."

"Lucky for Jared Mom used the gun Sunday afternoon," I mused. "But unlucky for the killer. If Mom and Dad hadn't gone shooting Sunday afternoon, the gun might have been gone for days—weeks, even, without either of them knowing."

Storm nodded. "Imagine how bad it would look for him if she hadn't. He had keys, he obviously would have known about the security lapses, and it's his aunt's gun. He had an argument with her that night. That's a pretty powerful circumstantial case."

"But he has an alibi—he was at Dominique's."

"It's pretty convenient, though." Storm laughed. "By giving him one, she's also giving *herself* one…*she's* the one who could have taken the gun—and she definitely had some issues with Tara. Suppose, for a moment, that Dominique took the gun. Maybe she wanted to kill Jared. He led her on, broke her heart, lied to her on more than one occasion, right? Sunday night, the Saints win the NFC Championship—which means the Saints are going to be feted and honored, and it looks like it'll be Tara Jared's taking around with him instead of Dominique. The gun is just right there in the junk drawer. She takes it, puts it in her purse, and it goes home with her. The next night, Jared shows up, wanting to talk to her privately. Here's her chance, right? So, she takes him upstairs…he tells her some lame story. She's in love with him, so she believes it—it's amazing the bullshit people in love will believe—and they have sex. He falls asleep—and there are Tara's keys right there on his key ring. She slips out with the gun, goes over to Poydras Tower, lets herself in to Tara's apartment, shoots her, leaves the gun, and gets out of there. Who's to know any different?"

"You *are* a good lawyer," I replied. "If I were on the jury, I wouldn't convict Jared."

"That's why I make the big bucks, Scotty." He shrugged. "They could be working together, for all we know. Dominique took the gun and gave it to him, and they alibied each other. Or you can argue the exact same story, only in reverse. Dominique took the gun to use on him, but he smoothes everything over with her, and when *she's* asleep he takes it, kills Tara, and comes back so he's there when she wakes up in the morning."

"Do you really think Jared's that smart?" I made a face. "Not the Jared I know. Besides, if Jared were using Dominique as his alibi, he would have provided one from the beginning."

He laughed. "No, I don't think he's that smart. But I'll be curious to hear what Jared says. Be interesting if he denies being with her, wouldn't it? I mean, I can see why he wouldn't want to tell anyone he was with her…but surely he had to know she'd eventually come forward."

The front door opened and once again, a cold blast of air blasted through the apartment before it could be shut again. I looked down the hallway and sighed with relief to see Colin walking down the hall.

Colin kissed me on the cheek—his lips were cold—and plopped down on the end of the couch, unzipping his leather jacket. "How are you feeling?"

"I'm really tired of everyone acting like I'm an invalid," I said sharply. "I hit my head. Big fucking deal—don't say a word, Storm," I warned as he opened his mouth with a grin. "What did you find out, Colin?"

"You're not going to believe this, but every single person

at that party had a reason to kill Tara Bourgeois." He shook his head. "I swear to God, it's like *Murder on the Orient Express*."

"You're kidding." I exchanged a look with Storm.

"I wish I were," he replied. He pulled his notepad out of his coat pocket. "Gia Romano, believe it or not, was actually in the Miss Louisiana pageant—she was Miss Slidell." He sighed. "Gia was the favorite going in—it was really down to between her and Tara, no one else was close. But on the final night, Gia was sabotaged. Her dress was torn—she had to get a last-minute replacement dress that didn't really fit right, and she tripped on the hem. Her guitar strings were broken—and while she was able to restring the guitar, she was so rattled she messed up her song— and she wound up falling completely apart in the Question. She wound up third runner-up…after it was over, a stage hand told her he'd noticed Tara alone with her guitar. She confronted Tara, who admitted sabotaging her…but there was nothing Gia could do at that point."

"Is that really a reason to kill someone?" Storm asked.

"If you take into consideration Gia entered the pageant primarily because she needed the money for college, yes, it is." Colin said, his face grim. "She had to drop out, and now she's working in a tanning salon, trying to save enough money to go back to college."

"But why wait, what, a year and a half?" I pointed out.

"True." Colin shrugged. "And there's her roommate, Mike."

"Surely he wasn't in the Miss Louisiana pageant." Storm joked.

"No, she just got him fired." Colin shook his head. "You know, the more I hear about Tara, the more I think she got what she deserved."

"Nobody deserves to be murdered, Colin," I objected, stifling a yawn. The Vicodin was making me sleepy.

"She did—she was a horrible person." Colin made a face.

"Mike was hired by the pageant officials to keep her in shape—he had a very lucrative business as a personal trainer out at Airport Fitness—and he was doing very well. He's gay, by the way— and after the big brouhaha at the Miss United States pageant, he refused to keep training her."

"And who could blame him?" I yawned again. "If she were my client, I would have quit, too."

"Unfortunately for Mike, the gym owner didn't know he was gay," Colin went on. "Tara complained to him, and got Mike fired. He lost his entire clientele."

"Seriously?" I couldn't believe what I was hearing. I spent the majority of my twenties working as a personal trainer. Granted, the gym I worked at was on the edge of the French Quarter and probably about fifty percent of the clientele were gay—but it was hard for me to imagine *any* gym owner firing an employee for being gay.

Colin nodded. "He's been trying to build his business back up at this gym over on St. Charles Avenue—but he's been in pretty dire straits for a while. He had a car repossessed, and that's partly why he moved in with Gia. He couldn't afford to live on his own anymore."

Storm whistled. "And he just happens to be in a band with a girl who was also in the Miss Louisiana pageant with Tara." He shook his head. "I see what you mean about *Murder on the Orient Express*."

Colin started going down the list, ticking off motive after motive. "The only person I spoke to without a connection of some sort to Tara is Lurleen Rutledge."

Storm's phone started ringing. He got up and walked into the kitchen.

Colin sat down on the sofa with me. "Are you sure you're okay?"

"My shoulder is the main problem—it's really sore and

stiff." I sighed. "I really must have landed on it funny. I took a Vicodin, and it's made me sleepy."

"I'm so sorry. I probably yanked it too hard when I pulled you out of the way." He leaned down and kissed my forehead. "But all I could think was—"

"You can give me a massage after Storm leaves." I winked at him. "And I'm sure Frank's going to need one when he gets home."

"You have no idea how much I miss you both when I'm not here—"

He was interrupted by a shouted obscenity from the kitchen. "Are you all right?" I shouted as Colin and I exchanged puzzled looks.

Storm walked back into the living room, his face mottled with anger. "That was Venus on the phone."

"Calm down," I advised.

Storm just gave me a look and poured more Johnnie Walker into the glass he'd been using. "You're not going to believe this."

"Believe what?"

"Mom's gun was also used to kill Marina Werner."

CHAPTER NINE

ACE OF CUPS, REVERSED

Hesitancy to accept the things of the heart

I woke up the next morning just before seven.

I slipped out of bed and pulled on some sweats before heading into the bathroom to do my usual just-woke-up routine. I could smell the coffee brewing from the kitchen—I'd remembered to set the timer before going to bed for a change—and it drew me in. I moved my shoulder around a bit. It was a little stiff, but it didn't hurt anymore. I sighed with relief.

After Storm got the news about Mom's gun, we'd sat around and tried hashing out different theories of the crime. Knowing Mom's gun had been used to kill Marina Werner certainly changed everything we'd already been thinking about the case—and meant starting over from scratch.

The two murders were definitely connected, but how?

The obvious connection was the anti-gay rally—Marina was an organizer, Tara was the headline speaker—but I hadn't found anything to connect anyone at Mom and Dad's party to both women.

"Besides Mom and Dad," Storm pointed out, only half joking. "This would look really bad for them if we hadn't all been there while someone was killing Tara."

We got absolutely nowhere.

Storm had finally gone home shortly before Frank got home from Biloxi. Colin and I had to go over everything again with him. We stayed up a little while longer, but I could barely keep my eyes open. Frank was also exhausted both physically and emotionally, and so we finally decided to just hit the sack and start fresh in the morning.

Steam rose from my coffee mug as I headed to the desk. It was freezing in the apartment, so I turned on the heat for a little while to take the edge off.

I sat down and started doing some research on Marina Werner.

I was on my third cup of coffee when I finally exhausted all avenues of online research.

She wasn't, I thought as I printed out my summary of her life, particularly interesting. She was the oldest child of Dick Werner, founder and minister of the Dove Ministry of Truth out in Kenner on Airline Highway. She'd been in her early thirties, and according to the pictures I'd found of her online, not a particularly pretty woman. She had brown hair she kept cut extremely short, and rather plain, nondescript features. She wore glasses, had narrow shoulders and ample hips. She apparently favored knee-length skirts, blouses, jackets that matched the skirts, and sensible flat-heeled shoes. She worked as the treasurer of the Ministry, had a business degree from the University of New Orleans, and had pretty much been her father's right hand in the Ministry from the day she graduated from college. She'd never been married even though she was in her late thirties—which I found a little odd. *Why wasn't she married?* I wondered, peering at the best photograph I'd found of her online, from the Ministry's website. Granted, I didn't believe a woman was worthless unless she was a wife and mother—an archaic mentality of the patriarchy—but her father was the minister of a denomination of Christianity that was all about "traditional values."

Surely her father would have pressed her to get married?

She was the product of an early first marriage to a Rebecca

L. Burleson—they'd apparently been very young when they married. The divorce (so much for traditional values!) came not long after he started the Ministry, and he hadn't waited long after the divorce was final before marrying his current wife, Mary Ellen Kirkwood, with whom he had three sons. The oldest was apparently taking over some ministerial obligations from his father—rather creepily, his name was actually Dick, Jr., but he went by DJ.

DJ was obviously the favored child, probably because he was going into the family business. His picture was everywhere on their website, most often standing between his parents. Like his father, he had a big toothy smile and what Mom always called "God's hair," a full head of thick hair sprayed rigidly into place. There were some shots of him in khaki slacks, a polo shirt, and a hard hat working on a construction project—a homeless shelter in Kenner.

Are there a lot of homeless people in Kenner? I wondered as I stared at his picture. He was in pretty good shape—something you couldn't really tell in the shots of him wearing suits and ties. His chest looked well developed, his stomach was flat, and definition showed in his biceps as he swung the hammer.

He was good looking if you liked that type.

I didn't.

I clicked on the page marked *The Ministry's History.* Dick had started preaching, apparently, in a small town out in Plaquemines Parish. He eventually heard the call to move his ministry to Kenner, where he and Mary Ellen had bought an old abandoned church on Airline Highway and founded the Dove Ministry of Truth. The page read like a press release, written in breathless prose with lots of exclamation marks and claims of MIRACLES!!! and GOD'S HAND showing itself. It made me want to throw up, but still—I had to give them credit. Twenty years ago, they opened their church with just five parishioners, and they had built it into a rather impressive megachurch with thousands attending services in person and who knows how many hundreds of thousands more watching on television.

They certainly knew how to market and promote their brand of snake oil.

I couldn't help but be amused as I noticed that Mary Ellen Werner's hair had also gotten bigger and her make-up thicker over the years. It was almost as though the Ministry's growth could be measured in the size of her hair and thickness of mascara. Her hair, though, was truly impressive—and had to be at least part wig. The most recent photo I could find on the site was from DJ's wedding last summer to a woman who looked barely out of her teens. She was pretty enough, and all smiles as she looked up adoringly at her newly wedded husband—who was smiling at the camera instead of at his wife.

Mary Ellen's hair was a masterpiece, though. The curls were piled up at least three inches tall on top of her head, and more curls cascaded down over her shoulders and down her front—and probably in the back as well.

I was so fascinated by Mary Ellen's hair that I almost missed Tara Bourgeois standing on the other side of the bride.

Tara was wearing a frilly dress that was sea foam green and completely unflattering, and was holding a small bouquet of flowers as she gave the camera a forced pageant smile.

It was a bridesmaid's dress if I'd ever seen one.

I leaned back in my chair. Well, it only makes sense, I thought. Tara was from Kenner, it's not much of a stretch she would go to services at the Dove Ministry of Truth. But if she was a parishioner there, wasn't it kind of shitty to make them pay her to speak at their homophobia rally?

I distinctly remembered hearing Mom say the Dove Ministry was paying Tara ten grand to talk about the "Homosexual Agenda."

I got up and refilled my coffee cup. I could hear someone in the bathroom brushing their teeth, so I started another pot brewing before I walked back into the living room. I sat down on the couch.

Whoever killed both women could have just been targeting them because of their anti-gay stance.

In which case, it was logical to assume that Peggy MacGillicudy was next on the hit list.

But Mom's gun was the murder weapon. That meant the killer had been at Mom and Dad's on Sunday night.

That was a chilling thought.

Frank sat down next to me, yawning as he set his coffee mug down on the table. He glanced at the print-out of the Marina research. "You're getting started early." He stretched and put his arm around my shoulders.

"Yeah." I put my head down on his shoulder. "Turns out, Tara knew Marina—at least, she knows Marina's brother and his wife—she was in the wedding party." I shook my head. "But who at Mom and Dad's was connected to both women? It just makes my head hurt, Frank."

"There might be another connection between them we haven't found yet," Frank pointed out, picking up his coffee and taking a big drink. "We didn't even know the murders were definitely connected until last night. And you know better than anyone else online research isn't as good as old-fashioned legwork. How's your head this morning?"

I felt around until I found the knot under my curls. "It feels like it's gone down some—and I don't have a headache. My shoulder's a little tight, but it's okay."

"Glad to hear it." He stretched and I could hear his back cracking. "I'm kind of stiff today myself—was a hell of a practice yesterday. I wish I didn't have to go back over there today." He made a face. "I'd rather stay here and help you guys crack this case." His face darkened. "It really pisses me off someone used Mom's gun to kill people."

"I wish you didn't have to either—but it's not every week you get a title shot." I patted him on the leg. "What time do you have to be over there today?"

"I've got to be there at eleven." He frowned. "I have a photo shoot." He rolled his eyes and laughed. "Did I really just say that?"

"You said it, supermodel." I grinned at him. "I have to say, though, it doesn't feel right investigating a case without you helping out."

He grinned back at me. "Let me go hop in the shower—I think I hear Sleeping Beauty rustling around in there—and I'll make us all breakfast."

I watched him walk out of the room and was about to reach for my coffee cup when I noticed my laptop was still sitting on the end table where I'd left it when Storm showed up yesterday. *Oh yeah, I was researching Lurleen Rutledge*, I thought as I reached for it. *Not much point in finishing that—I can't imagine a gallery owner's widow having a reason to run around killing homophobes.*

But when I touched the computer, it whirred and the screen came back to life. It was set to go to sleep if there wasn't a keystroke in five minutes—and the search engine where I'd plugged Lurleen's name into had continued to search when I put it aside.

I looked at the screen and let out a gasp.

Lurleen Rutledge had been born Rebecca Lurleen Burleson and had married Dick Werner when she was nineteen.

Lurleen Rutledge was Marina's mother.

"Frank! Colin!" I shouted, bringing them both on the run. "Lurleen Rutledge was Marina's mother. Look!" I pointed at the computer screen.

"I'll be damned." Colin whistled.

"But why would she kill her daughter?" Frank made a face. "And Tara?"

"I don't know," I replied. "But we need to find out."

An hour later, Colin and I said good-bye to Frank as he left for Biloxi. We waved as he drove the Jaguar out of the parking lot. "I wish he didn't have to go," I said wistfully. "It just doesn't feel right investigating a case without him."

Colin nodded, slipping his hand into mine and squeezing it. "Yeah, well, this is a chance for us to work together—so let's make the most of it. Off to Lurleen's?"

"Too early," I replied. It was just past nine. "Let's drop in at the Devil's Weed and talk to Emily some more about her band mates—maybe she knows about a connection one of them has to Marina."

"Sounds good," he replied.

We walked out of the lot and headed for Royal Street. "Besides," I said as we walked up Barracks Street, "Emily mentioned that Lurleen sometimes came in for coffee in the mornings, so it wouldn't hurt to be there if she happens to stop by today."

The morning was cold and damp, and I shivered as we walked. It started raining just as we got to the Devil's Weed. I sighed in relief as we opened the door and stepped in. The warmth inside felt great. Emily was behind the counter reading *Gambit Weekly*, and there was no one else inside.

"Hey, guys—you're out and about early this morning!" She smiled weakly at us. She turned away from the counter and poured us two large cups of dark roast. But when I got to the counter, I could see her eyes were puffy and red.

"Emily, are you okay?" I asked, worried.

She gave a little shrug of her shoulders. "I had a really rough day yesterday." She sniffed again, her eyes welling with tears. She reached for a tissue and blew her nose. "I got some bad news."

"Oh, sweetie," Colin said, and I took her hand, giving it a comforting squeeze. "Do you want to talk about it?"

She bit her lower lip. "And I did something really, really stupid." She wiped at her eyes. "I don't know what to do."

I said sternly, "Get some tea, sit down, and tell us what's wrong."

She poured some hot water into a large mug and stuck a tea bag in it. She came out from behind the counter and sat down with us at a table.

"I did something really stupid," she said, looking down in her cup. "And now I think it's—" She bit her lip again. "I think I'm going to be in a lot of trouble."

"Emily, we'll help you, no matter what it is," I reassured her.

"I'm the one who took Mom's gun," she said in a half whisper.

Colin and I exchanged horrified glances.

"Emily," I said slowly, "*you* were the one who took Mom's gun Sunday night? You lied to me yesterday?"

She nodded and wouldn't look me in the eyes. "Technically, I didn't take it Sunday night, it was Monday morning. But yes, Scotty, it was me." She took a deep breath. "But I didn't mean to kill anyone! I didn't kill anyone! That's what I don't understand." Her voice shook and her eyes filled with tears. "When you asked me about it, you told me it was the gun used to kill Tara Bourgeois, and I couldn't believe it. I didn't kill her, Scotty. I didn't kill anyone. I didn't even know Tara Bourgeois. I don't know how the gun got there. You have to believe me!"

"We believe you," Colin said in his most reassuring voice, glancing at me. "But you have to tell us what happened."

"I feel so stupid." She wiped at her eyes again. "A couple of weeks ago, I met someone at our show at the Spotted Cat."

The Spotted Cat was a music club on Frenchmen Street in the Marigny District. The place had been packed, Emily explained, and the band had never sounded better. "We were rocking." A faint smile played at her lips. "And there was a woman in the audience. Every time I looked over at her, she was staring at me. And whenever our eyes met, she winked at me.

"I haven't seen anyone, you know, since Mickey dumped me," Emily went on. Mickey had been this rather large butch Emily had dated for a little under a year, and the relationship had abruptly ended the previous summer. "So, when we were done with the set I was kind of in the mood to be flirty, you know, so I went out to her table and introduced myself. She bought me a glass of wine, we talked, and one thing led to another…"

It was hard not to grin, but Emily wouldn't have appreciated it. Emily, for a far-left almost socialist lesbian, had very old-fashioned opinions about sex. She didn't judge other people for being sexually active, but for herself, well, she didn't believe in falling into bed with someone she'd just met, or picking someone up in a bar. She had to be in love before she had sex with someone.

I didn't trust myself to say anything, but Colin came to my rescue.

"That's not like you, Emily." He said.

"I *know*!" She started crying, enormous deep sobs that shook her entire body. She kept wiping at her face. "I'm…suh-suh-suh-sorry guys…I…I…"

I put my arm around her and she put her head down on my shoulder. Colin and I looked at each other helplessly. I patted her head until she finally got control of herself again.

"Sorry." She blew her nose and gave me a grateful smile. "I know what you're thinking. But no, we didn't do anything but hold each other that first night. It felt so right, you know? She was so funny, and smart, and we finished each other's sentences, and so we started seeing each other. We talked on the phone every day whenever we could steal a minute, and I fell in love." She hung her head. "I'm such an idiot."

"Don't beat yourself up," Colin soothed. "Everyone makes mistakes, Emily."

"But I was beginning to wonder about things, you know." She took a deep breath. "There were long stretches of time when I couldn't talk to her, when she wouldn't return my calls, you know? At first, I thought well, of course it must be her job."

"Her job?"

"She told me she was an accountant." Emily nodded. "But you know, it was weird—there were *nights* she wasn't available to talk to me, and some weekdays when she was. I started getting suspicious, like thinking maybe she was married and had kids or something"—that very thing had happened to her a few years earlier—"but she always had an answer any time I'd ask her— you know, she always had the answer, the perfect response to my question."

"Which of course only made you more suspicious," I added, winking at Colin, who looked puzzled.

"So, Sunday morning she walked me to work before she went home," Emily went on, her eyes welling up with tears. "She told me she was leaving town that day on business—some big audit or something in Dallas, and she'd be gone for ten days, but she promised to call me whenever she could." She took a deep breath. "I was a little late that morning, and there was a customer waiting. When Reena saw the customer, she turned white and just said good-bye—no kiss or anything, just ran off down the street. It was weird."

I closed my eyes. I knew exactly where this was going. "Was the customer Lurleen Rutledge, by any chance?"

Emily goggled at me. "How did you know that?"

Even Colin was staring at me. "Never mind, just finish your story."

Emily swallowed. "Yes, it was Mrs. Rutledge, and she was

a lot friendlier than she usually is—I really thought she'd read me the riot act for being late and making her wait, you know, but she didn't, she was really nice. She even hung out and talked to me while I was brewing the coffee and getting the shop ready to open. It was strange." She gulped again. "And then, that night at the party, Mrs. Rutledge took me aside at halftime and started asking me all kinds of questions about Reena."

Colin closed his eyes and tilted his head back. "Reena's real name was Marina Werner."

Emily bit her lower lip, but it didn't work. She started sobbing again.

So Marina Werner was a closet lesbian, I thought. That probably explained why she'd never gotten married.

"She told me…" Emily snuffled and wiped her nose. "She told me the woman I was seeing was actually Marina Werner, the woman who was helping organize the Protect Marriage rally, the daughter of that horrible homophobic minister at Dove Ministry…"

Bet she didn't tell you she was Marina's mother, though.

"I was in shock. I didn't believe her. But she pulled out her iPhone and went online, did a Google images search, and sure enough, there she was. My Reena, the woman who spent the whole night telling me how much she loved me and wanted me to move in with her, was that horrible woman." She covered her face in her hands and started sobbing again.

I got up and got her some fresh tissues. By the time I got back she had managed to get hold of herself again. "I wasn't thinking, Scotty, you have to believe that. I think I went out of my mind. The whole second half of the game all I could think of was how she'd used me, mocked me, the whole time we were together she was laughing at me behind my back…so when the game was over, I went into the kitchen and put Mom's Glock in my bag, and I went home."

"So how did—"

"The next morning I went over to her house." Emily went on like I hadn't said anything. "I was just going to get my stuff, you know, and leave her a note. Imagine my surprise to find her there! She hadn't left town—I don't know why I thought that wasn't a lie, but it was, I'm so stupid—she couldn't see me all week because *she was going to be too busy with her fucking rally.*" She gulped. "She was shocked to see me, of course, and we had a horrible argument. And of course, I had the stupid gun in my bag. I got so mad I took it out and shook it at her. She tried to take it from me and it went off!"

"Well," Colin said, "it was an accident, Emily, you didn't mean to—"

"I didn't *kill* her." She looked at him as though he were insane. "The bullet went into the mirror over the couch and broke it. I think we were both so shocked we just stood there for a minute… and all I wanted to do was get out of there, so I turned and ran out the front door, jumped in my car, and headed home." She sighed. "It wasn't until later that I realized I didn't have the gun—I must have dropped it in her house. I didn't know what to do. What if she pressed charges? What if she had me arrested? I didn't know what to do, guys, I thought I was going to lose my mind. I didn't know if I should call her, I didn't know…" Her voice trailed off. "And then yesterday you came down here asking all those questions about the gun. I'm sorry I lied to you—but when you said the gun had been used to kill Tara Bourgeois…"

I closed my eyes and replayed our conversation. "You thought I was asking because you'd taken the gun to Marina's."

She nodded. "And when you said it had been used to kill Tara, I didn't know what to think, other than somehow Marina had done it. I—I didn't know what to do." She grabbed my hands. "Scotty, I didn't kill Marina. I didn't kill Tara. I know it looks bad, but I never intended to kill Marina. I'd forgotten I even had the stupid gun, and then…oh God, I've made such a mess out of things."

The bell over the front door rang, and we all turned.

It was Venus Casanova and Blaine Tujague, homicide detectives with the NOPD.

"Emily Hunter?" Venus asked as they walked toward the table.

"Yes?" Emily replied, standing up.

"We need you to come down to the precinct and answer some questions." She nodded at Colin and me. "Colin, Scotty."

Emily gave me a terrified look. "Scotty?"

"Don't worry." I already had my cell phone out and was dialing Storm. "I'll have Storm meet you there. Don't say a word until he gets there, okay?"

CHAPTER TEN

FIVE OF WANDS

Strife, legal troubles

"Right now, she's pretty screwed," Storm said with a sigh. "One of the neighbors heard a shot and saw Emily leaving—got her license plate number."

"And didn't call the police?" Mom asked. "Who hears a gunshot and doesn't call the cops?" She rolled her eyes.

We were gathered around one of the bigger tables in the Devil's Weed. Mom and Dad both looked tired—I'd run upstairs and woken them up hours before they usually got up. Despite the copious amounts of coffee they'd downed since then, they were still tired and grumpy. Once Storm arrived from the police station, they'd closed the shop.

"It was *Kenner*, Mom. She thought it was a car backfiring. People out there aren't as familiar with gunfire as we are here in the city," Storm answered. He shrugged. "Hard as it is to believe, most people wouldn't recognize an actual gunshot if they heard one—they think it sounds like it does on television or in movies. It wasn't until the police came snooping around that she remembered."

"But she made a note of Emily's license plate?" Dad frowned. "Why would you do that?"

Storm rolled his eyes. "She's part of the neighborhood watch group." He shrugged. "And no, the irony that she couldn't recognize the sound of a gunshot didn't escape me."

"But she only heard the one shot?" I asked. "She didn't hear another one?"

"Shortly after Emily left, she ran her morning errands." He shook his head. "Like I said, Emily's really screwed. But at least they found the bullet she admits to firing. Anyway, the bail hearing will most likely not happen until later today."

"We'll post her bail," Dad said without a moment's hesitation. "No matter how much it is, we're good for it."

"This is all my fault." Mom slammed her fist down on the table, making our coffee mugs jump. Coffee sloshed onto the table. She ran her hands over her head. "If I'd just kept the damned gun locked up like I should have, she couldn't have taken it. And maybe both those women would be alive. How could I be so irresponsible?"

"It's not your fault, Mom," Colin replied. "How were you supposed to know someone would take your gun? And use it?"

I shivered. "I don't like the idea you can't trust people who come into your home. Besides, the whole point of *having* a gun in the house is to protect yourself. It's not like a burglar is going to just sit around waiting for you to unlock your gun case."

"I suppose." Mom didn't look mollified. "It's just so unlike Emily. I mean, she *hates* guns, absolutely hates them."

"I can't imagine how she must have felt." As soon as the words left my mouth, I could have bitten my tongue off. I glanced over at Colin, who just gave me a sad smile.

Of course I knew exactly how she'd felt.

During the last Mardi Gras before the levees failed, we'd gotten involved in a murder investigation so complicated and involved I still couldn't wrap my mind around it. At its conclusion, we'd all been led to believe Colin was the mastermind behind a massive criminal conspiracy that spanned several continents and left behind a stack of bodies. We'd eventually discovered he was innocent—several years later.

So, yes, I could relate to how Emily must have felt Sunday night when she found out the truth about Marina Werner.

"I am sick to death of these self-righteous homophobes turning out to be self-loathing closet cases," Mom said angrily.

"The good news is they're only charging her with Marina's murder. But you can bet your ass they're going to try to pin Tara's on her, too." Storm finished his coffee. "Her alibi is pretty solid, but they're going to try to poke holes in it." His face got grim. "I'm not worried—I'm pretty sure I can get the charges dismissed once the bail is set."

Fortunately for Emily, she'd been rehearsing with Huck Finn until around one in the morning, after which they'd gone to the Clover Grill for something to eat before hitting the pub for drinks until around four in the morning. All three of her band mates were willing to say so in court.

"The best-case scenario, in my opinion, would be if they did charge Emily with Tara's murder," he went on, his eyebrows coming together. "Two murders committed with the same gun in less than twenty-four hours, but they only try her for one because she's got a solid alibi for the other? The district attorney would be *insane* to proceed in that case." He got a smug look on his face. "I'd have the jury so confused they'd never convict."

"The best-case scenario would be for us to find the real killer," I replied. I glanced at Colin, and he gave me a slight nod. "Did any of you know that Lurleen Rutledge was Marina Werner's mother?"

"What?" Mom spluttered, her eyes bulging. "Are you serious?"

I nodded. "It's true. Lurleen was Dick Werner's first wife."

"I can't believe it—she was married to that monster? You think you know someone—I've known Lurleen for, what? Fifteen, twenty years, maybe? I thought Philip was her only husband. And she never told me she had children—never mentioned it." Mom turned to Dad. "Did you know, dear?"

Dad shook his head. "She never said anything about it to me."

"Well, she was at the party Sunday night." I leaned on the table. "I'd say she's probably the only person there besides Emily who knew Marina—and where she lived."

"How could any mother kill their child?" Mom replied, looking back and forth between Storm and me. "It's so unnatural."

"Unfortunately, it happens every day—not every mother has your maternal instinct, Mom." Colin got up and took a bottle of water from the refrigerator next to the espresso machine. "Do you mind giving Lurleen a call, Mom? We've rung her buzzer a few times, but she doesn't answer."

"She might not want to see anyone—I know I'd want to be left alone if one of my children—I can't even say it." She shuddered and clasped my hand. She pulled her cell phone out and hesitated. "You know, it might be a better idea to call Cara, her assistant—if Lurleen is grieving…"

"That makes sense." Colin turned his chair around and straddled it.

Mom scrolled through her address book and placed the call, putting the phone up to her ear. "Cara? Hi, it's Cecile Bradley, how are you doing, dear?" She winked at me. "Yes, I know, it's terrible, that's why I'm calling…how is Lurleen doing? Uh-huh, yes, I can imagine. Is there anything I can do? No, I insist, it isn't any trouble." She glanced over at the pastry cabinet. "We've got a wonderful crumb coffee cake with raspberry in…I'm sure Lurleen will love it, I ordered it with her in mind…no, seriously, it's no trouble…I can't get away from the shop right now, but I can send Scotty over with it in a few minutes…yes, he's right here and he doesn't mind at all." She gave me another wink and a thumbs-up. "All right, I'll send him right over. And please, if you can think of anything…and please let Lurleen know all she has to do is call. All right, darling." She disconnected the call and made a face. "For the record, I hated doing that. But if it'll help Emily…" She stood up with a sigh. "Let me wrap the crumb cake up."

A few minutes later, Colin and I were walking across the street with the boxed cake. It had started raining again. Colin held an enormous umbrella over both of us, but my pants still got soaked before we got under the cover of the balcony on the opposite corner.

Lurleen Rutledge had a huge apartment on the third floor of the building directly across Dumaine Street from the Devil's Weed. Mom once joked that her glassed-in balcony gave Lurleen a gorgeous view into Mom and Dad's apartment. I'd never actually been inside Lurleen's place, but it had been featured once in *Crescent City* magazine. It was gorgeous, and had been exquisitely decorated by one of the top interior decorators in the city. It was a little overdone for my taste, but I didn't have to live there, either.

We rang the buzzer, and were rewarded with an answering buzz as the steel front door unlocked. I winked at Colin as we walked into the large entry way. The floor was black and white parquet marble, and a hanging staircase stood opposite a door that must lead into the jewelry shop on the first floor. The stairs were polished and gleamed in the light from a massive chandelier. We walked up the steep stairs to the second floor landing. There was a black wood table with an enormous flower arrangement next to a door with a 2 on it, and a huge window at the opposite end looking onto Royal Street. There was another hanging staircase directly over the one we just came up. We walked around and started up the second set of stairs.

"How on earth do people get furniture into these places?" Colin asked when we were about half the way up.

I laughed. "They pay people to do it for them."

"Of course they do," Colin sighed as we got to the top. This landing was the duplicate of the one below, down to the flower arrangement. There was another flight of stairs to the fourth floor, but the door marked 3 was slightly ajar. I walked over and knocked—which made the door swing open.

"Hello?" I called softly, stepping inside. "It's Scotty, delivering the coffee cake. Hello?"

The room just inside the door was a dining room. The walls were painted a deep emerald green. The floor was hard wood polished and buffed so that it shone in the light cast by a large chandelier. A dark mahogany dining table was centered directly under the chandelier. A white lace tablecloth ran lengthwise down the center of the table. A golden bowl with apples and pears sat in the middle, with golden candlesticks holding long white tapers on either side. There was a matching sideboard against the opposite wall. A golden candelabra stood in its center with three lit white tapers dribbling wax mounted in it. Off to our right was a large doorway leading into the darkened living room. A figure was sitting on a white leather sofa, dressed entirely in black.

I assumed it was Lurleen—but I wasn't really sure what to do next.

I heard Colin softly shut the door behind us and was about to ask him what we should do when a door on the left popped open. Cara White, also dressed completely in black, waved us toward her with a warning glance into the living room. Careful not to make a sound, we crossed the dining room and went through the kitchen door.

The kitchen was enormous. There was a double sink, marble top counters, and dark wood cabinets running all the way to the high ceiling. In the center was an island with a surface that looked like it was made out of cutting board. Stainless steel refrigerators took up the entire left wall, and there was a huge stove along the wall it shared with the dining room. A complicated-looking coffee machine took up most of the counter on the right wall, and there was a door at the end of that counter. It was open, and I could see a small sitting room just beyond.

Cara White was a small woman. She couldn't have been five feet tall or weighed more than ninety pounds. She was almost birdlike in her movements, with almost child-sized hands. She wore her light brown hair cut in a short bob, and gold-rimmed glasses perched on her long nose. Her lips were thin and her chin pointed. She wasn't wearing make-up on her pale skin, and three moles ran in almost a straight line down the left side of her face. She could have been any age from thirty-five to fifty. She took the box from me, placed it on the center island, and untied the string. "Would you like some coffee, Scotty? I just made a fresh pot." She gave a weak smile to Colin, holding out her hand. "I don't believe we've met. I'm Cara White, Mrs. Rutledge's assistant."

"Colin Cioni," he replied, bowing over her small hand and pressing his lips to it. "My condolences." She blushed with pleasure and preened a little bit.

I was frankly a little overcaffeinated, but if it would get her talking I could force down yet another cup. "Sure, some coffee would be nice." I gave her a sympathetic smile. "How is she doing?"

She inclined her head in the direction of the living room. "Did you see her?" She asked, getting down two more china cups from a cabinet directly over the coffeemaker. She sighed. "Poor thing." She filled the cups, placed them in matching saucers, and set them down on the island. I added some cream and a packet of Sweet'n Low to mine. I took a sip and somehow managed to keep my face inexpressive. It was so strong I'm surprised it didn't permanently stain the inside of the cup.

"Wonderful." I smiled back at her, setting it down in the saucer.

"Just give me a second, okay?" She cut a piece of the coffee cake and lifted it onto a small plate. She poured about half the pot of coffee into a carafe and put everything onto a silver tray.

She picked it up and backed into the door, which swung open behind her. She gave us both a wink before she vanished through the doorway.

"Nice place," Colin whispered. "I take it the late Mr. Rutledge was pretty well fixed?"

I nodded. "I guess so—this place wasn't cheap. His gallery was ridiculously expensive—I went there once for a fund-raising party they hosted for the NO/AIDS Task Force while he was still alive, and the cheapest thing I could find was about twenty-five grand." I made a face. "Obviously, I didn't buy anything."

The door opened again as Cara came back in with a long-suffering sigh. "Be sure to thank your mother for me again." Cara poured another cup of coffee and took a sip. She sat down on a bar stool and gestured for us to also sit. "That was very kind of her." She shook her head. "Lurleen is taking this really hard. I guess I shouldn't be surprised—but they were estranged, you know. They hadn't really spoken in years. I don't think Marina ever set foot in here. But still—I'm sure Lurleen thought—you never think"—she lowered her voice to a whisper—"that your daughter is going to be *murdered*." She shivered dramatically.

"How sad." I forced myself to take another sip of the jet-fuel coffee. "I'm sure whatever the problem was seems so unimportant now."

Cara nodded. "I can't imagine not speaking to my mother. I mean, yes, she's annoying and controlling, but she's still my mom, you know?" She hugged herself.

"Do you know what caused the estrangement?" Colin asked, finishing his coffee.

Cara refilled his cup without being asked. I made a mental note to make sure I didn't finish mine. It was much stronger than I preferred—and a second cup would probably give me a heart attack. "She never really told me, but I'm pretty sure it was because of the divorce." Cara cut herself a piece of the cake and licked the knife before tossing it into the sink. "Her ex-husband had sole custody of the kids and rarely let Lurleen see them when they were growing up."

Kind of like how Jared never got to see his mother very much growing up, I thought.

"She tried, I know she tried." Cara shook her head, making a tsking noise. "Every year, I send them packages on their birthdays and at Christmas. They always, without fail, get sent back. Can you imagine? So terribly sad."

"No. No, I can't." I picked up my cup, but set it back down. There was no way I was taking another sip of that coffee.

"There's a memorial service tonight, at that Dove Ministry out in Kenner." Cara made a face and whispered, "That awful Reverend Werner told Lurleen she wasn't welcome. Can you imagine? And him a man of God."

I was just about to ask another question when the door swung open.

As a rule, Lurleen Rutledge was the epitome of the well-put-together New Orleans lady of leisure. But now she looked—disheveled and disastrous. She wasn't wearing any makeup, and her eyes were bloodshot and swollen. Her auburn hair, always regally styled, was in a stunning state of disarray. She was wearing a black sweatshirt over a pair of black jeans. Her feet were bare. "Scotty. Colin." She was holding her plate in her left hand. She tried to smile but the result was just a sad baring of teeth. There was a bit of the raspberry filling in a corner of her mouth. "That was so kind of Cecile. I…I don't…" She started to choke up but took a deep breath and regained control of herself. "I don't know how to thank her."

"I know this is a terrible time, Mrs. Rutledge, but Scotty and I are looking into what happened to your daughter," Colin said gently. "Would you mind answering a few questions?"

She sagged a little, but nodded.

We followed her back through the dining room to the living room. She plopped down on the sofa, and we each took one of the wingback chairs on the other side of the coffee table from her.

"I'm so sorry, ma'am," I said.

"Thank you." She took a deep breath. "All I can think of is the lost years…" She picked up a framed photograph from the cushion next to her and handed it over to me. It was an old photo of a young boy and girl, dressed in their Sunday best. "Weren't they adorable?"

"Yes." I handed it over to Colin, who made appropriate noises. "I don't understand, Mrs. Rutledge—"

"Lurleen," she interrupted me with that terrible smile again. "Call me Lurleen, please."

"Cara said your husband had sole custody of the children," I went on, and as soon as I said it could have bitten my tongue off. It generally wasn't a good idea to tell someone their assistant gossips about them.

She nodded. "Yes." She sighed and rubbed her eyes. She took a deep breath. "Dick divorced me for adultery. It wasn't hard to convince a judge in Plaquemines Parish I was a whore and an unfit mother." She made a face. "It didn't hurt that there were pictures, and I'd left him and was living with another man." She gave me that horrible smile again. "Does that shock you? It was a different time—though every time I go back there, it doesn't seem to have changed much. My first husband was a monster."

You don't have to tell me, I thought, thinking about the rally he was helping to produce.

"I wanted to get out of my parents' house," she went on. "Great reason to get married, right? Dad drank and smacked us all around. Dick was nice to me, really nice. His dad was a preacher—he did a lot of traveling, and Dick wanted to be one, too. Dick was good—at the time he was a good man, you know? He wanted to marry me—I would have slept with him, you know, I didn't care, but he thought it was a sin, we had to wait till we got married. We got married the day after we graduated from high school…I think I got pregnant that same night. Marina was born almost exactly nine months after our wedding date. I had Bobby about ten months later." She sighed. "I wasn't even twenty, trying to take care of two babies while Dick tried to get going as a preacher. We were so poor I bounced a check for a can of tuna once. That was the first time Dick hit me."

Cara brought the coffeepot in and refilled everyone's cups. As soon as the kitchen door shut behind her, Lurleen started talking again.

"I thought a man of God wouldn't have the devil in him, the way my daddy did, you know? But after a couple of years, I would have rather been married to a man like my daddy—he might have smacked us around when he was drunk, but he was good to us most of the time. Dick started getting funny ideas about God, you know? He started to believe he was a prophet, and that God spoke through him. Disobeying him was disobeying God. He started a small congregation of his own in Rouen, little better than snake handlers, really, but people liked what he had to say, I guess." She took a drink. "I began to think about killing myself, you know. I loved my kids, but I hated my life. Anything had to be better, you know. And then I met Dudley Rutledge.

"I don't know what he saw in me—I still don't, not to this day, I don't know what he saw in me. But he was so kind, and loving. I know it was crazy, I know it was wrong, but he started driving out to Rouen to see me. He loved me, he wanted me. I didn't know how to act. I just didn't care about anything. And finally, I came back to New Orleans with him. Dick was furious, he threatened me—and somehow he got pictures of me with Dudley. I guess he hired a detective, I didn't care—he filed for a divorce. Dudley got me a lawyer, we fought with everything we had but we lost. We lost the kids. I was morally unfit to be a mother. And his congregation—they all testified against me, for him. They said I lied. Even the kids—my own children—

testified that they didn't want to be with me, that he'd never hit me, that I was a sinner and was going to hell and they didn't want to be around me. It broke my heart, but if I stayed, I'd die. I had to choose between my children and my life. I chose my life, God help me. And my children stayed with him, being poisoned against me every day of their lives."

"That's horrible," Colin said in a choked voice. I stole a glance at him—his face was mottled, which meant he was furious. Having lost his mother and siblings to a terrorist bombing when he was little more than a teenager in Haifa, nothing enraged him more than anyone who separated a mother from her children.

"I tried, you know." She swallowed. "I sent them presents for their birthdays, for Christmas—but they were always sent back. I always assumed it was Dick sending them back—but when they were adults and had their own homes, the presents were still sent back. My children hate me. They don't want anything to do with me because I'm a sinner." She barked out a harsh laugh. "You can imagine my surprise Sunday morning when I saw my daughter holding hands with Emily, kissing her right in front of the Devil's Weed, right there for God and everyone to see. The look on her face…" She started to laugh but it turned into a sob. "It was like she'd looked right into the face of Satan himself. She ran away. I should have just let it go…but no, I couldn't." She covered her face in her hands. "I called her. I taunted her. 'Do you think your father will approve of your lesbianism more than he did my adultery?' Yes, those were the things I said to my daughter. The last time I spoke to my daughter. Instead of trying to help her, of being there for her…I knew how much pain she had to have been in, how conflicted. I'd been there myself…and now…" She removed her hands from her face. "I'm sorry, I know I haven't been much help to you…would you mind? I think I need to be alone."

CHAPTER ELEVEN
THE MOON
Unforeseen perils, deception

We went down the stairs in silence.

"I think we need to go to that memorial service tonight," Colin said as I opened the door to the street.

My mind was still reeling from Lurleen's story as I stepped out into the cold. The rain had stopped while we were inside. The wind had picked up again, though. I shivered and turned the collar of my jacket back up to shield my neck. "Do we have to?" I asked.

Colin nodded. "Yeah, we do. If at all possible, we need to talk to Reverend Werner, maybe the brother, DJ, too."

"And tell them what, exactly?" I made a face. "Hi, we're trying to prove Marina's lesbian lover didn't kill her, can we have a few minutes of your time, please?" I rolled my eyes. "Yeah, I'm sure they'll drop everything and talk to us. We'll be lucky to get out of there with our lives."

He gave me a look. "We'll be a little more subtle than that, Scotty. We'll come up with a good cover story." He winked at me. "It's what I do, you know. One doesn't infiltrate a jihadist terrorist cell wearing a Star of David pendant."

"Well, duh." I stuck my tongue out at him. Not the most mature response, to be sure, but I couldn't think of anything else. "How are we going to get there? Frank's got the Jag."

"We'll borrow Mom's Prius," he said and started walking back toward the Devil's Weed. I groaned and hurried after him.

He rapped on the door and Mom let him in. Everyone was still sitting around the table where we'd left them.

"Did she like the cake?" Mom asked as she locked the door behind us.

"She loved it. Mom, can we borrow the Prius? We're going to run out to Kenner and do some nosing around at Marina's memorial service, see what we can find out—and Frank's got the Jag," Colin asked in a rush.

Mom nodded. "The keys are hanging on the rack upstairs." She wagged a finger at him. "I'd better get it back in one piece."

"How did it go with Mrs. Rutledge?" Storm asked.

"You tell them while I get the keys," Colin replied, heading for the storeroom door.

I sat down and gave them a brief sketch of the sad story of Lurleen's divorce and her volatile relationship with her daughter. When I was finished Mom said angrily, "That sorry son of a bitch. I could shoot him myself."

"Not really the time to make death threats, Mom," Storm replied with a crooked grin. "Fortunately, your gun is in police custody."

She gave him a sour look. "Cute. But how could anyone…" Her voice trailed off. She bit her lower lip and took Dad's hand. "Your father."

Dad nodded, a sad look on his face.

"What are you talking about?" I was puzzled.

"Jared," Dad said quietly. "Papa Bradley pretty much drove Jared's mother out of his life."

"Aunt Bethany." Storm barked out a laugh. "Papa Bradley bought her off years ago, Scotty. That's why she hates all of us."

"She took the check," Mom snapped. "No one forced her to take it, you know." She looked at me, then at Storm. "Papa Bradley doesn't have enough money to buy my children away from me."

"You weren't married to Skipper, either," Dad replied with a sad sigh. "MiMi told me—oh, it doesn't matter anymore. It was a long time ago, and Skipper's different now."

"What are you two talking about?" I was completely lost. "I don't understand."

Dad looked at his hands. "Skipper used to get violent when he was drunk, Scotty. He used to—he used to hit Bethany. She left when she"—he swallowed—"when she had a miscarriage."

Mom's face went white, red, and then back to white again. She got out of her chair, walked over to the counter, and whirled around. "Are you telling me Skipper caused her miscarriage?"

"That's what MiMi said," Dad said miserably. "Skipper denies it, and Papa and Bethany won't talk about it. It's why she left."

"And she left Jared behind?" I choked the words out. "Wasn't she—"

"That's why Papa had him committed." Mom ran her hands over her head. "I cannot believe you never told me any of this. Why, John?"

"Because I didn't know for sure, Cecile." He looked so miserable I felt bad for him. "All I know is what MiMi told me, and you know she's not reliable." He shrugged.

"Poor Jared," Mom said as Colin burst through the door with the keys.

"What's going on? What did I miss?" He looked from Mom to Dad to Storm and finally at me.

"I'll tell you," I said, standing up. I just wanted to get as far away as possible. Colin nodded and followed me out the front door. As we walked quickly back to our apartment, I filled him in on the little family revelation he'd just missed.

"Poor Jared," he said as I unlocked the gate and we walked to the back of our building.

I didn't say anything as we went up the stairs. It was hard for me to process, really. Uncle Skipper had always smelled of liquor—I couldn't remember ever being around him when he wasn't drinking. It was just one of those things, like the sun comes up every morning and the river flows into the Gulf. Uncle Skipper always drank. I'd never seen him violent or angry, though—not once. But how old was I when Bethany left him? I barely remembered her from my childhood.

But what I really didn't want was to feel sorry for Jared.

As I changed into a black pair of slacks and a white shirt, I tried to remember if I'd ever liked Jared when we were kids. I couldn't. He was always spoiled, and blameless—even when he did something wrong, the rest of us were blamed "because we were older and knew better." He cried whenever he wanted attention, or when the older kids didn't want to do something he wanted to—which never failed to bring an adult on the run. The adult inevitably would hug and pet Jared while scolding us.

And he just got worse as he got older, I thought as I knotted a black tie. But am I being fair or holding on to childhood grudges?

I didn't remember Uncle Skipper being committed.

What had Mom called it—"the revolving door of stepmothers"?

I grabbed my black leather jacket and sat down on the couch. I got the cards out, shuffled, and laid them out on the coffee table. I frowned. The meaning was inconclusive, which was kind of annoying.

"Come on, Scotty," Colin called down the hallway. "Let's get going—we're going to have to deal with traffic as it is."

We hurried down to the lot on Chartres Street where Mom parked the Prius. It was getting dark, and cold rain was pouring down in sheets. By the time we were safely inside the car, my pants were soaked through from the knee down. My teeth were chattering. Colin started the car and turned the heat up full blast. We headed out of the Quarter to the I-10 on-ramp beyond Armstrong Park. As we headed around the curve, I could see rush-hour traffic was barely crawling.

"Do you really think anyone at Dove Ministry is going to talk to us?" I said to break the silence, which was starting to get on my nerves. "What should our cover story be?"

"Don't turn around, but I think there's a car following us," Colin said, glancing into the rearview mirror again.

I felt my stomach drop, and I shivered. "Are you sure? I mean, the traffic is pretty thick."

"There's a midsize car back there. It followed us all the way up Dumaine and onto the highway." He shrugged. "Sure, it's rush hour and a lot of people are heading out to the 'burbs, but it's still kind of curious. I have a gut feeling about it—and my gut feelings are never wrong. It could be the same car that tried to run us down yesterday. It's the same type."

It was taking all of my self-control not to turn around for a look. I glanced into the sideview mirror right outside my window. It was speckled with moisture, and all I could make out in the gloom was a row of headlights.

But if Colin said someone was following us, someone was following us.

I closed my eyes. *Don't panic, don't worry about it—Colin is a trained operative. If you're going to be followed by bad guys, who better to be driving than Colin?*

So instead of worrying I started trying to put the pieces together.

What Lurleen Rutledge had told us was a pretty awful story, but at the same time her alibi was Cara, and vice versa—and how trustworthy was that? Her story had rung true—but wasn't it also entirely possible Lurleen had not called her daughter but had gone out to her house to confront her? And if she arrived after Emily had left the gun, she could have just as easily shot her own hypocritical daughter—the tears and the grief wouldn't be any less real.

So, I couldn't cross Lurleen off the list of suspects. Cara could also have done it, but I didn't see a motive for her. Her only connection to Marina was through Lurleen, and she had no connection to Tara.

That was the other thing—Tara. Both women had been killed with the same gun, both women were involved in planning this big homophobic rally. Maybe the killer was some gay man or lesbian who'd finally had enough and decided to kill them both.

I reached down and turned on the radio, which was set to WWNO, the station from the University of New Orleans. WWNO was devoted to all things New Orleans and was affiliated with NPR. The newscaster was talking about some bill going before Congress—some reform bill for Wall Street that obviously had no chance of being passed or implemented.

The car continued creeping forward, and out of the corner of my eye I could see Colin occasionally looking back into the rearview mirror. He signaled and changed lanes as we went around the turn just past the Superdome. I started to ask if he still thought the car was following us but thought better of it when I noticed his lips were compressed into a tight line.

That wasn't a good sign.

"An anti-gay marriage rally planned for this Saturday in New Orleans will continue, despite the murder of one of the chief organizers and one of the speakers," the monotone-voiced woman said. I turned up the volume.

"Peggy MacGillicudy, the executive director of Protect American Marriage, released a joint statement with Reverend Dick Werner of the Dove Ministry of Truth, a megachurch based in Kenner, a suburb of New Orleans. MacGillicudy and Reverend Werner are going forward with the rally despite what they call 'the recent tragedies perpetrated on our movement by the Homosexual Agenda's terrorists.' The Louisiana governor is considering calling out the National Guard for fear of violence at the rally."

Colin hit a button and the station changed to one playing soft jazz. "That bullshit makes me sick," he said in a low voice, glancing again into the rearview mirror. Traffic was moving a little faster now—about twenty miles per hour. "Homosexual terrorists, my ass—that stupid bitch should head to the Middle East sometime if she wants to see some fucking terrorists."

"You know, that same thought has crossed my mind, Colin," I replied, looking out the window. "If it weren't for Mom's gun, it wouldn't be that far of a reach to think it could be just that— some gay or lesbian who got sick of the persecution, of the hate, wanting to get some of our own back."

"That MacGillicudy woman and Reverend Werner should just be glad that most gays are law-abiding," he went on grimly. "How many teenagers have killed themselves because of things those two have said? How many gays have been beaten or killed by thugs thinking they're doing God's work? Those two just egg that kind of shit on, and when it happens take no responsibility for it." He glanced in the rearview mirror again. "They should be grateful their churches aren't being bombed and no one opens fire at their stupid hate rallies."

Time to change that subject, I thought. "The thing that I don't get about all of this is the gun." I scratched my forehead. "How could someone have known Emily would leave Mom's gun at Marina's? No one could have. Someone went over there, saw the gun, and seized the opportunity? And then figured, what the hell, maybe I'll get a chance to kill Tara, too? It doesn't make any sense."

"That's because you're trying to make sense out of something that doesn't make sense." Colin shrugged. "Criminals aren't in their right minds as a rule, Scotty, and what they do doesn't make sense. A lot of things don't make sense in this world. That's why there's religion. People can't make sense out of a senseless world, so they decide it must be part of some big master plan they can't comprehend, and have to put faith in the unknown that there's a reason for it all."

"That's kind of cynical."

"Maybe. But isn't it cynical for Werner and MacGillicudy to manipulate other people's beliefs to advance their own agenda?" Colin's knuckles whitened on the steering wheel. "Religion is supposed to be a comfort, you know? Not a reason to kill."

A suicide bomber had killed Colin's mother and siblings when he was in his late teens. That was why he'd joined the Mossad in the first place. He'd eventually tired of the violence and resigned—and eventually wound up going to work for Blackledge.

I touched his arm, and his hands relaxed on the steering wheel. He glanced over at me and smiled. He looked into the rearview mirror and frowned. "The car's still back there, about two cars back, keeping pace with us but always staying two cars behind us."

I swallowed. "The traffic should let up after the Causeway interchange. Maybe you can try to lose him then."

"I'm not sure we should lose him," he said idly.

I didn't like the sound of that. "Why not?"

"Doesn't it make more sense to catch him?" He gave me a sly wink. "That way we can question him, maybe get to the bottom of this whole thing. I'm pretty sure it's the same car that tried to kill us yesterday."

I bit my lower lip.

I've been in a car chase before, and it's not a lot of fun. But given how heavy traffic was, I didn't think there was much of a chance of it happening until we passed Causeway Boulevard—and we would be taking the Clearview exit a mile past it. I scrunched down in my seat and turned the vent so the hot air was blowing directly at me. I glanced in the sideview mirror again, but all I could see was a long line of headlights behind us.

"We'll be getting off at Clearview, right?" Colin looked over at me as we slowed to about five miles an hour again. "That's the best way to get to Airline Highway, right?"

"Yeah. What are you thinking? Or do I want to know?"

Colin laughed and patted my leg. "Don't worry, Scotty, I know what I'm doing." He looked in the rearview and let out a breath. "Well, I guess I was wrong—they're getting off here."

I exhaled and my entire body relaxed. I looked out the window and saw a couple of cars shoot past us down the Carrollton exit. The traffic started picking up speed, and we shot around the first part of the S curve that took the highway through the Midcity, City Park, and Old Metairie neighborhoods.

We actually made it to the Clearview Parkway exit in a little less than ten minutes, which was a surprise. I directed Colin to take the Huey P. Long Bridge exit that pointed us straight into Kenner. The traffic was still heavy and slow as we turned right onto Airline Highway and came to a dead halt.

"Wow." I said, straining to see ahead of us. "That's the church lot up ahead to the left—I think that's why everything's backed up."

There was a uniformed cop out on the highway directing traffic into the vast parking lot of the Dove Ministry of Truth. He waved us on with the glowing cone in his hand, and we headed into the crowded parking lot. A massive electric sign was flashing MEMORIAL SERVICE FOR MARINA WERNER TONIGHT. A lot of people in yellow slickers were directing cars into parking places. The parking lot was packed with cars. Everywhere I looked people were sloshing through the inch or so of water on the pavement to get to the church. Someone directed us to a space, and Colin turned the engine off.

"So, what's our cover story?" I asked.

"If anyone asks, we're private eyes Marina hired." He winked at me. "And we can't say more than that. That should put the cat among the pigeons, don't you think?"

"Yeah." I got out of the car and opened my umbrella. The rain was still pouring down, and I took a deep breath as I looked at the Dove Ministry of Truth.

I'd never even been past the Dove Ministry before. I never

have occasion to be on Airline Highway—it's out of the way from the Quarter to the airport. As cold water soaked through my shoes, socks, and pants legs, I was beginning to be sorry I came this time. I felt queasier the closer I got to the building. It was a huge structure of brick, glass, and steel, maybe two or three stories tall. On the front was an enormous steel cross with several spotlights directed at it. I shivered, and not just from the cold.

A Christian church had never given me such an unpleasant feeling before.

I'd gone to Catholic school until college, and had attended enough Masses and prayer services to last a lifetime. I'd been to the Episcopalian services with my Bradley relatives. Every time, the most sense I'd ever gotten was something benign and peaceful.

But this place was setting off alarms in my soul.

Once we went through the glass doors into the crowded foyer, I could hear an organ playing "Nearer My God To Thee." My stomach was churning, and despite the cold I could feel sweat forming on my forehead and under my arms. I slipped my jacket off and draped it over my arm. An older woman, maybe in her late fifties, gray shot through her black bouffant, pressed a program into my hand. She smelled of roses, and she gave me a very sweet smile. "Bless you and thank you for coming," she said, patting my arm.

There were several sets of open double doors on the other side of the cavernous foyer. People were streaming through the doors. I bit my lip and followed Colin toward the doors on the far left. Everyone was so polite, and every so often I caught a glimpse of women who were softly crying to themselves.

It was so strange.

Had Tara and Marina really touched the lives of so many?

My phone vibrated in my pocket. I slipped it out and glanced at the screen. Colin's face grinned up at me, and across the bottom of the picture read the words: *Mass hysteria, you think?*

I slipped the phone back in my pocket.

The nausea I felt outside was getting stronger, and a headache was starting to form behind my eyes. I dry-swallowed and took several deep breaths as we entered the sanctuary. A chill ran through my body. There were rows and rows of hardwood pews, with red velvet cushions for the worshippers to sit on and more cushions on the back rests. Pockets on the backs of the pews held worn Bibles and song books. There were five aisles ending in several wide stairs, which led up to a pulpit. On the back wall behind the pulpit was another gigantic iron cross, with spotlights flashing different colors on it—first blue, then red, yellow and green. Massive candelabras stood on either side of the pulpit. Just to the right stood several risers, presumably for the choir. Throughout the sanctuary people milled about, removing coats and placing umbrellas on the floor, hugging and murmuring. The murmuring was low and quiet, almost unearthly. Colin and I slipped into a pew in the back, sliding to the opposite end.

"Are you okay?" he whispered to me as I spread my coat over my legs. "You look pale."

"Maybe I'm coming down with something," I whispered back. The headache and nausea were getting worse, and I rubbed my arms to try to warm them. I took a few deep breaths.

"We can leave if you want," Colin continued, his face worried. "You really don't look well."

I shook my head. "I'm fine," I lied. I wanted nothing more than to get the hell out of the Dove Ministry of Truth.

There was something definitely off about the place.

I closed my eyes and leaned my head back, pressing my forefingers into my temples. That sometimes worked for a headache, and the deep breathing seemed to be helping with the nausea.

I opened my eyes and looked forward. The different-colored lights were still flashing on the cross. It seemed *obscene* in some way to me.

A portly bald man in a black suit stepped out onto the pulpit, holding a microphone. "I'd like to encourage everyone to take their seats, please, so the service can get started."

The murmuring stopped and within a matter of moments everyone in the place was seated in a pew. I was amazed at how quickly and orderly it was accomplished.

I was about to say so to Colin when I caught sight of a familiar-looking head of thick blond hair in one of the front pews.

Father Dan? What the hell was he doing here?

I strained my eyes, trying to make sure it was him—but I couldn't be certain. The hair color was right, even the shape of the head, but he was almost fifty yards in front of me and I couldn't be sure unless I saw his face.

Colin pinched me so hard I almost yelped.

"Why did you do that?" I hissed, and he elbowed me in the side, I looked at him, and he was gesturing with his head. I turned and looked in the direction he was staring, to the front of the sanctuary but the opposite side.

My eyes got wide. "Enid?"

"What the hell is she doing here?" he hissed to me without moving his lips. "That is your aunt, isn't it?"

I nodded. She was standing at the side of the very front pew on the right side, dressed completely in black—a black turtleneck sweater over a knee-length black skirt and black hose. She was wiping at her nose with a handkerchief. As I watched, she sat down.

Enid was a member of the Dove Ministry?

I couldn't believe it—even though it explained her defense of Tara to Frank the other night.

How—and when—had this happened?

All the Bradleys were Episcopalians—except for our branch of the family. Storm and Rain had converted to Catholicism as teenagers, but Mom and Dad were Wiccans. Papa Bradley was as fervent an Episcopalian as he was conservative politically—he certainly would not approve of his daughter attending services at a megachurch.

But it also might explain just how Jared and Tara had met in the first place.

A group of men and women in purple and white choir robes with gigantic crosses slowly filed in from behind the pulpit and took their places on the risers. An organ began playing solemnly from somewhere—there wasn't one in sight.

The entire congregation rose in unison. Colin and I scrambled to our feet as another man walked out onto the pulpit and two enormous television screens lowered from the ceiling on either side. Suddenly the man's face appeared in extreme close-up on both screens.

The Reverend Dick Werner himself.

Werner was a short man and didn't miss many meals, from the looks of him. He had reddish-brown hair that was balding, and long frizzy reddish sideburns. He wore wire-framed glasses, and on the JumboTrons his dark eyes burned with a frightening intensity.

The headache, which had been subsiding, came back with a roar as he began speaking. "Brothers and sisters! Thank you for coming out for such a solemn, sad occasion as we pay tribute to two of our own, two who have fallen in the battle to save the world for our Lord and Savior, Jesus Christ!"

"Amen," the entire congregation said in unison.

"This is spooky," Colin whispered to me.

He wasn't kidding. It was spooky. It was like the entire crowd was trained to say "amen" in unison every time Werner paused for breath.

And he began to speak, talking about how his daughter and Tara were soldiers for Christ, trying to shine a bright light in the darkness created by the Homosexual Agenda. On and on, he ranted, with his audience chanting "amen" in unison as though on cue.

I felt sick, and sicker with every sentence he spoke.

Then he yielded the pulpit to Peggy MacGillicudy herself.

"This is a tragic day in the fight for God's truth, and preserving the United States of America," she said into the microphone.

I pushed my way past Colin, out of the pew.

My head felt like it was going to explode.

I managed to make it out into the foyer and into a stall in the men's room before I threw up.

I washed my face in the sink and rinsed out my mouth with cold water before heading back inside.

But they were singing "Amazing Grace," and the whole thing was over.

I made my way back to Colin as everyone was standing up. "Come on," I whispered. "I want to talk to Father Dan."

He looked at me in shock. "Father Dan's here?"

I nodded and started pushing my way through the crowd. I spotted his blond head moving to the front of the church—where Enid was standing with another woman I didn't recognize.

Father Dan grasped the arm of the woman.

She turned and looked at him, her face contorting.

She slapped him across the face and ran up the stairs of the pulpit with Enid at her heels.

Father Dan just stood there, looking after her, not moving as the place emptied of people.

"We need to talk," I said as I caught up to him.

There was a red handprint on his right cheek. He gave me a sad look. "Okay," he replied. "But not here."

CHAPTER TWELVE

THE LOVERS

The choice between vice and virtue

"Thank you." Father Dan smiled at the waitress as she put a cup of coffee in front of him. He took a sip. "I'm originally from Kenner, you know. I still have a lot of family out there," he said after she walked away. "I went to high school with Tara's mother."

"You mentioned that the other night," I replied.

We were seated in a booth at the Chili's Restaurant on Veterans' Boulevard in Metairie. Father Dan had told us to follow him when we left the church parking lot, and this was where he'd brought us. It wasn't very crowded—some of the booths were taken and several people were seated at the bar. We were in a corner by big glass windows that faced the parking lot. It was still raining, but the restaurant was overheated. Our jackets were piled in a corner of the booth, and I'd removed my tie. A waitress walked past us carrying a sizzling plate of fajitas. My stomach growled.

My nausea and headache had magically gone away as soon as I walked out of the Dove Ministry building, and I was starving. I hadn't eaten anything besides a piece of crumb cake at Lurleen Rutledge's, and that felt like it was a million years ago. I took a sip out of my iced tea. I looked down at my menu. I didn't care how many grams of fat were in it—I was ordering a bacon cheeseburger and fries.

Maybe even chili cheese fries.

He took another sip of his coffee and gave me a sad look. "Well, there was more to it than that, I'm afraid. I didn't just go to high school with Marilou—I knew her much better than that."

"You were friends?" I asked.

He shrugged and smiled. "I married her."

"You performed her marriage ceremony?" Colin said after a moment. I was too stunned to speak. *I couldn't have heard that right.*

Dan took another drink of his wine. He looked down at the table. "No, I mean I married her. Stood up in front of God and said the vows with her. Man and wife married." He swallowed. "Obviously, it was a huge mistake."

"But I thought—" I spluttered out, but stopped myself from adding *you're gay.* I didn't know that. Sure, Father Dan ministered to the queer community. Sure, I had seen him in gay bars, not wearing his collar. I'd seen him walking around during Southern Decadence without a shirt, in skimpy costumes on Fat Tuesday. But as far as I knew he'd never broken his vow of celibacy. I'd never seen him with his arm around another man, or kissing one. I'd never seen him leave a bar with a guy.

No—even if he was celibate, he still had to be gay.

Father Dan wouldn't bring his eyes up from the table.

"Do you guys need another minute?" our waitress said, and I almost jumped out of my skin.

"That would be great," Colin flashed his million-dollar smile at her. "Thank you."

Father Dan's face was a deep shade of red. "It's a long story—and you boys probably can't understand, but things were different back then." He ran his fingers through his hair. "Scotty, you grew up in a very loving and supportive environment. Orleans Parish has always been a lot more accepting of gay men than Jefferson Parish, and you couldn't have asked for better parents. Colin, I don't know what your family was like, but I can tell you—I grew up in a family where being gay—where being different—just wasn't possible."

So he IS gay, I thought with an inward sigh of relief. I didn't want to think my Gaydar was *that* far off.

"I kept praying for God to cure me, ever since I knew I was attracted to boys instead of girls," he went on. "But he never did—he never took it away from me, no matter how hard I prayed, no matter how many times I begged, no matter how good I was. Our priest—" His voice broke. "Our priest, Father Romano, kept hammering into me that it was a sin, and to read Job—that sometimes God tested us, our faith, and that this was a huge test, and that it was up to *me* to prove *my* faith to God."

"That's disgusting," Colin replied. "You can't pray away the gay."

Father Dan smiled weakly. "We know that now, Colin—but back then…" His voice trailed off.

"The Dove Ministry preaches that—they even have ex-gay workshops," I pointed out. "A lot of Christian denominations believe God and prayer can make you straight."

"Throughout history the word of God has been perverted by men," Father Dan replied with a sardonic laugh, "to fit their own agendas. I may be a priest, but even I have to admit the Catholic Church has been one of the worst offenders." He took a deep breath. "But the world was different then—things have changed so much…" He shook his head. "So, I did everything I possibly could to change. I dated girls, tried to not look at other boys with desire. Marilou…I convinced myself I was in love with her." His voice broke. "What I did to her was unforgivable. Absolutely unforgivable…I have never expected her to forgive me, how could she? All I can do is ask God to forgive me, and to give her the peace and understanding to do the same."

"How could you have married her?" Colin's voice was low. "That was so *selfish*."

"Do you think I'm not aware of that, Colin?" Father Dan's face flushed. "I am so ashamed of what I did to her. I don't expect you two to understand...how much I hated myself. How many times I thought about killing myself. When Marilou came into my life...I thought she was a sign from God. I thought God had answered my prayers. She was so beautiful, so sweet and loving...and a good Catholic." He closed his eyes and took a deep breath. "She'd even considered becoming a nun...I did love her, that wasn't a lie, you know. But I didn't love her the way a man should love a woman. I was just a teenager, and I thought...I didn't know the difference." He swallowed. "And when I see her now—like tonight, the bitter woman she is now—I *did* that to her, do you understand me? I've lived with that all these years." He took a deep breath. "I ask God's forgiveness every day."

"I'm not trying to be insensitive," Colin replied, "but I'm trying to understand. How can you have faith when one of the tenets of your religion condemns all gays and lesbians to hell?"

"*My* faith—I personally don't believe that, Colin." A faint smile crossed Father Dan's face. "The hierarchy of my church does. I just don't happen to believe that any human is incapable of error. The *humans* who run my church are capable of error, and are very capable of sin. History shows this, over and over again. Religion is often perverted to justify unspeakable acts and crimes—like war. How can a God who is about love and peace sanction war and wholesale slaughter of His children? He cannot. And I don't believe that some ambitious old man who plays politics and gets elected to sit on a throne in Rome somehow becomes infallible, that every word from his mouth on doctrine and matters of faith is indisputably correct, that he speaks for God. No one speaks for God."

"Careful—you're starting to sound like an Episcopalian," I said before I could stop myself.

Instead of being offended, Father Dan laughed and the flush faded from his face. "Scotty, you're incorrigible. But I pray every day for guidance. I question my faith daily. But it's not for me to understand God's plan for me. I refuse to believe God would turn His back on His children simply because of their sexual attraction to people of the same sex. A merciful, loving God would not do that. Man, yes. God, no." He spread his hands. "We are all God's creations, and my faith requires me to reject the fallibility of God. I do not believe same-sex attraction is Satan tempting us to turn away from God. I know, from my own experience, that I was *born* this way; so God created me as a gay man. He has a purpose. Rejecting that purpose would be turning my back on Him."

Our waitress materialized again. She was a pretty girl in her early twenties with brown hair and a round face. Her nametag said *Sheila*. "You gentlemen ready to order?" she asked, a pad in her hand.

"Nothing for me, but I would like more coffee." Father Dan smiled at her.

"I want the bacon cheeseburger, medium, and can I get chili cheese fries with it?" My stomach growled again. I hadn't even looked at my menu, but I ordered a bacon cheeseburger—every place like Chili's serves a bacon cheeseburger. Colin ordered the same—Father Dan asked for another glass of wine.

"So, yes, I dated Marilou when we were in high school. She was a wonderful girl, really, quite pretty. I could see a lot of Marilou in Tara, actually. Marilou was quite pretty, and she loved life—she just wanted to grab life with both hands and squeeze it dry. And when we—when we"—he swallowed—"when we were together, I got aroused." He whispered the word, his face flushing again. "So I thought the feelings I had—when I looked at boys—that maybe it was an aberration, just a phase I was going through."

I bit my lower lip. I remembered thinking the exact same thing when I was a teenager. I remembered wondering if all boys had the same feelings, just didn't ever talk about them or act on them. I remembered the first time I realized they didn't—it was horrible to know I wasn't like the other boys, that my sexual wiring was different. And he was right—I'd been incredibly lucky. My parents had been loving and accepting. They'd been excited about my being gay, rather than being horrified. They'd embraced my sexuality with a vengeance, joining P-FLAG, marching in Pride parades, and openly advocating and working for gay equality.

"After we graduated from high school, we both started going to UNO." He went on, his voice shaking. "It was at UNO I met a guy who was openly gay, wasn't ashamed to shout it to the world." He lowered his voice to a whisper. "But you have to remember—AIDS was ravaging the community in those days. There was no treatment. It was a death sentence, every diagnosis meant a horrible death…so little was known! My parents—my church—believed it was God's judgment on the gays, his terrible wrath on their sin. I was so afraid—I couldn't imagine what I would do if I got AIDS, but I wanted him, oh, how I wanted him!" His eyes got a faraway look in them. "He was so out and proud—I'd never known such a thing was even possible, you know? He used to wear a pink shirt that said 'I'm gay, get over it.' I couldn't believe anyone could have the courage to wear a shirt like that to school, to risk the abuse that must have come with it, you know what I mean? And I—I slept with him." He closed his eyes. "We used condoms, of course—but I was still terrified, absolutely terrified, that I'd have to explain to my parents, or to my priest, that I had AIDS. I hated myself so much for doing it, for enjoying it so much. It just felt right, I can't explain it better than that. It just felt right. Afterward I hated myself for giving into the sin." He swallowed. "I thought about killing myself, I didn't think I deserved to live, but I couldn't go through with it. But the guilt was so horrible. I decided to ask Marilou to marry me…I thought if I married her, you know, that would be the end of it. I thought—but it doesn't matter what I thought. It was such an incredibly selfish thing to do."

"It really was," Colin replied in a rather nasty tone. I kicked him under the table. He glared at me.

"I know it was," Father Dan said. He licked his lips. "I didn't think of her as a person, someone who had feelings, who deserved to be loved. I just thought of her as a solution to my problem." He sighed. "I hope someday God can forgive me. Marilou never has, and she never will. I can't blame her."

"That was the woman who slapped you at Dove Ministry, I take it?" Colin asked.

He nodded. "Yes, it was. We got married. She was so happy. And all I felt was trapped."

Oh, no. It came to me in a flash. "You were Tara's father, weren't you?" I asked slowly.

He nodded. "God help me, it didn't take long. After we got married I knew I had made a terrible mistake. But she was so happy—and I didn't know what to do. I prayed. I prayed a lot for guidance from God—but I sinned." He hung his head. "I thought"—his face contorted—"I thought it wasn't *cheating*, you see. The lies we convince ourselves are truths, so we can justify our own sins! I convinced myself that if I were with another man, it wasn't *really* adultery." He laughed bitterly. "The truth was, it was worse. At least to Marilou, it was. And if I hadn't been so selfish, so concerned with myself, I would have known that. But I wasn't thinking clearly. Obviously."

"Here you go, gentlemen!" Our waitress reappeared, placing our burgers down in front of us. I almost moaned with pleasure and my stomach growled so loudly I was afraid everyone in the place could hear it. "Can I get you anything else? More coffee?"

Father Dan nodded at her, and she swept away.

"She found out." He shook his head. "They always do, you know. I think it's possible I wanted to be caught—because I was taking some ridiculous risks. I'll never forget that day as long as I live." He stared off into space. "Marilou was at work—and so I had him meet me at our apartment. We were in the bed I shared with her. She left work because she didn't feel well. She found us—in our bed." He closed his eyes again. "As long as I live I'll never forget the look on her face. She became hysterical—as she had every right to. Tom pulled on his clothes and got out of there as she screamed at me, hitting me." He traced a finger along his front teeth. "She broke both of these teeth—she threw an ashtray at me and hit me right in the mouth. And then she left, went home to her parents. She wouldn't talk to me. She filed for a divorce and refused to ever speak to me again. And she was pregnant."

"Which was why she left work early that day to begin with," Colin prompted.

"When I found out, she told me it wasn't mine. But I knew Tara was my daughter, I always knew." He sighed. "She got married again before the baby was even born, you know, she married Johnny Bourgeois. He went to high school with us, too—he'd always had a thing for her, and now she was available. As for me…" He rubbed his eyes. "The only thing that got me through all of it was my faith, and I heard the call. I've been a priest ever since."

"It must have been horrible to hear Tara spout that homophobic nonsense at the Miss United States pageant," I observed.

"Until then, I was so proud of her." The waitress refilled his coffee mug, and he smiled his thanks to her. "I never knew her, you know. Marilou and her family made sure of that, and I don't know, maybe it was for the best. But I always kept an eye on her. I watched her grow up—from a distance. I think the proudest day of my life was when she became Miss Louisiana. I was there. I actually wept with joy when they put the crown on her head." He shook his head. "Pride is a sin, you know. But I never blamed Tara for the things she said, the things she did after the Miss

United States pageant. That was all Marilou. Marilou raised her to hate gays and lesbians, to think they were evil."

It's just the way I was raised, I heard Tara saying again in my mind.

"I just kept thinking if I could talk to her, make her see how wrong it was to hate people..." Dan finished his coffee. He pulled a twenty out of his wallet, and put it down on the table. "And now she's dead—and even after all this time, Marilou still can't forgive me." He stood up. "Enjoy your dinner, boys."

"Father Dan." Colin stopped him. "I know you were at Mom and Dad's the night Tara was murdered, but where were you on Monday morning?"

"You think I killed Marina Werner?" His eyebrows went up, and he laughed. "I suppose you have to ask. No, I didn't kill Marina Werner. I was at the Mission on Oretha Castle Hailey all morning, ministering to the homeless. You can check it out. Please do." He patted me on the shoulder and winked at Colin. "I'll see you boys later."

My mind was reeling, but I was so hungry nothing could stop me from devouring the bacon cheeseburger in a matter of moments. When all that was left was a puddle of ketchup and some French fry debris, I said, "He could have taken the gun."

Colin finished chewing the last bite of his burger and swallowed. "I don't see Father Dan killing Marina, frankly. You've been awfully quiet since we left the Dove Ministry, though. What are you thinking?"

"That place makes me sick," I replied as our waitress slid a small tray with the bill on the table. "And it was sickening the way Werner and that MacGillicudy woman are using the murders to further their own agenda."

"All zealots are like that, opportunistic." Colin slid an American Express card into the tray and took another drink of his iced tea. "It's reprehensible, but you have to admire how quickly they can think on their feet. They probably raked in about a hundred grand in donations for the church and her group tonight."

"False prophets," I said aloud, remembering the feeling I had while we were sitting in that awful place. "They prey on the weak, and then bilk them out of money."

"What I'm more curious about is why your aunt was there."

That jolted me. In my shock over the whole Father Dan thing, I hadn't given Enid another thought. "And she was right there in the front pew with Marilou Bourgeois," I said.

"And you said she said some homophobic things to Frank on Monday night." Colin smirked. "Just what is her connection to the Dove Ministry and the Bourgeois family, anyway? You know, she's the only person we know of who is connected to both victims."

"Enid couldn't kill anyone," I scoffed.

"You don't think she's changed since she had the gastro-bypass?" Colin asked as he signed the credit slip and put his card back into his wallet. "Frank does."

"He hasn't said anything to me."

"She's your aunt, Scotty." Colin patted my leg as I slid out of the booth and put my coat back on. "It's not cool to badmouth someone's relatives."

"Certainly not a problem with my crazy family," I retorted as we walked back out into the parking lot. "Frank knows that. So, what did he say?"

Colin shrugged as he started the car. Another car started farther down the row from us. His eyebrows came together as he peered out into the rain and shrugged again. "Frank said Enid was nuts but harmless before she had the surgery. After she started losing the weight and got her own place, she started changing. He said she was more mean-spirited and malicious than she used to be."

"That's because he didn't know her all that well before," I replied as he pulled out onto Veteran's Boulevard. "She's *always* been that way. She pretends like she's sweetness and light—all the little presents and the cards are just window dressing to cover what she's really like."

He made a U-turn and headed back for New Orleans. "What is it with you and her?"

I sighed and hit the button to make my seat recline. "She *is* mean, Colin. She always has been—she says incredibly mean things about other people to be funny. And the stuff she says is funny, but it's also mean and hurtful." I closed my eyes. "She used to do it to me all the time, and sometimes the things she said would really hurt my feelings. If I said anything, she would get all pouty and say she didn't mean it that way, she was just teasing, and on and on and on. But the funny thing I started noticing was she could say whatever she wanted to about someone else, and it was supposed to be funny. But if someone did the same thing to her, she would start crying."

"Could dish it out but couldn't take it?"

"Exactly. I don't remember exactly when it was, but she was at Mom and Dad's for dinner with everyone one night, and she started in on Storm. And you know Storm—he's kind of the same way, only *he* can take it when you tease him. And usually Storm just let her go—didn't say anything back, you know, just laughed and went along with it. But that night—I can't remember exactly what it was she said, but it really annoyed him for some reason, and he shot back at her in the same way—I think she was making fun of him because of gaining some weight, or something, and he just looked at her and said, 'Morbidly obese people really shouldn't mock other people for putting on a few pounds,' and she got all quivery and started to cry. 'I can't believe you're so mean,' she said, and then Mom just lost it completely."

"Ah, Mom." Colin laughed as he merged onto I-10.

"Yeah. Mom just went off, just read her the riot act up one

side and down the other, and then of course Enid finally got over her hurt feelings and said something nasty to Mom, and Mom told her to, and I quote, 'get your fat fucking ass out of my house before I rip off one of your enormous arms and beat you to death with it, you fucking hypocrite.'" I blew out my breath. "And of course, after she left everyone started comparing notes about her—and I've never really felt the same way about her since then. And after what she said to Frank the other night…"

"You think you can control your temper if we stop by there?" He glanced in the rearview mirror and frowned.

I turned and looked out the back window. "I wish you would stop doing that."

"I know, but I would swear there's a car following us—the same one that was in the parking lot at Chili's—and it looked like the one that was following us earlier."

"Which looked like the car that tried to run us over?" My heart started beating faster. I looked behind us again, but all I saw was headlights.

"I don't think we're in any danger," Colin replied, "but I don't like that someone is following us."

I closed my eyes and said a serenity prayer.

CHAPTER THIRTEEN
QUEEN OF CUPS, REVERSED
A woman whose imagination runs away with her

Aunt Enid lived on Coliseum Square in the lower Garden District. The house was a beautiful old Victorian mansion that had been split into apartments. A gallery ran around the entire first floor, and the left front corner of the house featured a round tower crowned by a witch's hat–style roof. The house itself stood three stories tall, and the second and third floors had small galleries as well. There was a large swimming pool in the fenced-in backyard, and bushes rimmed the front and side yards just inside a waist-high black wrought iron fence. It was painted a dark pink and stood on the corner facing the park. As Colin parked the Jag on the park side of Coliseum Street under a streetlight, I could see the park was completely empty except for a woman in a green raincoat walking a black Lab. It was a beautiful park filled with massive live oaks. The old-style lamps along the various paved walkways were all lit up. The rain had degenerated to a mist, which shrouded the park lights and gave them an eerie glow. The fountain was fully lit, and I could hear it splash as I got out of the car.

I'd only been to Enid's apartment once, shortly after she moved in several years ago. She'd called Frank and needed our help rearranging the furniture. I hadn't wanted to go, but Frank had insisted. She lived in a big, spacious, well-lit apartment on the second floor, which encompassed the front corner of the building with the tower. The tower room was, she informed us, her crafting room. The whole place was done in pastels—pinks, pale blues, lavenders. The walls were covered with framed prints of scenes from medieval literature—damsels in distress waving handkerchiefs at knights in shining armor, the Lady of the Lake rising from the water with Excalibur in her hands while Arthur knelt on the shore, Ophelia floating in her watery grave with flowers entwined in the hair spread out around her head like a halo.

That visit was in May, and while it was a lovely eighty degrees outside, her windows were all tightly closed. Walking into the apartment felt like stepping into a walk-in refrigerator—it couldn't have been more than a frigid sixty degrees inside. I was so cold I wished I'd brought a sweater. The apartment had been in complete disarray. There were dirty dishes and take-out debris all over the kitchen counters. The sink was filled with dirty pots and pans. Every garbage can was overflowing sides onto the floor. Empty boxes were scattered everywhere I could see. Those little Styrofoam packing beans and crumpled sheets of bubble wrap were all over the floor. We moved her couch a few times—it finally wound up back where it had originally started. Finished, we beat a hasty retreat, her insistence on having us over for dinner "once I'm settled in" ringing in our ears.

That dinner invitation had never come.

We went up the back stairs to the short covered gallery that led to her back door. Her car, a bright yellow Karmann Ghia, was parked in her spot, and all her lights were on. I hesitated for a moment before knocking on her door. I heard footsteps and the door swung open.

"What took you—" She stopped herself when she realized it was Colin and me. Her hand flew to her mouth. She'd changed into a pale blue cotton sweat suit. "What are you two doing here?"

"We were in the neighborhood and thought we'd stop by," I lied, plastering a smile on my face. "Can we come in? It's cold out here."

Her narrowed eyes moved back and forth from me to Colin. She stepped aside after a moment. "Of course." Her tone was pleasant but forced. "What a pleasant surprise!" She forced a big smile onto her face that didn't quite reach her eyes.

She was obviously not pleased to see us, and I wondered who she'd been expecting.

We walked past her into her huge living space. It was an enormous room, with lots of windows for light. All of her blinds were closed, and it felt like an oven inside. I felt sweat forming under my arms. She had the same prints on her walls, but the frames were now ornate and gilt. There were also pale blue velvet curtains at every window, tied back by gold cords ending in enormous gold tassels. The apartment looked like a hurricane had swept through it. There were newspapers and magazines piled on every available surface. Empty soda cans, wineglasses with a puddle of red wine in the bottom, empty wine bottles, and clothes were scattered all over the floor. There was barely enough room for one person to sit on the couch, which was otherwise buried in debris. There was also a strong odor of cat urine, and I noticed three cat boxes next to the refrigerator in the kitchen. An enormous white cat was perched on a pile of disheveled newspaper on the arm of the couch, looking at us with disdain before pointedly starting to clean himself.

She walked over to one of the armchairs and transferred the pile of debris from it to the top of another pile on the coffee table. The pile wobbled but didn't fall. She did the same to the other armchair, gesturing for us to have seats. "I wasn't expecting company or I would have picked up a bit," she said, smiling. "Promise me you won't tell anyone what a horrible housekeeper I am! Can I get you boys anything? Wine? Diet Coke? Tea?"

"Nothing for me," Colin said, gingerly picking his way through the debris on the floor to one of the armchairs and sitting down.

"Me, either," I replied, debating whether I wanted to sit down. I decided it would be rude not to, so I slid into the other chair. "We just ate at Chili's."

"I *love* Chili's!" she squealed, clapping her hands together. Colin gave me an odd look I couldn't interpret. "They have the best chicken Caesar wrap!" She licked her lips. "I'll have to head out there tomorrow and have one. Are you boys sure you don't want anything?"

"No, we're fine." I smiled back at her.

"I'll have some wine, if you don't mind." She hurried into the kitchen area and pulled the cork out of a half-empty bottle. She opened a cabinet and got down a tumbler, which she filled almost all the way to the top. She sat down in the clear area on the couch, holding the wine with one hand while she stroked the cat with her other hand. A wad of white cat hair drifted into the air before settling on the end table. "I'm sorry I've never had you boys over—I keep meaning to invite you, but then time just gets away from me!" she said, using her breathless little girl voice that raised my hackles. She reached over and stroked the enormous white cat. "Who's Mommy's little man?" she cooed as he climbed into her lap, purring. "Oh, who's Mommy's sweet kitty? Yes, that's my Harley."

Colin glanced over at me. I just gave him my *whatever* look as another cat, this one orange and white and weighing at least twenty pounds, leaped into my lap and started nudging my hand with his head.

"You pet him, Scotty!" Enid commanded, her eyes wide. "Jonah doesn't usually like people, you know. He must think you're *special*."

I started scratching the cat under his chin as commanded, and he closed his eyes to slits, purring. "Enid, I was just curious—how did you know Tara Bourgeois?"

Her eyes narrowed for a moment before widening again as she gave me an innocent face. "Well, I met her at the Ministry, of course. I know her mother, Marilou, quite well. She's one of my dearest friends. Such a wonderful, sweet woman, that Marilou. She's just devastated about Tara, the poor thing."

I took a deep breath. Jonah was now kneading my chest with his front paws, and the claws were piercing through my thin white dress shirt. "I didn't know you were a member of the Ministry," I said, trying to keep my voice neutral.

"Oh, yes, Scotty, I am." She clasped her hands together, like she was about to start praying. "The Ministry is just wonderful. Reverend Werner is such a Godly man. He truly communicates with God, you know."

I swallowed. "So, how did you wind up at the Ministry?"

She closed her eyes. "I remember it as though it was yesterday. It was when we evacuated for Katrina—we went to Atlanta and were staying at a Hotel Intercontinental. I had a terrible argument with Papa—I don't remember what it was about now, and it doesn't matter, I suppose…and I ordered a huge meal from room service." Her eyes opened, and she gave me a sly look. "I always took refuge in food when I was unhappy, and I was unhappy all of the time. You remember that, don't you, Scotty?"

I just nodded.

"I was flipping through the channels, hoping to find a movie or something, and I saw Reverend Werner on one of those Christian cable channels, talking about New Orleans, so I stopped and watched." She got a blissful look on her face again. "It was like he was talking directly to me, Scotty. And I knew God was going to save New Orleans because of men like Reverend Werner, and I decided right then and there to join his ministry when I got back."

"You've been going there that long?" I said, wondering why no one in the family had ever mentioned it.

"Well, no." She shook her head. "I backslid and forgot all about it. I kept wandering in the darkness. I was lost, Scotty, but now I'm found." She gave me a beatific smile. "You know what it was like for me, remember?" Harley jumped down from her lap as she shuddered. "It was so cold out there without God's love. I always knew something was missing from my life, you know, but I never knew what it was. And then I found God's light."

"But you're an Episcopalian," I replied, trying to make sense of this. "You went to church with Papa and MiMi every Sunday."

She made a rude noise. "Episcopalians. They're just Catholics without the pope. Idolaters." She shook her head. "There's nothing in that church for anyone. God has turned His back on that church—no one there heeds God's law anymore, and He has turned His back—and not just on them. No, sir! The Catholics, the Baptists, the Lutherans, the Methodists—all of them. They no longer follow God's law." She gave me a predatory smile. "But it's not like that at the Ministry. Dick Werner is truly a prophet of the Lord." She shook her head and made clucking noises. "It's just terrible about his daughter."

"You knew Marina?" This came from Colin. Yet another cat was at his feet—this one black with gold highlights.

"Oh, yes. Marina was one of my best friends." She nodded, wiping at her eyes. "Dear, dear Marina was closer to me than my own brothers. She was the first person to really care about me. She was the one who convinced me to get the gastric bypass, you know. She told me we needed to pray on it, and God would let me know what He wanted me to do. It changed my life."

I was confused. "I thought Aunt Leslie—"

"Leslie's nothing but a whore." She cut me off with a hiss. "She doesn't love Skipper. She married him for his money, to be in our family. That's a whore in my book. No, it was Marina and Marilou who convinced me to ask God where I should have it done, and it changed my life. No, *God* changed my life. My life now has purpose."

"You still haven't told me how you joined the Ministry." I lifted Jonah off me and set him down on the floor. He took off like a shot. I ruefully looked down at my black sweater, now covered in white cat hairs. I tried to brush it off to no avail.

"My car broke down." All the lines in her face smoothed out, and her eyes—her eyes took on an ecstatic look. "I was driving home from the airport—I'd just gone to that weight loss place in North Carolina and *gained* three pounds. I was upset and didn't know what I was going to do. And my car started overheating on Airline Highway—I don't even remember why I chose that way to come home, you know? It was like God was directing me. So I pulled into the next parking lot, and it was Dove Ministry." She smiled. "And my cell phone battery was dead so I couldn't call for help—God's handiwork again—and so I had to go knock on the doors. It was Marina who answered the door."

God's handiwork. Every time she said it, a chill went down my spine despite the overheated apartment. I was starting to sweat. *How can she stand this place being so hot?* I wondered.

"Marina could see I was troubled—and not just about the car. She took me into her office and got me a glass of iced tea. She told me she would call one of the members who was a car mechanic, and she did. But she could tell there was something else wrong, and she wanted to know." She gave me a glare. "She actually *cared*, which is more than I can say about my own family."

I dry-swallowed and bit my tongue. I didn't know what to say—I didn't want to start an argument with her. "So, Marina cared about you."

"Yes, she did, and I can tell by your tone, Milton Scott

Bradley, that you don't believe me!" She reached inside her sweatshirt and pulled out a gold cross inlaid with rubies. "She *gave* me this! For Christmas this year! And she always appreciated my cards and presents. No one else ever did! No one in my so-called family!" Her voice rose. "You think I don't know what my own family thinks about me?"

I snuck a glance at Colin. He wasn't looking at either one of us—he was looking around the apartment. "I'm sorry to interrupt," he said, standing up. "But I need to use the bathroom."

She waved at the hallway. "You can't miss it. The door's open." She watched him cross the room and once he went down the hallway, she hissed at me, "Isn't it bad enough your lifestyle is condemning you and Frank to hell, do you have to make it worse with *that* one?"

I gaped at her. I wanted nothing more than to slap the smug look right off her face.

"I learned the truth at the Ministry," she went on. "About everything. About how I was surrounded by vipers in my own family, every last one of them doing Satan's work, trying to turn me into a willing servant of the Evil One. That's why I was so unhappy, Reverend Werner himself told me so. Because I wanted to do good, because I wanted to do God's work, and my family were all agents of the devil."

"And so they convinced you to do the gastric bypass?" I remembered vaguely hearing about it when she'd had it done. I'd always thought it was Aunt Leslie who convinced her to have it, but apparently I'd heard wrong.

Although I could swear I remembered Aunt Leslie telling me about it—and I was pretty sure Leslie had stayed at the hospital with her.

"Reverend Werner told me the weight was a curse from the devil, because he knew I was good, and so he made me eat and eat so my health would be bad and I would die early—which was the only way he could win, the only way he could defeat the goodness in my soul." She sat back, folding her arms. "And I knew I was important to God, because why else would the devil want me to die? So I had the surgery so I could be healthier, have a longer life, keep doing God's work." Her face took on a beatific gleam again. "Marilou and Marina were right there with me through it all. Reverend Werner's face was the first one I saw when I woke up from the surgery." She made a face again. "No one from my family could be bothered."

No, I know it was Aunt Leslie who was there with you—even Mom and Dad visited you—you had it done at Touro, I remembered. I didn't correct her, though. "That's just terrible, Enid. I'm so sorry to hear that."

"My parents—Papa and Mama—they never cared about me. Ever. They didn't want me. I might as well have never been born as far as they were concerned! It was always Skipper this, Skipper that. And John—he used to love me, but then he married that devil-worshipping whore Cecile, and she turned him against me."

It took all of my willpower not to leap across the room and strangle her. *How dare you call my mother a whore? She's worth a hundred of you, you crazy bitch!*

"And you, too, Scotty." She gave me a sad look. "You were always such a sweet little boy, not like Storm and Rain. You and Jared were my little angels. But then you—you turned your back on God and became a homosexual. Jared was all I had left. So, when Marilou was so worried about Tara's getting back involved with that terrible boy—that Joe Billette—and I thought to myself, Jared's a good boy, a little misguided, Tara's the right girl to set him back on the righteous path—so I helped bring them together." She smiled, not looking at me. "They were such a beautiful young couple, too—they would have had the most beautiful children." Her face darkened. "Who knew that

Tara was such a sinner? Such a liar? But then Lucifer was the most beautiful of the angels, and look how *that* turned out. Poor Marilou—Tara just about broke her heart." She took a sip of her wine. "I would have never introduced Jared to Tara had I known what she was doing."

"And what exactly was she doing?"

"She was a fornicator—spreading her legs for any man who would give her the time of day." Enid put her glass back down. "But she's dead, and now Jared, my little angel, can find a really nice girl."

My hands were shaking from the effort to contain my rage. "You do know he's seeing Dominique DuPre, don't you?"

She gave me a puzzled look. "Dominique DuPre?"

I took a deep breath. "She's a singer, and owns Domino's, a jazz club on Bourbon Street." I added, with extra emphasis, "She's *divorced*."

Enid's eyes widened, and her hand flew to her lips. "Oh, no. That won't do. That won't do at all."

Colin walked hurriedly back into the living room. He picked up his coat and gave me a look. "Well, we really need to be going, Enid. Sorry to have just dropped in on you like this unannounced."

She looked relieved. I stood up and, with an effort, kissed her on the cheek. "Maybe we should have dinner sometime."

"Wait just a second." She rooted around on the coffee table and finally removed two food-stained pamphlets. She handed one to each of us. "Please, will you read these for me? And think about your lifestyle. Please?"

I looked down at it. *Why Homosexuals Are Condemned To Hell—But They Can Be SAVED!* I swallowed, resisting the urge to shove it down her throat. "Thanks." I shoved it into my jacket pocket.

She picked up her cell phone off the end table and was

playing with it as she walked us to the door. "Hello? Yes, I had some company, but they're just now leaving," she said into the phone as she closed the door. "Bye, boys."

On the landing outsider her door, we looked at each other just as it started raining again. Colin rolled his eyes and twirled an index finger around his right temple.

"Come on, let's get home," I said, grabbing his arm. "I feel like I need to take a long hot shower."

"A Silkwood shower, for sure."

We were halfway down the stairs when I heard a loud cracking sound, and Colin grabbed me. "Get down!" he half shouted, shoving me forward.

I lost my balance but managed to grab hold of the railing, catching myself a few steps down. Pain shot out of my knees, and I winced. "What the—"

"Someone's shooting at us," he warned, gesturing down the rest of the stairs. "Get down as fast as you can, and stay down. Try to get to the car if you can."

He pulled a gun from his coat pocket and clicked the safety off. He peered into the gloom.

My quad muscles screamed as I hurried down the stairs as fast as I could, crouched down to make a smaller target. I heard another shot and a thud a few moments later as the bullet embedded itself into the railing about where I'd just been a few seconds before. I somehow made it down and crouched down on the wet cement in front of a Honda Accord. I glanced back up at Colin. He hadn't moved.

I peered around the Accord. The street was pretty well lit, but it was starting to get misty, creating weird glows around the streetlights and creating shadows. I looked across the street but could see nothing. There was a big house on the corner with a gallery wrapped around the first floor, but it was completely lit up. All the windows in the house were dark, though. I looked up to the second floor. No gallery, and all the windows appeared to be closed.

So, the shooter had to be either on Coliseum Street or in the park.

I could hear my heart beating as I crept along the side of the Accord toward the street, keeping myself shielded entirely by the car. When I reached the end of the car, I looked back up at where Colin was still crouched on the stairs. He was looking in the direction of the park as well.

I slowly let my head around the back end of the car.

I could see a vaguely human shape underneath a huge live oak in the park.

I saw a flash, and a second later the sound of the gunshot reached me.

Behind me I could hear thudding steps running down the stairs.

I turned and saw Colin crab-walking across the cement toward me.

"He's under the live oak tree," I whispered. "Give me the gun."

Colin locked eyes with me. "Are you sure?"

I nodded.

He slipped me the gun. I stuck my head around the side of the car again.

Damn! The shape was gone!

"He's not there anymore," I said, just as Colin's cell phone began ringing.

There was another gunshot from the park, and I ducked back around the car.

I heard an engine start up and the squeal of tires as a car sped off. I looked back around in time to see the glow of red taillights go by on Coliseum Street.

"Nice work," Colin said into the phone, standing up. He put his phone away and winked at me, gesturing for me to stand up.

I did, and looked over at the park as two black shapes ran out of the park right for us, without a sound, at an almost inhuman speed.

I let out a deep sigh of relief as the shapes reached us.

"I love you guys," I said as I recognized them.

CHAPTER FOURTEEN
EIGHT OF SWORDS
Restricted action through indecision

"The driver got away," Rhoda Sapirstein said as she took her hood off, running a hand through her mop of curls. She was plainly disgusted. "The *coward*."

"I got a picture of his license plate with my phone," her partner, Lindy Zielinsky, said as she removed her own mask and shook out her long chestnut hair.

I'd first met Rhoda and Lindy during the Pleshiwarian case, when they'd swung from the roof of my building on ropes and come crashing through one of the sets of French doors leading out to my balcony. They were old friends of Colin's, and both were Mossad agents. Rhoda and Colin had actually gone through training together—and he'd trained Lindy several years later. Rhoda was originally from Haifa and had a thick Israeli accent to go with her devilish sense of humor. She was strikingly good looking, and her body was an impressive collection of lean muscle mass.

Lindy was American born and had a Texas twang when she spoke. Her family had immigrated to Israel when she was in her late teens. She was breathtakingly beautiful, with glittering green eyes and a heart-shaped face. She also had an impressive set of breasts. They weren't just partners as agents, but in their private life as well.

Colin called them the Ninja Lesbians, and I couldn't think of them any other way.

"Why didn't you tell me the Ninjas had our back?" I gave Colin a good smack on the arm. You couldn't ask for better backup than Rhoda and Lindy.

In the distance we heard the sound of approaching police sirens. Colin looked at me. "You'd better call Venus and get her down here on the QT."

I sighed and pulled out my phone. I do not take it as a point of pride that I have a New Orleans police detective on speed dial—and the feeling is mutual. She answered the phone with a long-suffering sigh. "Let me guess—bodies in your parents' living room again?"

"No, this time there's only one, and it's in Coliseum Square," I replied.

"I'll be right there. Do not move, do not touch anything, and don't get your story straight," she snapped before she hung up on me.

As I put my phone back into my jacket pocket, I glanced up at Enid's windows just in time to see the blinds close. *Interesting*, I thought.

Lindy and Rhoda led us back to the body, with Lindy keeping up a running commentary. "The car was a green Accord, just like you suspected, Colin, and yes, it followed you out to that church, then back to that Chili's place—which smelled incredible, by the way, I hope the food was as good as it smelled—and finally back here."

"You were following the people following us?" I gave Colin another dirty look. Seriously, would it have killed him to tell me they were protecting us?

Colin winked at me as Lindy nodded. "Of course. Fortunately when we got the call from Tel Aviv about being loaned out to Blackledge, we were already in the States."

"Yes, thank you for ruining our vacation in beautiful Palm Springs," Rhoda deadpanned, smacking Colin on the arm. "First one we've had in years, and of course we don't even get to relax in the sun for two full days before we get the call."

"Can I help it if I wanted the best?" He leered at her.

She smirked. "Well, it's true that we're the best, of course."

"Good work, thank you." Colin replied as we reached the body under the live oak.

He was lying facedown in the mud and was wearing all black. He looked to be about six feet tall or so, and in pretty good shape. He was wearing a black stocking cap on his head. There was a bleeding hole in his back and a pool of blood puddling in the dirt beneath him.

"Not a professional," Rhoda said contemptuously. "Definitely an amateur. He was easy to spot on your tail, and the shooting? Pfah." She pointed back to the house. "Look at the ridiculous angle he was trying for! He would have to be a trained sniper to make that shot—or incredibly lucky. And a trained sniper he was obviously not." She shook her head. "Why he did not wait makes no sense to me. Or why he did not lie in wait for you at the bottom of the stairs, where he could get off clear shot at short range—it makes no sense." She shrugged. "Amateurs."

I looked in the direction she was pointing and could see she was right. It was a ridiculous angle to try for. He could have easily hidden between the cars. From there, even if he opened fire when we came out onto the back gallery, he could have had a clear and easy shot.

I turned at the sound of footsteps coming up behind us on the sidewalk. Venus Casanova and her partner Blaine Tujague were coming up behind us. "How did you get here so fast?" I asked. "I didn't hear your car."

Venus' face was impassive. "We live on Coliseum Square." She gestured over her shoulder with her left hand. "Just a few houses down from here."

I did a double take. "Together?"

"Not that it's any of your business, but no—I live in the carriage house behind Blaine's house." She waved her hand. "That doesn't matter. So, what do we have here?" she asked, kneeling down next to the body as a pair of squad cars came racing around the corner at Martin Luther King. "Who shot him?"

"That would be me." Rhoda stepped forward, and nodded. "He was shooting at Abram and Scotty—"

"Colin," Lindy interjected, and Rhoda looked nonplussed for a moment.

"It's all right." Venus held up her hand. "I know his real name, but for simplicity's sake—and my case file—we'll just call him Colin, shall we?" She took her notepad out of her jacket pocket. "Blaine, you take the women. I'll talk to the locals." She gestured with her head to the left side of the tree. We walked over and waited while she gave the patrolmen instructions. As they started taping off the area, she walked across the wet grass toward us, an expectant look on her face.

"Scotty didn't know Lindy and Rhoda were trailing us," Colin said before either Venus or I could say anything. "I mentioned we were getting some backup, but I didn't tell him they were here."

"And why didn't you?" I glared at him. "You scared the crap out of me with all that stuff about the car following us, when you knew all along—"

"Stop!" Venus said in her "I've had enough of this crap" voice, holding up her hand. "This is my investigation and I don't want to hear any gibberish. Let me ask some questions—and I'm not going to tolerate any sidetracking, got it?"

We both nodded.

"First off, does this have anything to do with the Tara Bourgeois or Marina Werner murders?"

"I don't know," I replied. "I mean, I think so, but—"

"It's possible." Colin cut me off. "Yesterday a car tried to run us down on Bourbon Street—and today, when we drove out to the Dove Ministry, what appeared to be the same car followed us out there." He shrugged. "After we had dinner in Metairie, I thought I saw the same car following us down here. Turns out I was right—Rhoda and Lindy had that car in their sights the entire time."

"And what exactly are you doing down in this neighborhood in the first place?"

"My aunt Enid lives in that building right there." I pointed at the house. "Those are her windows on the second floor. We had some questions for her, and when we came out, this guy started shooting at us."

Venus' right eyebrow drifted up a bit, as did the right corner of her mouth. "An interesting woman."

To say the least, I thought. "She was at the memorial service tonight at Dove Ministry for Marina and Tara—we wanted to know why. Why weren't you and Blaine there? Don't the cops always show up at memorial services for the victim?"

Venus rolled her eyes. "We were ordered not to." She shrugged. "Even though the two cases are definitely linked by the gun, Kenner has refused to give up jurisdiction on the Werner murder. We're refusing to give up jurisdiction on the Bourgeois murder. We're kind of at an administrative standoff."

"Dear God," Colin replied. "What is it with Americans being so goddamned territorial? Isn't catching the killer the most important thing?"

"You'd think so, wouldn't you?" Venus smirked. "But that's a fight going on with the higher-ups—the ones who want to be on TV every chance they get. This is a big case, Colin. The Kenner detective in charge of the Werner investigation went to the Academy with me—I'm godmother to his kids. So we're sharing information." She glanced over as the crime lab truck drove up. "Don't go anywhere. Excuse me for a minute."

"Like we'd go anywhere," I muttered. On the other side of the live oak I could see Lindy and Rhoda gesticulating while they spoke to Blaine, who looked confused.

Then again, that was a pretty normal expression for him. He's not one of my favorite people.

"I think we should tell Venus what we know, trade information," Colin whispered to me.

"What do we know?" I looked at him. What the hell was he talking about? "And she's not going to—" I stopped talking as he got a smug look on his face. I knew that look.

"She will."

I sighed as Venus made her way back over to us. "Does the name Roger Kennicott mean anything to either of you?"

"Is—*was* that his name?" I shook my head. "I've never heard of him."

"Me, either," Colin said. "Venus, I think we should all pool our information—I can get a background on this guy a lot faster and more thoroughly than the NOPD."

Her eyes narrowed and she opened her mouth. She closed it again with a sigh. "And if I say no, you'll just make a call and I'll wind up having to anyway, right?" She sighed resignedly. "For the record, I find that to be incredibly irritating."

"Catching the killer is the most important thing, right?" I pointed out.

She nodded. "Go ahead, see what you can find out about him. His driver's license number is LA 1000352."

Colin winked at her and walked away from us, pulling out his cell phone.

"I'm sorry," I commented. "We must drive you crazy."

"Yeah, well—believe it or not, you're not the biggest pains in my ass." She laughed and looked back over at the body. Camera flashes were going off as the medical examiner poked around. "But Colin has resources I can't access, and like you said, catching the killer's the most important thing. I don't give a damn who gets credit, you know?"

"You'll get the collar, Venus," I pointed out. "We can't arrest anyone, after all. You don't really think Emily killed Marina Werner, do you?"

She sighed. "We had enough evidence to book her, Scotty. The district attorney's office is riding the commissioner's ass on this one. This has all the makings of one of those cases that'll go national if we don't solve it quickly. After the hurricane, with all the bad press the city officials got, and with crime on the rise again—" She sighed. "And of course, the Saints are getting the city a lot of great press. If we can't resolve the murders of two high-profile nationally known women—one of whom was dating one of the Saints—it's going to look bad. Really bad. Baton Rouge hasn't gotten in on the act yet, but the governor has national aspirations, you know. The last thing we need is pressure from upriver." She glanced at me out of the side of her eyes. "But off the record, no, I don't think she killed Marina Werner, and neither does my buddy in Kenner. She certainly didn't kill Tara Bourgeois—her alibi more than holds up." A vein started pulsing in her temple. "But it was the same gun that killed them both—your mother's gun." She sighed. "Every time the Bradleys get involved in one of my cases, it's worse than a goddamned migraine—no offense."

"None taken," I replied meekly.

"She's going to get a low bail, is my guess. She'll be out in the morning."

Colin came walking back over to us with a shit-eating grin on his face. "Blackledge is on it, Venus. They're going to e-mail me a report in a few minutes."

"Thanks, *Abram*." She gave him a mock salute.

"Looks like it'll be Agent Golden in your report after all, huh?" I sighed. "So, who are you really looking at for this?" There are benefits sometimes to having a superspy boyfriend when you're a private eye.

"I don't have any evidence, but my gut tells me there's

something not right about Joe Billette," Venus said slowly. "No alibi for either murder, and he had some serious issues with both women." She nodded. "You know, he was blackmailing them both. He admitted to demanding half a million dollars from Tara to make the sex tapes go away. Turns out Marina Werner made a down payment of a hundred thousand to him last week. She was supposed to make the last payment on Monday night—but she called him on Sunday afternoon to tell him she was finished with it all, she wasn't going to pay another red cent. He warned her he'd go public but claims she told him to do what he had to do, he wasn't getting another cent from her. He was furious, to say the least, and called Tara. He says Tara was stunned Marina had changed her mind, told him she would talk to Marina and resolve whatever the problem was."

"So, he was a blackmailer," I replied. It wasn't really much of a stretch to leap from blackmail to murder—but usually it was the *blackmailer* who wound up dead. "Wow, the first tape was released on Tuesday morning. He sure worked quick."

"Tara had until that morning to get the money to him," Venus went on. "Obviously, she was dead by then, so he went ahead and e-mailed the digital file to one of those tabloid shows when he didn't hear from her—they paid him a pretty penny for an exclusive." She shook her head. "He was pretty shook up when he found out she was dead." She made a face. "You know he actually asked me if I thought the value of the remaining tapes would go up because she was dead?"

"Ew," I said involuntarily. "What is *wrong* with people?"

"You tell me," she replied wryly as Colin's phone beeped. He excused himself and walked away. "So, what have you boys turned up?"

"We-ell," I said, thinking. I gestured over to my aunt's windows. "My aunt was at the memorial service. Apparently, she was friends with both Tara and Marina—that's how my dopey

cousin Jared met Tara in the first place, Enid set them up together."
I shook my head. "She's a member of the Dove Ministry."

"Those are some seriously whacked-out people," Venus
commented. "But what would—" She broke off as Colin came
walking back over, a big grin on his face. "What's the word?"

"Roger Kennicott is—*was*—employed as security at none
other than the Dove Ministry of Truth." He glanced down at his
phone again. "He has a record—nothing major, some assaults—
mostly bar fights—from when he was in his twenties. He was
dishonorably discharged from the military—I couldn't get those
records." He winked. "At least, not yet. But he went to work for
the Dove Ministry about four years ago, after doing a couple of
years for his last arrest. He's been clean ever since."

"Why was someone from the Dove Ministry following us?"
I turned and stared at the body. "And tried to kill us yesterday?
Why? What do we have to do with them?"

Blaine came walking over to us. Lindy and Rhoda were
standing, watching him, with their arms around each other. "The
car was registered to the Dove Ministry," Blaine said with a big
grin. "I got an APB out on it now." He gestured back over his
shoulder at the Ninja Lesbians and whistled. "Their story checks
out. We found a bullet in the railing of that building, just where
they said we would—and it's a slug from a Colt, which is what
the victim is carrying." He was bouncing on the balls of his feet.
"This is definitely linked to the Dove Ministry, Vee. I can't wait
to hear the good reverend try to talk his way out of this one."

"Don't call me Vee," she replied irritably. She filled Blaine
in on what Blackledge had dug up on Kennicott. His smile grew
wider and wider.

"Yes!" He did a fist pump. "Come on, let's get out there and
bring down some homophobe ass!"

I'd often wondered about Blaine's sexuality. During the
Mardi Gras case, he tried playing me by claiming we'd had a

one-night stand once—and I almost fell for it. After that, I'd been sure he was straight—and that was, I realized, part of the reason I didn't care for him. I didn't appreciate some straight cop playing gay to weasel his way into my confidence.

But if he was gay—I felt myself softening toward him.

A little.

"All we can do is question him," Venus replied. "We don't have proof that Kennicott was acting on his orders."

"According to Kennicott's financials, some major funds were moved into his account yesterday morning," Colin interrupted. "A hundred thousand, to be exact. We don't know yet where it came from"—he frowned down at this phone—"but they're working on tracing it."

"I bet you anything it was from one of the Ministry's accounts." Blaine started bouncing again, a big grin on his face.

Venus frowned at him. "We don't know that. You need to calm down—until we have proof, there's not a damned thing we can do."

A theory started forming in my mind, and all the scattered pieces began fitting together. I looked up at my aunt's apartment. She was standing in one of the tower's windows, looking down at us, talking into her phone.

"The thing that's been confusing us all," I said slowly, "is the issue of Mom's gun, right? It was used in both murders, so we have been working on the assumption that the same person killed both women."

They all turned and looked at me. "Go on," Venus replied.

"But we also originally assumed whoever took the gun was the killer, and we were wrong about that," I pointed out. "We now know Emily was the one who took Mom's gun, but she didn't use it. She took it over to Marina's to confront her. It went off, she got scared and left—and also left the gun behind." I kept staring up at Enid in the window. She was talking, very agitated.

"Marina was originally planning to pay off Joe Billette—and then on Sunday, she changed her mind and called it all off. That couldn't have made *Tara* very happy. Joe told Tara on Sunday night she had until Tuesday morning to finish paying him the balance—and Tara didn't have that kind of money lying around, right? So, where would she get the money from?"

They just kept looking at me.

"Well, Peggy MacGillicudy and her group *might* have that kind of money," Colin said dubiously.

"But if you were Tara, would you ask her for it? Think about it—would *you* ask the group that's promoting you and getting you on every talk show in the country to pay off someone blackmailing you with sex tapes? Too big of a risk, I'd think, and I'm pretty sure Tara would have thought that, too. So ask yourself this question: If I were Tara, what would I do?"

"Well, the first thing I'd want to do is find out why Marina changed her mind." Venus looked around all of us. "Wouldn't you?"

"Makes sense." Blaine nodded.

"So why *did* she change her mind?" Venus asked. Colin just grinned at me.

"Marina spent Saturday night with Emily Hunter, and Sunday morning she walked Emily to work," I went on. "Her mother saw her. Her mother saw her *kiss* Emily. After years of being rejected by her daughter for being a sinner, for committing adultery, lo and behold, her sinful mother *finds out she's a lesbian*! And human nature being what it was, her mother couldn't resist mocking her.

"So, here you have Marina. She's a closeted lesbian whose father is one of the biggest homophobes in the country. His church—which she works for—is just as homophobic and is hosting a big anti-gay rally this coming weekend in conjunction with a national anti-gay group. Marina is about to be outed. She's about to lose everything. But she also knows PAM's spokesperson is a big phony, and she's about to buy off the blackmailer who could expose Tara—with church funds, most likely.

"Marina knows the church will turn on her. She knows her father will turn on her. She's about to lose everything. And I think, that Sunday afternoon, Marina had an epiphany.

"I think Marina finally came to terms with who she was." I took a deep breath. "And she decided, at long last, to do the *right* thing. She wasn't going to pay off Joe Billette. She was going to let him expose Tara—hey, if she was going to lose everything, so should Tara. It would be her coming-out present to the world. So she told Billette she wasn't going to pay him. He told Tara she needed to come up with the money herself."

"That wouldn't sit well with Tara," Colin said, catching on. "Not with her big book release coming up."

"Exactly. Now, imagine you're Tara again. It's Sunday night. You're going to be on every major talk show in the country to promote your new book. You're in the Superdome watching the most important football game in the history of New Orleans— and if the Saints win, you're going to go to all the celebrations on Jared's arm—it's the culmination of all your ambitions, everything you've been working toward for months."

Colin jumped in. "Only she's about to lose it all because of Marina, the person she thought would help bury her past once and for all. What a night of hell that must have been for her—Jared even said she was acting funny."

I nodded. "So what do you do if you're Tara? She had to confront Marina, ask her why she was backing out, why she wasn't paying Joe off—try to convince her to give him the money. Everything was crumbling around Tara—this was worse than just being publicly embarrassed, remember. She was going to become a laughingstock, the punch line for every comedian in the country. So, Monday, she gets up and goes over to Marina's. Emily had already left. I imagine Marina, who was already an emotional wreck before Emily went over there, was pretty fucking distraught. They had a confrontation of sorts—maybe Marina told her the truth, we'll never really know. But at some point, Tara picked up Mom's gun and shot and killed Marina. She took the gun and got the hell out of there.

"But now she was really screwed. She still needed the money. Where could she turn? Who could give her the money and save her ass? She couldn't ask Peggy MacGillicudy for the money. She couldn't ask Reverend Werner. Her mother certainly didn't have the money. She sure as hell couldn't ask my cousin Jared. The way I see it, there was only one person she could logically ask."

I looked from Venus to Blaine to Colin. They stared back at me, not saying anything, even Colin, who raised one arm in a "so?" gesture.

I pointed up at my aunt in the window. "My aunt Enid."

CHAPTER FIFTEEN
THE FOOL
A promising new beginning

"Enid?"

I couldn't help but grin at the incredulous look on Colin's face. "Yes, honey, dear old Aunt Enid. We've been looking, almost from the beginning, for someone who was connected to both Marina and Tara." I started ticking things off on my fingers. "Who introduced Tara to Jared? Enid. Who just told us Marina Werner was 'like a sister to her'? Enid again. Who did Tara know who had access to the kind of money she needed? Bingo—Enid." I glanced back up at her window. She was still standing there, only she'd turned her back to the window. She was still talking on her cell phone. "She has a Bradley trust fund, just like I do—only hers is way bigger than mine. Enid told us Marilou Bourgeois, Tara's mother, was a dear friend, too. So who else would Tara turn to in her hour of need?" I shook my head. "I don't think Tara went to Marina's planning to kill her—I do think she just went there for answers. But she was in a highly emotional state— everything she'd worked so hard for was about to blow up in her face—and Marina was also volatile. We'll never know what happened that morning, since they're both dead, but we do know when Tara left, Marina was dead. And Tara brought the gun back to her own apartment."

"So, you think there were two killers, is what you're saying?" Blaine asked. "Tara killed Marina, and someone else killed Tara."

"That's exactly what I think." I swallowed. "We've all been going crazy trying to find a double murderer—but I believe there were two killers who just happened to use the same gun. That's why we can't find someone to fit both crimes! Everyone who might have killed Tara had an alibi for Marina's murder, and vice versa." I looked back up at the window. "But I think the person who can answer the rest of our questions is Enid."

"You don't know who killed Tara?" This was from Venus.

I shook my head. "No, I don't. But I have a feeling Enid just might—I think Enid knows a lot of things she isn't telling anyone." The lights in Enid's apartment went off. "What the—?" As soon as the words came out of my mouth, I saw her coming down her back stairs in a hurry. "Where is *she* going?"

"Come on!" Colin took off running across Coliseum Street. After a moment's hesitation, I ran after him.

Colin got to her just as she was getting into her car. I heard her snap, "Let *go* of my car door!" When I came up she gave me a beaming smile. "Scotty, will you tell your friend to let me go? I have to be somewhere, and I'm really in a hurry." She scowled at Colin. "You're really being *rude*."

"I'm really sorry, Enid, but we have to ask you some more questions." I smiled back at her, hoping my friendly tone was just as insincere as hers sounded.

Her eyes narrowed. "I've already answered your questions, and you've wasted enough of my time tonight already," she snapped, tugging on the car door again. "I have nothing else to say to either one of you. Now let me go or I'm calling the police."

"No need—we're right here, ma'am." Venus flashed her badge as she walked around me. "Now, you need to step out of the car."

"I know my rights! I don't have to talk to you!" Her eyes flashed crazily. "If I'm not under arrest, you can't detain me! Now get out of my way!" Her voice kept rising with every word.

"Get. Out. Of. The CAR," Venus said through gritted teeth. "NOW!"

Instead, Enid turned the key and revved the engine. Colin stepped to the inside of the door and tried to reach over the steering column to shut the engine off. But as he leaned inside the car, Enid slammed the gearshift into reverse and shoved her foot down on the gas pedal. The car flew backward. Blaine, who'd been standing behind it, barely had time to jump out of the way. He hit a slick spot on the pavement and his feet went out from under him as the car, its tires squealing loudly, spun while Enid turned the steering wheel hard.

The car slid sideways into the street and Colin came flying out. He hit the pavement with a sickening thud and his head bounced.

He didn't move.

Everything seemed to be moving in slow motion. I started running toward Colin, but it took forever. My legs felt like they were mired in molasses. Enid's back tires spun and squealed as she slammed the car into drive. The door swung shut and I saw a triumphant smile on her face as I reached Colin and knelt down. His eyes were closed.

Out of the corner of my eyes I could see movement. As I fumbled for my phone I saw two black figures run out from the park—and I heard gunshots. I turned my head and saw Enid's car go around the corner—but it was out of control. It was spinning and weaving from side to side and then it disappeared from my line of vision. There was a loud crash and the sound of shattering glass. The two black figures—who had to be the Ninjas—dashed off down Coliseum Street. I heard Venus swear loudly and she ran past me, her gun drawn. On my other side I saw Blaine sitting up groggily, shaking his head.

Colin opened his eyes with a moan.

"Are you okay?" I gasped out as I punched the keypad of my phone.

He winced as he sat up. "I'm okay, but my head hurts—it hurts like a bitch. Don't call nine-one-one, I don't need an ambulance."

I could hear the operator saying something. I disconnected the call. "Are you sure?"

"Now you know how I felt the other day," he said. He moved his arms and legs and winced again. "I think I may have cracked a rib." He started gasping a bit. "That fucking hurts!" He winked at me and grinned. "You should see your face! Seriously, Scotty, I've had worse happen. This is nothing."

"I'll be right back." I said. I hurried over to where Blaine was sitting up. "Blaine, are you okay?"

His eyes looked a little glassy and unfocused, but he nodded. "Yeah—I just bumped my head and got the wind knocked out of me. Did they get that crazy bitch?"

"I'm going to go check on that right now, if you're sure you're okay?"

He waved his hand, and I walked quickly down to the corner.

Enid's car had jumped the curb and smashed head-on into a live oak tree. Steam was rising from the crumpled front end of the car, and I could see the windows had all broken or cracked from the impact.

Enid was sitting on the sidewalk across the street, her head down. Venus was kneeling beside her. Lindy and Rhoda walked up. "Nice shooting," I said.

Lindy grinned. "Thanks." She shrugged. "Shooting out a tire isn't much of a challenge."

"Can you two do me a favor?" When they nodded, I went on, "Can you go make sure Colin's okay? He was in the car when she took off, and fell out—he hit his head and thinks he cracked a rib, but he doesn't want an ambulance. I want to go talk to my aunt."

Rhoda's jaw set. "No ambulance? We'll see about that."

I could hear Enid talking in her little-girl voice as I walked up. She glanced over at me and away quickly, but not before I saw her nose was bloody and her upper lip was swollen.

Venus nodded at me and said, "You almost ran over a cop, and Colin Cioni could have been killed by your recklessness. That's two counts of attempted murder right there, Ms. Bradley."

Enid choked back a sob. "I don't know why I did that. I don't. I'd never hurt anybody."

Venus looked like she wanted to slug her. I held up my hand and winked at her. I knelt down. "Enid, can I ask you some questions?" I said in a soft, friendly voice.

She looked at me, tears running down her cheeks. "Scotty, you know I'd never hurt anyone on purpose!"

"Of course not," I cooed back at her. I forced myself to take her hand. "It must have been such a shock when Tara told you she'd killed Marina."

"It was an accident." Enid's voice was muffled, but she sounded defeated. "She didn't mean to kill her. She just went over there to find out why Marina wasn't going to pay Joe Billette the money." She shook her head. "It didn't make sense to me, either. Marina wouldn't return my calls, so I told Tara I'd take care of it. I made the arrangements for the wire transfer to his account from mine." She sobbed again. "But he called me, you know. He e-mailed me one of the recordings." She lowered her voice. "I couldn't believe what I was seeing! She was a *nasty* girl, Scotty—just nasty. She was—she was doing the devil's work. I couldn't let that go on. So I canceled the wire transfer."

She wiped at her eyes. "A girl like that—she had to be stopped. It would only be a matter of time, you know. She liked being looked at, she liked being recorded. That nasty Joe Billette told me so when I talked to him. He said she needed to be stopped, that I'd better be prepared to keep paying people because she'd just do it again and again, that he wasn't the only one out there with recordings like that...I couldn't believe my eyes. I called her, told her I wanted to talk to her. Jared had already left—they'd had a big fight."

"Why did you want to talk to her?" I asked, squeezing her hand.

"I had to tell her." She gave me a look that chilled me to the bone. The façade she hid behind was cracked, and this was the real woman—someone I didn't know. Someone I didn't want to know. "She wasn't going to marry Jared. She was going to be exposed. And she killed Marina, my friend Marina. So when she let me in, I told her. Everything. She was going to be exposed, and she needed to turn herself in for Marina's death. I told her she had to come clean, it was the only way she could save her soul." Her face hardened. "She started screaming at me, calling me names. She told me horrible lies about Marina." She shuddered. "She told me Marina was a lesbian, and that was why she decided not to pay Joe Billette off, that she was going to come out and leave the church! Can you imagine? What a horrible person that Tara was."

There were some inconsistencies in her story, but I decided to let her just keep talking.

Tara shook her head and laughed her breathy little-girl laugh. "As if Marina could be a lesbian! Her father was a man of God, she was raised in the Ministry! I picked up the gun and told Tara to shut up. She started calling me names—so I shot her." She smiled at me. "She needed to be shut up, you know. I couldn't let her spread those lies about poor Marina. I wiped the gun off and left."

"You knew Marina was dead before you went over to Tara's?" I asked gently.

She scrunched up her face and thought for a moment before answering. "No, Tara told me when I got to her apartment she'd actually killed Marina. Because she was a lesbian."

"Is that what made you so angry with Tara?"

"No. I told you, she was telling lies!" she snapped angrily.

"And when Jared told me he'd hired you and Storm to protect him, well, I couldn't let you find out the truth about any of this. You'd never understand. You'd use Tara's lies against us. I had to protect the Ministry!" Her face reddened and she spat the words at me. "You're a *sinner*."

"So you paid some of the Ministry's thugs to try to kill me and Colin." I stood back up. I gave Venus a look, and she nodded.

"Enid Bradley, you're under arrest for the murder of Tara Bourgeois…"

I walked away back up Coliseum Street, my stomach churning.

My own aunt had paid someone to kill me.

Because I was a sinner.

As I walked, I remembered what she'd been like when I was a kid. She'd always been happy, it seemed, and always in a good mood. She was always ready to play games, always up for going to the movies or renting some. She'd always been fun.

But it had all been a façade. Underneath, she'd been desperately unhappy. As she got older, it got worse.

And now—well, I'd be really surprised if her lawyer didn't plead diminished mental capacity.

It started raining again as I got back to where the Ninjas and Colin were leaning against Mom's Prius. Rhoda was bandaging his ribs.

"She confessed," I said with a sigh. I felt really tired and wanted nothing more than to go home and get in my bed and sleep for about a week. "She killed Tara. She paid Kennicott to kill me."

"I'm sorry, Scotty." Lindy put an arm around me. "It must be hard."

"I'll be okay." I forced a smile. "I mean, it's sad, but I lost my aunt a long time ago. I just want to go home."

"How's Blaine?"

"He was just shook up a bit," Colin replied. "Come on, let's go home and get out of this rain."

Colin passed me his phone with a smirk. "Check out this e-mail."

I looked down at the screen and read:

Confirmed: money transfer into Kennicott bank account came from a Whitney National Bank account in the name of Enid Elizabeth Bradley. There are some other suspicious activities on the account as well. There is a pending transfer in the amount of $400,000 to an account at Metairie Savings and Loan under the name of Joseph R. Billette. This transfer was initiated on the afternoon of January 23, but was canceled on the morning of January 24.

So there it was in black and white.

"Forward it to Venus," I said wearily. "And let's get out of here."

We told Venus we'd come by the police station and make formal statements in the morning. She nodded, but pointed at Rhoda. "You need to come down to the station now." She held up a hand as Lindy and Rhoda both starting protesting. "I'm not charging you, but it would be my ass if I didn't get your statement tonight." She waved at the body being loaded into the coroner's wagon. "You did shoot someone, after all. And we got the driver, too—he got picked up out on Airline Highway—and he's willing to talk." She sighed. "Sorry about your aunt, Scotty."

I just nodded and walked back through the rain to the Jag.

"Are you really okay?" Colin asked as I started the car and pulled away from the curb.

"Like I said, I'm just really tired. Let's just get the car back, give Mom her keys, and go home."

We rode the rest of the way in silence. We trudged around the corner and up the back stairs to Mom and Dad's apartment. When I unlocked the back door, Mom came running. "There you two are!" She looked from me to Colin and back again. "We've been so worried—what's happened? You both look terrible." She lowered her voice. "Frank's here."

"What?" I asked.

"When he got back from Biloxi, he got worried and came over here."

I walked past her into the living room, and Frank jumped up. "Scotty!" He threw his arms around me and crushed me in a bear hug. "I was so worried…"

"Why didn't you call?" His arms felt so good around me I didn't want him to ever let go.

"I—" He sighed and kissed the top of my head. "If you guys were out working on the case, I didn't want to interrupt. I mean, you were with Colin, so—" He looked over my shoulder. He let go of me and hugged Colin, who winced.

"Easy there, big guy." Colin gently pushed him away. "I cracked a rib."

"What happened?" Dad asked, putting down the pipe he was loading.

Even though I just wanted to go to bed, we sat down and told them everything.

"Enid better hope I never get my hands on her," Mom said grimly. "And Father Dan was Tara's father? Wow. You think you know somebody."

The back buzzer rang, and Dad walked through to the kitchen.

"I think we should feel sorry for Enid, despite everything." I replied. "She's not in her right mind—who knows how long she's been unstable? Who paid enough attention to her to even notice?"

"It's hard for me to believe she's a killer," Mom replied. "A mean-spirited, small-minded backstabbing bitch, yes. But a killer? That's a bit of a stretch for me, I have to say."

I took a deep breath. "It's sad more than anything else. She really thought she was doing a good thing by playing matchmaker for Jared and Tara. But when she found out about what Tara was really like, she couldn't stand the thought of Tara marrying her little angel."

"I wasn't going to marry her."

I turned and stared at my cousin Jared. He looked like he'd just gotten out of bed and hadn't bothered to wash up. He was wearing a ratty-looking pair of jeans with rips here and there, and a Tulane sweatshirt under a leather jacket. There was stubble on his face and his curly hair was a mess.

"What are you doing here?" I asked.

He ran one of his big hands through his messy hair. "I heard about what happened. With Aunt Enid." He plopped down on the couch. "I wanted to make sure everyone was okay." He looked over at Colin. "Are you okay, Colin?"

"He's fine." I crossed my arms. "Who told you?"

"Aunt Enid called." He swallowed. "She didn't want to call MiMi or Papa, so she called me. I had no idea…" He swallowed again, looking at each of us in turn. "She was—so unbalanced." He buried his face in his hands. "This is all my fault."

You're taking responsibility for something? I did a double take, not quite sure how to react.

And then I remembered about his mother and Uncle Skipper, and softened a little bit. *It's been hard for Jared*, I reminded myself, *and that's why the adults cut him so much slack when we were kids. Besides, we're adults now.*

"Have a seat." Mom patted the sofa next to her.

Jared sat down. "None of you—none of us—would have been involved in any of this stupid shit if it weren't for me being such a coward." He covered his face in his hands and leaned forward onto his knees.

I folded my arms. "You mean about Dominique, right?"

He nodded.

"Dominique?" This was from Dad. "What does she have to do with any of this?"

"He's been seeing her," I said before he could open his mouth. "For quite some time. But he didn't want anyone in the family to know." I sat down and leaned back. "That's why he trotted good ole Tara out for Papa and MiMi's consumption."

"Enid found out. I don't know how she did, but she knew. After the Atlanta game, she invited me over for dinner. She told me—" He took a shaky breath. "She told that Papa and MiMi—and Dad—would never approve. Papa would cut off my trust fund, cut me out of the family."

"That's not true," Dad said. "Sure, they wouldn't have been happy about it at first, but they would have never cut you off. Never."

"Seriously, Jared, they might have gotten angry with you—and maybe Papa would have cut off your trust—but they would have gotten over it eventually." I forced a smile onto my face. "He cut mine off when I dropped out of Vanderbilt." *Of course, it took nine years before he released it again, when I turned thirty.*

He looked at me, and the pain in his eyes wounded me. "Why wouldn't I believe Enid? She's the only person in the family who's ever cared about me." He went on in a rush, "I never see my mother. Even now that I'm grown, she doesn't want anything to do with me. Dad and MiMi are always drunk. And Papa—" He shook his head.

I was so shocked I couldn't speak.

He looked at Mom. "Anyway, Enid told me she knew the perfect girl for me, the former Miss Louisiana, and she would set me up with her. She said Tara was just the kind of girl Papa and MiMi would approve of." He scowled. "I figured I could show Tara off as my girlfriend but keep seeing Dominique. It was stupid."

"Jared—" I started to say but he cut me off.

"I was scared, okay?" he snapped. "None of you know what it's like, you know?" He glared at me. "You want to trade places with me, Scotty? You want to grow up with my dad and the stepmom of the moment?"

"Well, when you put it that way," I said slowly, "no, not really."

"That's what I thought. You don't know how lucky you guys have it. Papa wrote you off a long time ago, Uncle John, Aunt Cecile—no offense, but you know what I mean." He had the decency to blush. "So your kids—they never had to put up any of the shit I had to. 'You're a Bradley, Bradley men do this, Bradley men don't do that, Bradley men play football, Bradley men...'" He shook his head. "Nothing's good enough for him. 'Well, Southern Mississippi isn't a major school, but a football scholarship is a football scholarship.'" He leaned forward. "I fucking hated playing football. Hated it. I would have quit in high school, if I could have."

I bit my lip. Maybe it did kind of suck to be Jared. "But why do you play now? No one's making you play anymore."

He sighed. "It's all I am now." He shrugged. "I don't really mind it anymore. I stopped minding at USM."

Maybe if I were Jared I'd be kind of an asshole, too.

"Enid—she was the closest thing to a real mother that I had." His face twisted. "And it turns out she's crazy as a loon, of course. And Tara—sure, she was pretty enough, and she was pretty hot in the sack—"

"We really don't need to know about that side of her," Mom interrupted.

He blushed again. "Yeah, sorry. But she never stopped

talking. Ever. And all about herself. I couldn't stand it, you know. But Papa loved her, just thought the sun rose and set out of her ass. And the longer it went, the worse it got. I didn't know if I was ever going to get out from under. I didn't want to bring her to that dinner on Monday. Papa suggested it, but it was Enid who pushed it. Enid told her about it, didn't even give me a chance to decide one way or the other." He glanced at Mom. "That was kind of awesome when you slugged her, Aunt Cecile."He looked back at me and Storm. "That was really what we fought about that night. I didn't tell you the whole story. That night I was finished with her. I was going over there the next morning to get my stuff, give her back her keys, and I was going to tell Papa about Dominique—after the Super Bowl." He swallowed again. "And when I saw her lying there—and the gun—I knew it was yours, Aunt Cecile. But the gun wasn't the only thing I took." He reached into his jacket pocket and pulled out a baggie. Inside it was a gold cross encrusted with diamonds. "This was in her hand. It's Enid's."

"So you *knew* Enid killed her?" I blurted out. I was furious. "You do know she tried to kill me and Colin, right? If it weren't for you, none of us would be involved in any of this mess!"

"Technically, that's not true, dear," Mom replied. "He didn't have anything to do with Emily taking my gun over to Marina's. We still would have been involved."

My head was starting to hurt. "But…"

But what was the point?

I looked around at everyone's faces and decided to let it go.

Sometimes you have to just let it go. You can't sit around playing "if only."

The most important thing was that the killer was under arrest and the case was closed. Emily was cleared. And Jared—well, we might not ever be close. We might not ever be friends, for that matter. But I didn't resent him anymore, and that was progress of a sort, right? Maybe he wasn't so bad.

I took a deep breath and crossed the room to where he was sitting.

I stuck out my hand.

He smiled and took it.

Well done, Scotty, I heard the Goddess whisper inside my head. *Well done.*

EPILOGUE

Enid's lawyer did argue diminished mental capacity, and any number of therapists agreed that Enid's ability to differentiate between right and wrong was more than slightly skewed.

The anti-gay marriage rally was canceled, much to Mom and Father Dan's delight. The scandal of Marina's closet lesbianism was lost in the scandal over the release of more sex tapes featuring the late, unlamented Tara Bourgeois. But within a few days, another Hollywood celebrity went into rehab and everyone forgot about Tara Bourgeois.

"She'll be lucky if she winds up an answer in Trivial Pursuit one day," Frank said a few days later.

It was sad, but it was certainly true.

We all drove over to Biloxi the next Saturday night to watch Frank's title shot. The place was packed, which kind of surprised me. Frank looked incredible as he walked to the ring, every muscle pumped and oiled, in his black trunks with a silver lightning bolt on the front. His black boots were polished to a fine shine, and his black knee pads only made his amazing legs look even sexier. Colin squeezed my leg so hard I almost cried out. The champion, a lean kid in his early twenties with long hair and red tights, gave Frank a pretty rough time for a while—but Frank eventually rallied and just kicked the crap out of the kid. In and out of the ring they fought until finally Frank rolled him onto his shoulders and the referee slapped the mat three times.

Frank was world champion—at least of the Gulf Coast Wrestling Alliance.

Colin and I made him wear the belt to bed that night.

Over the next week, nothing mattered but the Super Bowl. Someone took the banner out of the hands of the gold statue of Joan of Arc on Decatur Street and replaced it with a Saints flag. It was unbelievable; the Super Bowl was all anyone could talk about all week. The *Times-Picayune* could have been renamed *The Saints Daily Bulletin.*

And on game day, Colin, Frank, and I walked over to Mom and Dad's. This time, there wasn't a party. It was just us, and somehow that was better, I thought.

We all cheered when the Saints, our boys, took the field. "There's Jared!" I shouted, pointing out his number, and we all cheered again.

We were all so nervous, we just kept talking—nervous chatter that really didn't mean anything. It was just so strange that the Saints were there, playing on the biggest stage in American sports, where none of us ever thought they would be.

The game started.

It seemed to speed by, as the Colts built a 10–0 lead, and the Saints came back to make it 10–6 at the half. Halftime seemed to last an eternity. "We have to give them the ball back," I moaned as the teams took the field for the second half. "COME ON, DEFENSE!"

I couldn't believe my eyes as the Saints went for an onside kick. *Who does that in the Super Bowl?* I thought as the pile of players around the ball fought and clawed while the officials tried to separate the crowds. "Come on, come on, come on," I was whispering over and over again, and I saw an official signal Saints ball.

I jumped to my feet and screamed—and outside I could

hear cheers echoing through the French Quarter. When the Saints scored to take a 13–10 lead, we all leapt to our feet again, screaming—and again we could hear the noise and cheers from all over the city. Fireworks exploded, horns honked and we were all hugging each other and cheering.

Of course, the Colts scored again to go up 17–13. But by now, I could feel it. I didn't want to say it out loud—it's crazy, but I was afraid if I spoke the words aloud it would jinx them; the gods would punish us for hubris—but I felt it in my heart, the unthinkable: *My God, we are going to win this game.*

Another field goal by Hartley, who set a new Super Bowl record; three field goals over forty yards, and the Saints were back within a point, 17–16.

There was yet another explosion when Saints tight end Jeremy Shockey caught a pass to go ahead 22–17. This time, the cheers outside were so loud it sounded more like sonic booms echoing throughout the city. When the two-point conversion failed, I thought, *Okay, we can win this 25–24.* Then the call was challenged, and when it was overturned for 24–17 lead, my whole body was trembling. I was sitting between Frank and Colin on the couch, and I was squeezing their hands so hard I was afraid I might break bones. But I couldn't help it. I couldn't let go, I couldn't stop squeezing—and frankly, they were squeezing me back just as hard as the Saints kicked off to the Colts again— and the Colts started marching steadily down the field. Peyton Manning looked unstoppable. There was no question in my mind they were going to tie the game. The ball was snapped, and perhaps the greatest quarterback of all time went back to throw again. A man got open, and he let the pass fly.

And somehow, Tracy Porter read the route, jumped in front of the receiver, grabbed the ball out of the air, and took off for the end zone.

We were screaming.

When the Saints cornerback reached the thirty yard line and

it was obvious no one was going to catch him, I choked up. Tears started flowing as I somehow managed to say, "We're going to win the Super Bowl."

Colin and Frank and Mom and Dad and I danced around the living room, jumping up and down and just screaming, high-fiving each other until our hands stung.

And again, we could hear the noise of everyone else in New Orleans. There was an incredible booming roar outside, coming from every direction. It was almost like rolling thunder—and there were times I swear I felt the entire city shaking. I have never heard anything like it in my life; an entire city cheering at the same time. I got goose bumps. Fireworks, horns, and human voices shouting as loudly as they could.

And the clock began to run down.

And finally, unbelievably, improbably, the time ran out and the Saints were the champions of the Super Bowl.

And it sounded as if an entire city sent up a cheer as one throat, as though in that one shimmering, glorious instant the entire population ceased to be separate entities but somehow became one mind, one emotion, one expression of sheer, unadulterated ecstasy that was better than any mind-altering substance I've ever taken.

For that all too brief moment, a diverse and complex city all shared an extraordinary bond.

And it became possible to dream again, because there was proof again, finally, that dreams could come true if you chased them hard enough.

Tears streaming down our faces, our arms around each other, we watched the trophy presentation. Our bodies were all trembling.

Outside, the biggest party in the history of the city of New Orleans began. Fireworks boomed over Jackson Square. The cannons on the riverfront roared. And the sound of the crowds outside—if I live to be a hundred, I will never again hear such a magnificent sound—the loudest sound of joy in recorded history.

It was another lost night. We went out into the crowds and joined the celebration. More and more people poured into the Quarter all night long—I don't think I've ever seen the French Quarter that full of people even on the most crowded Fat Tuesday. Bars were giving away drinks. Champagne corks were flying. Second lines snaked through the streets.

No one knows how to party like New Orleans.

We finally made it home around eight in the morning.

"You guys want to head out to the airport to wait for them?" I asked as I started a pot of coffee, just in case. "I'm dead tired, but I'll go if you guys want to."

Frank and Colin exchanged a look. "We-ell," Frank said slowly, "that would be fun, but we could just go to the Saints victory parade tomorrow night."

"And I was thinking it would be fun to celebrate in our own way." Colin winked at me.

I turned the coffeemaker off and smiled at the two men I was so blessed to have in my life. "Let's go, then."

I truly am blessed, I thought as I followed them into the bedroom. *Thank you again, Goddess.*

About the Author

Greg Herren is the award-winning author of ten mysteries for adults and two young adult suspense novels. He has published hundreds of articles and short stories in various markets. He is a member of the Authors Guild, International Association of Crime Writers, Mystery Writers of America, Sisters in Crime, Horror Writers of America, and Novelists, Inc. He is currently serving as a board member of the Southwest Chapter of the Mystery Writers of America. He works as an HIV educator and lives in New Orleans. He blogs at scottynola.livejournal.com.

Books Available From Bold Strokes Books

Darkness Embraced by Winter Pennington. Surrounded by harsh vampire politics and secret ambitions, Epiphany learns that an old enemy is plotting treason against the woman she once loved, and to save all she holds dear, she must embrace and form an alliance with the dark. (978-1-60282-221-4)

78 Keys by Kristin Marra. When the cosmic powers choose Devorah Rosten to be their next gladiator, she must use her unique skills to try to save her lover, herself, and even humankind. (978-1-60282-222-1)

Playing Passion's Game by Lesley Davis. Trent Williams's only passion in life is gaming—until Juliet Sullivan makes her realize that love can be a whole different game to play. (978-1-60282-223-8)

Retirement Plan by Martha Miller. A modern morality tale of justice, retribution, and women who refuse to be politely invisible. (978-1-60282-224-5)

Who Dat Whodunnit by Greg Herren. Popular New Orleans detective Scotty Bradley investigates the murder of a dethroned beauty queen to clear the name of his pro football–playing cousin. (978-1-60282-225-2)

The Company He Keeps by Dale Chase. A riotously erotic collection of stories set in the sexually repressed and therefore sexually rampant Victorian era. (978-1-60282-226-9)

Cursebusters! by Julie Smith. Budding-psychic Reeno is the most accomplished teenage burglar in California, but one tiny screw-up and poof!—she's sentenced to Bad Girl School. And that isn't even her worst problem. Her sister Haley's dying of an illness no one can diagnose, and now she can't even help. (978-1-60282-559-8)

True Confessions by PJ Trebelhorn. Lynn Patrick finally has a chance with the only woman she's ever loved, her lifelong friend Jessica Greenfield, but Jessie is still tormented by an abusive past. (978-1-60282-216-0)

Jane Doe by Lisa Girolami. On a getaway trip to Las Vegas, Emily Carver gambles on a chance for true love and discovers that sometimes in order to find yourself, you have to start from scratch. (978-1-60282-217-7)

Ghosts of Winter by Rebecca S. Buck. Can Ros Wynne, who has lost everything she thought defined her, find her true life—and her true love—surrounded by the lingering history of the once-grand Winter Manor? (978-1-60282-219-1)

Who I Am by M.L. Rice. Devin Kelly's senior year is a disaster. She's in a new school in a new town, and the school bully is making her life miserable—but then she meets his sister Melanie and realizes her feelings for her are more than platonic. (978-1-60282-231-3)

Call Me Softly by D. Jackson Leigh. Polo pony trainer Swain Butler finds that neither her heart nor her secret are safe when beautiful British heiress Lillie Wetherington arrives to bury her grandmother, Swain's employer. (978-1-60282-215-3)

Split by Mel Bossa. Weeks before Derek O'Reilly's engagement party, a chance meeting with Nick Lund, his teenage first love, catapults him into the past, where he relives that powerful relationship revealing what he and Nick were, still are, and might yet be to each other. (978-1-60282-220-7)

Blood Hunt by L.L. Raand. In the second Midnight Hunters Novel, Detective Jody Gates, heir to a powerful Vampire clan, forges an uneasy alliance with Sylvan, the Wolf Were Alpha, to battle a shadow army of humans and rogue Weres, while fighting her growing hunger for human reporter Becca Land. (978-1-60282-209-2)

Loving Liz by Bobbi Marolt. When theater actor Marty Jamison turns diva and Liz Chandler walks out on her, Marty must confront a cheating lover from the past to understand why life is crumbling around her. (978-1-60282-210-8)

Kiss the Rain by Larkin Rose. How will successful fashion designer Eve Harris react when she discovers the new woman in her life, Jodi, and her secret fantasy phone date, Lexi, are one and the same? (978-1-60282-211-5)

Sarah, Son of God by Justine Saracen. In a story within a story within a story, a transgendered beauty takes us through Stonewall-rioting New York, Venice under the Inquisition, and Nero's Rome. (978-1-60282-212-2)

Sleeping Angel by Greg Herren. Eric Matthews survives a terrible car accident only to find out everyone in town thinks he's a murderer—and he has to clear his name even though he has no memories of what happened. (978-1-60282-214-6)

Dying to Live by Kim Baldwin & Xenia Alexiou. British socialite Zoe Anderson-Howe's pampered life is abruptly shattered when she's taken hostage by FARC guerrillas while on a business trip to Bogota, and Elite Operative Fetch must rescue her to complete her own harrowing mission. (978-1-60282-200-9)

Indigo Moon by Gill McKnight. Hope Glassy and Godfrey Meyers are on a mercy mission to save their friend Isabelle after she is attacked by a rogue werewolf—but does Isabelle want to be saved from the sexy wolf who claimed her as a mate? (978-1-60282-201-6)

Parties in Congress by Colette Moody. Bijal Rao, Indian-American moderate Independent, gets the break of her career when she's hired to work on the congressional campaign of Janet Denton—until she meets her remarkably attractive and charismatic opponent, Colleen O'Bannon. (978-1-60282-202-3)

The Collectors by Leslie Gowan. Laura owns what might be the world's most extensive collection of BDSM lesbian erotica, but that's as close as she's gotten to the world of her fantasies. Until, that is, her friend Adele introduces her to Adele's mistress Jeanne—art collector, heiress, and experienced dominant. With Jeanne's first command, Laura's life changes forever. (978-1-60282-208-5)

Breathless, edited by Radclyffe and Stacia Seaman. Bold Strokes Books romance authors give readers a glimpse into the lives of favorite couples celebrating special moments "after the honeymoon ends." Enjoy a new look at lesbians in love or revisit favorite characters from some of BSB's best-selling romances. (978-1-60282-207-8)